FEB 2 1 2013

W9-DBP-201

4 copies

Julian Solo

Julian Solo

Shelly Reuben

DODD, MEAD & COMPANY
NEW YORK

Grateful acknowledgment is made for permission to reprint lines
from "My Heart Stood Still" by Richard Rodgers and Lorenz Hart.
©1927 WARNER BROS. INC. (Renewed). All rights reserved.
Used by permission.

No part of this book may be reproduced in any form
without permission in writing from the publisher.
Published by Dodd, Mead & Company, Inc.
71 Fifth Avenue, New York, N.Y. 10003
Manufactured in the United States of America

First Edition

1 2 3 4 5 6 7 8 9 10

Library of Congress Cataloging-in-Publication Data

Reuben, Shelly.
    Julian Solo.

    I. Title.
PS3568.E777J8   1988   813'.54   87-33168
ISBN 0-396-09283-7

To the Reubens:

My parents—Ghita and Sam
My uncles and aunt—Mike, Jack, and Libby
Thank you for my soul.

I am a fortunate man.

My guilt or innocence is currently being considered by a grand jury hearing of my peers; my mother is probably dead; my father has, for a long time, been dead; and my stepfather is certainly dead. But . . .

But, I am twenty-one years old, strong, and all of this is taking place in America, where, despite the unpredictability of our jurisprudence system, I have a reasonable expectation that I will not be mob-lynched. Also, I am surrounded by people who love, like, or are at least pledged to assist me. Me, being Mathew Wylie, offspring of the union of Martin and Cynthia, stepson of Julian Solo, a.k.a. "the Accused."

My attorney, Dominic D'Amato, is certainly pledged to assist me, and may someday even come to like me. As he has glowering black eyes, a glowering black disposition, and a vague aroma about him of garlic and breath mints, I shall not actively strive for his love. I shall, however, continue to seek out his approval, since my life is in his hands.

Also, since the one activity in which I can engage at present, and of which my attorney not only approves but actively encourages, is the composition of this journal, I herein record all of the thoughts, memories, feelings, and discoveries that led to the fatal night in question.

I have, assisted by my friend and inspiration, Detective Michael Laffy, stolen, borrowed, or otherwise absconded with notes, memoranda, diaries, and journals belonging to friends, family, enemies, or acquaintances of mine who were involved in this case, but who are not themselves accused of anybody's murder.

Those with whose love I have stated that I am surrounded are the aforementioned Detective Laffy; my mother's friend and my "aunt," Nancy Lee Meyers; and Dr. T. Gideon Humphries.

These three individuals being the extent of my "luck," I shall focus the remainder of these memoirs on the circumstances that resulted in my present misfortune.

The events in question began slightly less than a year ago, on January 15, 19—. At that time, I had been out of college for over six months, but still didn't know what to do with my life. A part of me inclined toward business, where I was fairly certain I could become successful; yet another part of me yearned to do my small part toward improving the human condition.

I am embarrassed to admit that despite all that has happened, I can still understand and identify with those humanitarian yearnings of my youth, and have not yet been able to dispel the notion that man is essentially good, noble, and heroic.

Dr. Humphries, with his benevolent disposition and almost *metaphysical* cheerfulness, has contributed somewhat to my refusal to give up on man. More significant, though, is my mother. When one is nurtured, guided, disciplined, inspired, encouraged, and loved by a heroine of the first magnitude, it becomes difficult, if not impossible, to deny man's potential. As my mother once said, "If a teacher demonstrates to you your capacity, you then have two choices. Either you can achieve it, or you can kill your teacher."

Mother was given to dramatic pronouncements, a characteristic that I fear I may have inherited.

But to get back to my story, I had spent the seven months since my graduation working for a graphic arts company that produced mail order catalogs. I had begun as a glorified messenger. After two weeks, I was promoted to the stock room, where I unpacked, inventoried, repacked, and delivered the merchandise to the studio where it was photographed for the catalogs. After photography, I had it all returned from the studio, where I then unpacked, inventoried, repacked, and shipped the same merchandise back to our clients.

Within a month of my promotion, I was promoted again, this time to assist the account executives in coordinating all of the photography, copy, artwork, paste-ups, and mechanicals that were involved in the preparation of a catalog. Finally, in December, I was promoted once more, to junior account executive, with a substantial increase in salary and responsibility.

At this point, I thought it would be wise to resolve my career conflict before I was appointed chairman of the board. (That's supposed to be humorous.)

The direction in which my humanitarianism leaned was, at that time, medicine. Detective Laffy had told me that several police- and firemen he knew were retiring with their pensions after twenty years, and taking up nursing as a second career.

Since men were successfully invading this formerly female-dominated profession, I thought that I might become a nurse, or, perhaps, a physician's assistant. I ruled out becoming a doctor because I could not see myself spending another six years in school.

In fact, I wasn't even about to go back to college to study nursing unless I was certain beforehand that the career was right for me.

Therefore, I took a leave of absence from my job, and decided to spend the subsequent six months living off my savings, doing emergency room volunteer work in the local hospitals and researching career opportunities. (I also intended to read a lot. Among other things, everything Sir Arthur Conan Doyle ever wrote.)

Once, when I was endeavoring to explain my state of mind to my mother as "trying to find myself," she grimaced and said, "Mathew, it's so common for a young man to be trying to find himself. Why don't you think of yourself as larval, in the process of a more or less stressful molt."

So there I was at twenty-one years of age: independent (I had my own studio apartment on West Eighty-third Street), somewhat lonely (no beautiful fairy princess had yet deigned to honor me with her beneficence), confused, eager for life . . . and molting.

It was at this stage, and in this state, that I first encountered Julian Solo.

Julian is the kind of man one reads about but never actually meets. He is the man sipping Courvoisier on the deck of a yacht; the gentleman whose white cuffs beneath the sleeves of his tuxedo always seem to be whiter; whose pants' creases seem to be more sharply edged; and whose shoes always seem to retain that perfectly buffed but not-too-polished look that we lesser mortals can never achieve.

Everything that Julian Solo was took the cliché out of elegance and gave it back its status as an ideal. Julian's hair was thick, wavy brown, and fox-silver at the temples. His forehead was high; the skin was tight and unfurrowed, like a smooth band of flesh stretched across his brow.

His features were classic. Aquiline nose. Square jaw. Ice-blue eyes. He was slightly taller than medium height, taut and slender. I once saw him in formal dress: black tux, diamond cuff links, patent-leather shoes. Although he was moving slowly and gracefully toward a limousine, I evolved an image of him then, not as a man opening up a car door for a beautiful woman, but of a man, in formal dress, running forward at an even, relaxed pace, with a javelin held loosely in his hand. And, just before he reaches the limousine, he straightens up, snaps his wrist, and releases the javelin with an explosive force.

The javelin, of course, hits the target, whatever that happens to be, and then Julian ushers the beautiful woman into the back seat of the limousine and is driven away.

4

This is the image I still retain of Julian Solo; it was not, however, my first impression of him. The first time I actually saw his face, he was dead.

On January 18 of this year, almost one entire revolution of this, our earth, around the sun, when I had an eager appetite for living a life about which I had little knowledge, and when I was standing at approximately this very same spot (give or take a few perturbations) in our solar system, Julian Solo was standing in front of the main library building on Forty-second Street and Fifth Avenue. Immediately after the traffic light changed, and just as he stepped down from the curb, a bicycle-riding messenger swerved out of traffic to avoid an oncoming car, and crashed into Julian Solo. Julian was propelled by the impact back into the very same car that the messenger had successfully managed to avoid.

A theologian might describe the incident as an example of God stealing from Peter to give to Paul, or God's right hand not knowing whom His left hand is pushing in front of a bumper.

Regardless of the philosophic meaning of the accident, its immediate outcome was the brake-screeching delivery of Julian Solo's unconscious body to the emergency entrance of the hospital at which I had begun volunteer work on that very same day.

Now, hospitals do not ordinarily perform operations, nor do they usually do any but the most imperative procedures, in the small trauma room on the ground floor of the emergency ward. My supervisor at the time described this room's function as a place through which the most serious cases travel, or in which the most serious cases die . . . something resembling a nondenominational purgatory in which the surgical resident (Saint Peter) guards the pearly gates to the operating rooms on the eighth floor.

Even the defibrillators in the trauma room are used only in the event that the resident feels the patient wouldn't make it as far as the elevators without them.

Usually one of the surgical assistants or emergency room nurses assists the resident in the trauma room, if a patient gets wheeled in there. My first day at the hospital, however, the combination of a flu epidemic and a Long Island Railroad strike had so depleted the emergency room's staff that when Dr. Beale whizzed past me behind the stretcher carrying a newly arrived accident.victim, his one hand reached out immediately for the emergency room crash cart (which contains all of the medication and equipment necessary to instantly resuscitate a patient), and his other hand as immediately reached for me.

My memory of the next half hour is of a surrealistic semi-detachment in which I seemed to be performing in slow motion, and on command, while at the same time I seemed to be outside of myself and watching myself perform. I was ordered, during those terrifying minutes, to hand Dr. Beale a wide variety of instruments, to wipe off perspiration, to press clamps, to sponge blood, to wait, to hold, to plunge, and to pray. I do not pray, by the way. I am not a religious man. I was, until I was sixteen years of age, at a picnic to which I had invited Sharon Calvert, the all-A physics genius from my high school. Whatever had possessed me to invite her to a picnic sponsored by my religious youth group is beyond me, unless I figured that somewhere between her A's and her glorious auburn hair, she cultivated lusts.

Regardless of my motives, Sharon, between a piece of fried chicken and three-bean salad, forever upended my theological inclinations by asking me if God, being omnipotent, could create a stone too heavy for Him to lift. Just as that was the extent of my romantic interlude with Sharon Calvert, so was it the end of my romantic interlude with God. I had started my piece of chicken a theist, and ended it an atheist. *Sic transit gloria*.

Even so, on that first day in the trauma room, after Dr. Beale exposed the chest of the patient and then seemed almost to slam the shock paddles of the defibrillators against his heart, I found myself staring at the monitors over the bed,

6

wishing, shoving with my whole heart and mind against that stream of light on the screen. Pushing against it with every fiber of my will to please, oh dear God, to move. To move up and down in that hectic, jagged, ugly-beautiful, fragmented pattern across the monitor that means Life. Live. Live. Please live, I beseeched that static line that jumped with vitality only when Dr. Beale administered another shock. Live. Live. God damn you, Sharon Calvert. I wanted this man to live.

But the thin, illuminated line across the monitor lay flat against its own horizon, and Dr. Beale lifted the shock paddles away from the chest for the last time. Just as he was about to pull the sheet up and over the handsome, austere, but dead face lying tensely before me, Bernice Kaiser, the emergency room surgical assistant, called Dr. Beale to the next bed, where a stab victim was apparently bleeding to death.

Dr. Beale moved across the room. I stayed with my patient—for he had unalterably become mine in that mystifying half hour where I had linked my spirit and vitality to his inert form. I did not feel grief or sorrow as I stared down at him. I felt, rather, a dispassionate curiosity, the way one might imagine himself lingering intently over the individual objects in a room where he had either suffered greatly or exulted.

So did I stare down at Julian Solo, noticing the fine sheen of moisture just beneath his hairline, the smooth surface of the skin over his eyelids, the sharp declination of his nose to his nostrils. The straight, firm lips, clenched, it seemed, in death, as though against . . . Against what, I wondered. What, after dying, was there left to fight?

I lifted my hand to touch the lips, and then I don't know why I did what I did, but my hand, as though on a mission of its own design, inched its way down the side of the dead man's face to the temple, the ear, and then along the side of the neck, where it held. Waiting. Pressing. Perhaps even massaging. I do not know what instinct impelled me to explore in this way. Nor do I know why—or if—I held any hope.

But I continued to press my fingers against the artery in Julian Solo's neck, and I waited, and after several seconds or minutes or clusters of minutes, I thought I felt something beneath my fingers, and my eyes flicked over to the dead man's face, which remained tense, but which seemed, now, even tighter and more drawn, as though some internal force were pushing outward against the skin. I felt no pulse beneath my fingers, but I felt that tension against the air. Against Julian Solo's skin, and in his unmoving lips.

It was then that I thought I felt the pulse. I looked quickly down at my fingers. I shifted my eyes quickly back to his face.

Julian Solo's eyes were open.

He lived.

Letter dated January 16, 19— to Julian Solo, from Dr. T. Gideon Humphries, chief of psychiatry at Roosevelt Island Psychiatric Hospital.

So, my dear friend Julian!

You have decided to defy all medical, theological, and physical sciences by refusing to die, as any well-behaved body must, if its heart has stopped beating.

Can you see in me, Julian, my secret delight that the willful insubordination that you bring to your management of our Psychobiology Department, you are now inflicting on the realm of mortality itself? Let some other doctors, for a change, put up with your imperturbable iconoclasm.

Does Julian Solo live like other people live?

No, indeed. Our Dr. Solo not only makes up his own rules, he redefines the very concept of rules with his energetic disregard for the *integration* of the various sciences.

Therefore, should Julian Solo die like other people die?

No, indeed. In fact, this difficult, argumentative, and purely delightful genius can live forever, and with my blessings, yet, as far as I am concerned.

I don't know how you did it, Julian, but congratulations!

And for heaven's sake, stay in bed. I can assure you that the Psychobiology Department is not about to go anywhere without you.

As your immediate superior, my instructions to you are: Rest. Eat well. Maybe flirt with a few nurses. And don't worry about anything. We miss you, but for a few weeks we can manage without you very good.

Note dated January 16, 19— to Julian Solo accompanying a flower arrangement, from Melanie Graice.

Dear Dr. Solo:

Don't worry about anything at the lab. I canceled all of your appointments this week, and have arranged for two of the graduate students to feed the mice and clean up their cages.

If you need anything at all or would like me to stop by, call at any time. My home phone number is easy to remember: 226-33—, and I am always either at the office or at home, if you should need me.

Don't hesitate to call, and my best wishes for your speedy recovery.

P.S. I'll call tomorrow to see if you need anything.

Letter dated January 18, 19— from Mathew Wylie to his mother, Cynthia Wylie.

Dear Mother:

Thank you for your cheerful letter, which I received three days ago. I'm sorry I didn't answer sooner, but I have been busy with my job at the hospital and with my absorption in a new friend I made there.

Mother, meeting this man has put me face to face with a power stronger than any I have ever encountered. I am talking about the Will to Live, and a man named Julian Solo whose will to live was so strong that it literally overcame death.

I was in the operating room both when Dr. Solo "died," and when many minutes later he came back to life. And now, I am often by his side as he regains his strength, coordination, and health.

Since his miraculous revival, he has been interviewed, photographed, celebrated, and studied, all in the confines of his hospital bed, and all, on his part, with great amusement.

Hysterical ladies and pretentious professors are already writing and telephoning him about his "Life After Death" experiences or his "Out of Body Transcendence," and I have heard him give somber and completely nonsensical explanations of his "death," inserting vivid descriptions of his reunion, approximately three and a half inches above the electrocardiogram, with his dearly beloved and dead paternal grandmother, who was "beckoning him to the other side." I fear Dr. Solo's sense of the ridiculous is coming into conflict with these earnest but foolish folk, and as of this writing I have already heard Dr. Solo describe his afterlife in seven different ways. (Aunt Sybil reaching out her arms to him from the other side of a bridge; a long tunnel at the end of which is a beautiful light; laughing children and butterflies in a field of intoxicating fragrances; etc.)

My new friend appears to be compensating for his idleness in bed by tweaking a few brains here and there.

As to what really went on during that passage of time when he was dead, he has not told me anything except that when one's heart has stopped beating, the blood stops flowing, and when the blood stops flowing to the brain, it becomes oxygen-starved, and, in his words, "Of course one will hallucinate."

Although Dr. Solo tries to appear insouciant about this incredible experience, I believe that it has affected him profoundly, and I often walk past his room on an errand, only to see him writing furiously in a small notebook. His response to my questions about these notations was that he was recording his pulse, respiration, blood count, etc., for some research he was conducting. Research on what? I could not get him to say.

Other than that, nothing new has happened here. How are things going with Nancy Lee? I find it practically impossible to imagine her gurgling and cooing over an infant, but as I have the same difficulty imagining you having done so over me, I suppose anything is possible.

How is the baby? *What* is it? I sent it an allegedly non-sexist mobile, with teddy bears (I'm gagging on my pencil as I write this), ballet slippers, rocket ships, bucking broncos, and flowers. Presumably, if the child stares at it long enough, either he'll grow up to be an astronaut who does a mean tour jeté, or she'll be a cuddly botanist who can break horses.

But don't forget to tell our erstwhile adventuress that if she'd had the intelligence to fall in love with an easterner, I might have reluctantly considered baby-sitting for her heir on remote and unpredictable occasions.

That's all, except that Laffy sends his usual cow-eyed love (the man has no dignity), and I like my new apartment very much. Once one realizes the advantages of cockroaches and claustrophobia over birdsong and breezes, his "is the earth and everything that's in it, and—which is more—I'll be a man, your son!"

Now, it's *your* turn to write.
Love.

Letter from Cynthia Wylie to her son Mathew, dated January 22, 19—.

Dear Matt:
Hello my darling child. When I get home, I'll ask Alberto for some industrial strength roach killer for your new apart-

11

ment. I'm sure he must know about such things, as we never see any bugs either in the piano showroom or downstairs in storage.

Now, for the gossip.

Nancy Lee's baby is a girl, and she has a name—Judy. She is very cute, and gurgles and cries and burps and drools with delightful abandon. No question, she will grow up to be a Scarlet Woman.

I do very little helping out around here, and am probably not justifying my existence as a guest. But Nancy Lee still refuses to let me go home, and has insisted that I stay another week.

Therefore, would you please call up Mr. Sudan and tell him that I won't be back until February 3 after all. Daniel Tuffo can cover for me in the showroom tomorrow. Daniel offered to cover for my students, too, if any should have any questions, so you can give out his number if they phone you. Also, please call up Lillian Chen and Ralph Bromberg to cancel their piano lessons. Their numbers are in the red book by the telephone. And water my plants a day early, so that you can make all of the calls in time. Since I am always brainwashing the children *never* to miss a piano lesson, be sure to dramatize my plight when you talk to them. Best friend just out of the hospital; her husband confused; her child neglected; and so on.

As a matter of fact, I am having a ball. I have already been to the Getty Museum, the Norton Simon Museum, and the Los Angeles County Museum. I have seen the ocean, the *Queen Mary*, and Disneyland. And between jaunts, Nancy Lee and I do a considerable amount of giggling, a pastime completely inappropriate to both our age and our exalted degree of sophistication.

I adore Nancy Lee's husband David. He is a gentle, intelligent, loving, and kind man. He is madly in love with Nancy Lee, and doesn't seem to mind me a bit. He, unfortunately, doesn't curb Nancy Lee's natural inclinations to matchmake, and yesterday declared himself to be looking for a husband for me.

When I protested that I was perfectly happy being a decrepit old widow, he declared that my happiness had nothing to do with it. His daughter needs a great uncle. (You have apparently been appointed uncle.) And so I must remarry.

Now, young man, as to your new friend who has defied death, I must tell you that the subject of willing oneself to live has always intrigued me.

I don't know if I ever told you this story about Thomas Jefferson, but when he was a very old man, and dying, he literally willed his life to continue through the night and until the following morning, and when he uttered his last words, they were, "This is the fourth." He had determined to prolong his life until the fiftieth anniversary of the adoption of the Declaration of Independence.

And did you know that John Adams also died on the same day? July 4, 1826. His last words were, "Thomas Jefferson still lives."

Chilling, isn't it?

I think that great love for life, for an idea or an ideal, for another person, and perhaps even for oneself and one's unfinished tasks, can make a person summon from within a strength, a drive, a compelling and dynamic *force*, which can literally defy or overcome death.

I have never read any studies on it, but I would venture to suggest that such survivors (or perhaps *re*vivers as in your friend's case) are generally strong and/or great individuals. A man who could conceive of such a magnificent document as the Declaration of Independence, who could preside over the birth of our nation . . . such a man could make death wait for him.

Even your grandfather, whose greatness was in his spirit rather than his deeds, Grandpa waited until I had arrived at the hospital before he died. His doctor had called me three days before, but Manhattan had been completely snowed in. He told me that my father wouldn't last the night, but he did.

And the next night. And when I finally got to the hospital on the third day after his call, Dad saw me come into the room, and his eyes touched mine, and then he died.

Man can make death await his bidding, of that I am sure. But how? And how long? And in what manner? That I do not know. That is for the scientists to discover.

But it is intriguing, isn't it? And I don't wonder at this budding friendship that has begun with your personal Lazarus. I do wonder, though, how you can have suspected that he wasn't really dead at the time. Perhaps his skin had a certain patina? Or perhaps your beggar wishes became horses . . . and they rode.

In any event, my son, I congratulate you on your new friend. Now, for the mundane. Do you still like your job? Have you bought curtains for your front (and only) room? Are you taking your vitamins? Looking both ways before you cross the street, and . . . still regularly falling into unrequited love?

Don't forget to water my plants and call my students.

Love, and numerous hugs and kisses.

P.S. Nancy Lee says that your mobile is insane, and that she wouldn't trust a deranged mind like yours to baby-sit for her "heir" even if you weren't two thousand miles away.
P.P.S. Tell Laffy to take you out to dinner one night this week.

Letter from Mathew Wylie to his mother, Cynthia Wylie, dated January 22, 19—. This letter crossed his mother's letter in the mail.

Dear Mrs. Wylie:

You now owe me two letters. My diligence in corresponding with a woman old enough to be my mother astounds me!

The reason for my tasteless zeal is the gentleman of whom I spoke in my last epistle, Julian Solo.

Guess what? He wants to buy a grand piano! And guess what I told him my dear, dilapidated old mother does for a living?

Isn't that wonderful! Your prodigal son walks blithely into an emergency room, wherein he befriends a corpse who promptly comes back to life and orders a piano.

Will wonders never cease? Perhaps I am good for something after all.

In any event, Dr. Solo is leaving the hospital next week, and has asked if he can call you at the showroom after you return so that he can make an appointment to select his baby grand.

If I don't get a letter from you by tomorrow morning, I'm going to assume that the Comparachicos got you, and panic, and, despite my aversion to telephones, I will call you, and stammer incoherently for three minutes, sounding dreadful and pathetic, and your maternal heart will break.

Otherwise, God's in his heaven, and all's well in the world.
Love.

Letter from Cynthia Wylie to Mathew Wylie, dated January 25, 19—.

Dear Matt:
I tried to call you all last night. What's wrong? Where were you? I'm sure I'll reach you on the telephone this morning, but I'll write this anyway, as I'm terribly concerned after receiving your last letter.

What's all this nonsense about calling yourself my prodigal son? Why, you're no more prodigal (Do you even know what it means? Did you look it up in the dictionary?) than I am. How dare you malign yourself in such a way. How dare you say of yourself "Perhaps I am good for something after all"? What balderdash! What nonsense!

You are intelligent, gentle, curious, ambitious, hardworking, and you have a wonderful, vital, questioning mind.

15

In fact, Mathew, everything that has anything at all to do with your essentials . . . your core . . . your inner self and being—all of those qualities are truly both excellent and admirable.

Your problem, which I detect between the lines of your letter, is neither psychological nor philosophical. Your problem is called "being twenty-one." The twenty-ones are a terrible time during which everybody else has a girlfriend (or a boyfriend); in which everyone else has read more books, knows bigger words, has had deeper thoughts and more elegant sufferings; and during which everybody, without exception, is poised, sure of himself, has chosen the right career, and is already the boy or girl success of the decade . . . except yourself.

Oh, Matt, how well I remember being twenty-one. It's the year after which (so I thought) all great authors, poets, and pianists had already had their first books or poems published, or performed their first solo concertos at Carnegie Hall. It's the year in which the world whizzes by on jet airplanes, while you walk, and think that you crawl.

It's a year in which none of what you suspect about others and expect from yourself is either true or valid.

Give yourself allowances for all of the changes that are occurring in your life. Don't compare yourself to imaginary overachievers who, if they had accomplished the triumphs you ascribe to them, would be dead at twenty-three from sheer exhaustion.

Please look at the facts. You are just out of college. You have just taken your first apartment, and you are on a sabbatical from your first job. You are not yet certain to which career you wish to dedicate your life, but you are actively exploring the choices that you do have. You are paying your own way in the world; you are not mooching off anybody. And you are growing both intellectually and socially.

So try to be a bit easier on my only son. You are doing and feeling so many things for the first time. Give yourself enough room, time, and perspective to catch up with yourself.

Now, I shall try again to reach you on the phone, and end this letter telling you that you are a wonderful man and a wonderful son. I am profoundly proud of you, and love you very deeply.

P.S. Don't forget to water my plants.
P.P.S. I will be home on Wednesday, but don't have your friend call me about the piano until after February 10. I shall have caught up with my work by then.

Narrative by myself—Mathew Wylie.

I will take a moment here to digress from these correspondences in order to briefly clarify for you who is who and what their relationships are to one another.

You already know who I am. Mathew Wylie. The Accused.

Dr. T. Gideon Humphries is the chief of psychiatry at the Roosevelt Island Psychiatric Hospital, where Julian Solo worked.

Dr. Humphries is also a professor at the Herbert Fischman Medical Center, where he teaches courses in forensic psychiatry and philosophy. Next year for the first time he will teach his new course, entitled Pathological Philosophy, an endeavor he describes as "a major breakthrough in studies about diseases of the mind."

Dr. Humphries's specialty is the psychopathic personality, a specialty in which he asserts that he became involved by error. When he was a medical student, the administrative department of his school mistakenly scheduled him in an abnormal psychology class—he had intended to specialize in glandular biochemistry—and through that class he became inadvertently fascinated with the "ebbs and flows," as he calls them, of human behavior.

If one believes Dr. Humphries, he then went on, also inadvertently, to get his Ph.D. in psychiatry, to write three

17

books on psycho/sociopathological behavior, to build up and then depart from a lucrative Gramercy Park practice, and to become installed as chief of psychiatry at the Roosevelt Island Psychiatric Hospital.

Dr. Humphries is approximately sixty years old. His ethnic and racial backgrounds are a mystery to me. He is a small man, under five feet four inches, with a very narrow head, and cognac-colored skin. His face puts to mind one of those darkly varnished apple carvings, with features seemingly whittled deeply into angular planes. His nose is small and pug, with horizontal nostrils. His lips are full, but his mouth is narrow. His teeth are white and perfect. Probably dentures. His jaw is long and squared off. He has a white fringe over his ears, but his shining brown skull is bald. His eyes are hazel, with yellow specks around the pupils. The whites of his eyes are snow-white, like those of a newborn child. His voice is creaky, a little bit higher on the register than most male voices, but nice. Gentle and strong and homey, without being placating or condescending. If my old collection of Kipling poems, in its battered leather binding, with its gold embossed lettering, jagged pages, and feathering of dust could talk, that volume would sound like Dr. Humphries's voice. Benignly wise, unselfconsciously aged, and very probably uttering something about who was a better man than whom, Gunga Din. Dr. Humphries's accent and speech patterns? European? Yiddish? Midwestern? Northern black? It's anybody's guess, and any guess would probably be as right or wrong as the next one.

Julian Solo once speculated that Dr. Humphries could not have come into being unless his grandmother had been a Negro, his grandfather a Cherokee Indian, his father French Canadian, his mother a vaudeville comedienne, and his nanny a Talmudic scholar.

It was Dr. Humphries who hired Julian Solo when the two of them met at the Thirty-Sixth Annual Conference of Psychiatrists in Austin, Texas.

Dr. Humphries had read a paper on the role of philosophy in the study of mind diseases. His point was that a man's behavior, attitudes, mental health, and mental illness are all determined by his consciously and unconsciously held philosophy. And that the unreducible primary in psychiatric studies is not the *psychology* of man, but the *philosophy* of man, from which many of his psychological characteristics are derived.

At that same conference, Dr. Julian Solo read a paper on the latest psychobiological studies of brain activity during acts of violence of two different types—assault and self-defense.

Although each had heard the other speak, it was Julian Solo who was the most impressed with what the other man had to say. Initially, he sought out Dr. Humphries after the day's activities, ostensibly in order to probe more deeply into the philosophic aspects of mental illness, but actually "because Dr. Humphries seemed to me to have an overabundance of the rarest of all human qualities: cheerful and uncomplicated sanity."

Only when it became obvious that Dr. Humphries had already left the hotel did Julian Solo also depart to tour the small city of Austin. And it was just thirty minutes later that the two men met, hunched over a glass cabinet in the O. Henry Museum (a frame house preserved as it had been when the author lived there), and exchanged introductions.

A mutual affection for the delightful logic and predictable symmetry of William Sidney Porter's short stories led them to a shared dinner, during which they discussed opera (Julian loved it; Dr. Humphries would listen to it, but could not watch it), ballet (Julian liked classical and modern; the older man liked only classical), the cinema (each preferred the days when more was implied and less shown), and religion (man's earliest and least successful attempt to explain the universe, according to both).

By the time coffee was served, they were discussing their respective specialties, and Julian had made up his mind to apply for a research position at Dr. Humphries's institution, not knowing that Dr. Humphries had already decided that the younger man would be an excellent addition to his staff.

"What I *admired* the most about Julian," Dr. Humphries later told me, "is the appetite of his intellect, his genius in thinking and then proving what has occurred to nobody else, and his hunger for knowledge. What I *loved* about my friend, however, is his truly magnificent ego. Julian is an individual so flamboyant in his self-love and so greatly enamored of his own capabilities that he is above ugly emotions like cruelty and to indulge in pettiness. He is so far superior to his peers that he is not jealous, and he does not want to compete. He thinks only of others, hello, who are you, excuse me politely, but I am in a hurry, and please could you get out of my way."

Julian Solo came to work at the Roosevelt Island Psychiatric Hospital as a research scientist when he was thirty-nine years old. He managed to obtain funding from the Space Medicine Institute Division of Research Studies to finance his inquiry into that section of the brain called the hippocampus, and how the hippocampus responds to memory formation and novelty.

Since many aspects of Dr. Solo's history are interesting, and result in his ultimately inheriting The House on Shore Road (I always think of it in Capital Letters), I will relate them here.

Julian Solo graduated from college at eighteen years of age and promptly entered and graduated from medical school. Despite his youth, he eventually managed to attract patients to his surgical practice, and within four years he was being referred to as "that charming young doctor on Madison Avenue" by the wealthy disfigured, the critically ill, and the merely ailing.

At the age of twenty-seven, Julian attended an opening night performance of *The Man with the Glass Heart*, during which prima ballerina Nastasha Kiralova danced the role of Panache with heartrending virtuosity. Before the first scene of Act I was over, Julian was unconsciously ascribing to Nastasha Kiralova all of the brave, ebullient, and heroic qualities with which the ballet's author had imbued the character Panache.

Several weeks after this performance, Julian Solo married Nastasha Kiralova for the simple reason that Nastasha Kiralova was . . . is . . . magnificent. I have seen her dance on three separate occasions: once in the role of Juliet, once as Giselle, and once as the White Swan. She is, even today, an evocation of the sublime.

When Nastasha Kiralova dances, one has to fall in love with her. One has no choice. It is a matter of logical consequences, rather than emotional responses. Just as one plus one equals two; and just as sunrise follows sunset; and just as what goes up must go down . . . so, when Nastasha Kiralova dances, one falls in love. A. B. C. Simple. Inevitable. Irrevocable.

But the ability to inspire love does not guarantee that the love is either deserved, warranted, or sustainable. "The problem," Julian Solo once stated, "was not that I thought I had married Panache. It was that I *had* married Nastasha."

The marriage lasted exactly two years. "It took me ten seconds to fall in love with her, and one and a quarter years to realize that although she had the body of an angel, she had the soul of a thug."

Julian Solo was divorced at twenty-nine years of age. At thirty, he returned to his studies to get his doctorate in psychobiology. And at thirty-three, he inherited and moved into The House on Shore Road.

Julian did not marry again in the seventeen years following his divorce, because "next time, if there is one, I shall require the *soul* of an angel, and let the bones fall where they may."

The house that Julian inherited is a curious residence, alluring and forbidding at the same time. It was built after the First World War by Julian's great uncle, Howard Craven Solo, and it stands at the crest of the hill where Shore Road overlooks the Verrazano Narrows. From the window seat in the living room, from the master bedroom, and from the lab-

21

oratory, the view of the Verrazano Narrows Bridge is breathtaking.

The house itself is built of crude stones, mortar, and stucco. The roof is thatched, the kind my grandfather would have called "a wraparound job" and I would call "a Hansel and Gretel," because it seems to flow cozily over the superstructure of the building and then tuck itself neatly in around the eaves.

The old-worldly exterior of Julian's inheritance, with its gently curving roof, its three acres of lawn and garden, and its air of fairy tales and childhood fantasies, draws one to it as would an enormous blazing fireplace.

Other qualities of the house, however, make one hesitate and square his shoulders before entering. Around the entire property stands a six-foot-high spiked wrought-iron fence; and the windows of the house are small, overburdened by the bulging proximity of the surrounding stone, like half-lost eyes in the fleshy face of a man who has taken too much cortisone.

The size of The House on Shore Road is also both forbidding and inviting. There are three wings that come off the main section, and a complete, attached guest house in the rear, which Julian later used as his office and laboratory. A two-car garage is located beneath the guest house, and directly in front of the garage doors, Uncle Howard had installed an electronic, remote-control turntable. This enables the driver both to enter and depart from the narrow enclosure with his car always facing forward.

The house's interior is evocative of neither fairy tales nor childhood. Rather, it is weighted down with joist-beam ceilings, lancet and lobated arches, bull's-eye leaded glass, armorial friezes, and escutcheon motifs on each of the six chimneypieces embedded throughout.

On acquiring ownership of The House on Shore Road, Julian Solo's first act was to remove all of the wall friezes and fireplace escutcheons and donate them to the Brooklyn Museum of Art. "Uncle Howard may well have been a financial genius," he commented at the time, "but his taste was obviously in the homes he built rather than the one he inhabited."

Julian's great uncle, Howard Craven Solo, had earned his fortune in the early 1900s as a real estate tycoon. Long before the Levitts, the Stuyvesants, and the Foresgates, Howard Craven Solo had successfully built and promoted Cravencrest, a development of six hundred homes in Albany, New York; Craventown, a community of attached vacation homes in Amityville, New York; and Craven Valley, a collection of fifteen very expensive estates designed by five of the decade's top architects, in Lawrenceville, New Jersey.

Howard Craven Solo lived a life of, by, and for his work. He had married as a young man . . . because she was there. His wife and the dull, devoted daughter of this passionless union had both predeceased him.

Other than his work, Howard Craven Solo loved only two people in his lifetime. One was Miriam Breitch, his ancient, faithful bookkeeper, who had an incisive mind and who, I am told, annually did a blackface impersonation of Al Jolson singing "Swanee" at the office Christmas party, prior to lapsing into an alcoholic stupor and another 364 days of genteel remorse.

The other person he had come to love was the grandson of his identical twin brother Donald Solo. Donald, a chemist, had married a woman named Gertrude Little when he was forty years old and she was twenty-eight. Gertrude was also a chemist, and between visits to Bunsen burners and test tubes, they produced one child whom they named Julian. This Julian, who was *our* Julian's father, grew up to be literate, charming, intense, extremely handsome, nonmathematical, and passionate.

One of his passions was justice, and when Julian Sr. was twenty-one years of age, he joined the Royal Canadian Armed Forces to fight the Nazis before war was declared in this country. When he was twenty-six years old, Julian Sr. marched into Czechoslovakia as a member of the Allied Forces that liberated Auschwitz. One year later, once more a civilian but more

23

broodingly intense than ever, Julian Sr. wrote and published the novel *Indelible Acts*, based on his wartime experiences.

Indelible Acts became an immediate best-seller, and almost as immediately, Julian Sr. began to drink . . . and to disappear. When he was twenty-eight, and after he had disappeared for over five months, he returned to his parents' home with a bundle in his arms which he introduced as his child. He explained to Donald and Gertrude that he had conceived the child with a woman, the identity of whom he would (or could) neither describe nor disclose, and that the child's name was Julian Jr.

After the introduction, and with the help of his parents, Julian Sr. began the rearing process of his son, loving the boy with a fierce, protective, and proud passion that terrified the older Solos, as they feared that so great a passion might easily burn itself out.

Julian Sr. never grew bored with Julian Jr., however, possibly because he had never grown bored with himself, and the boy's features, form, and manner so closely resembled those of his father. Julian Sr. persisted in this love for his child for the next five years, during which time his periods of absence and his addiction to liquor both increased.

When, at the age of thirty-three, Julian Sr. died of alcoholism, his second novel was still unwritten, and the mother of his son was still and would always remain unidentified. Therefore, at five years of age, Julian Solo Jr. went to live with his grandparents in their Princeton, New Jersey, home, from which they commuted to the Welbourne Sanders Laboratories in Lawrenceville, where Donald Solo worked in the research department and Gertrude Solo worked in product development.

After a reasonably uneventful childhood, Julian became an orphan again at the age of fifteen, when his grandparents never returned from a seminar in Baltimore, at which they contracted the then still-unidentified Legionnaires' disease, and died.

Within a week of their deaths, Julian's great uncle Howard Craven Solo, Donald's twin brother, came to the rescue with the offer of neither a home nor an outstretched arm. He suggested, rather, that they meet.

"Come to my office, and we'll discuss your predicament."

"What exactly *is* my predicament?"

"You have no home and no family."

"I have you."

"Not until I say so."

A week later, Uncle Howard said so. When Julian was seventeen, Uncle Howard legally adopted his great nephew, and Julian had a new father. And when Julian was thirty-three years old, and Uncle Howard was negotiating to build one-hundred-acre tract homes in heaven, Julian Solo inherited The House on Shore Road.

Transcript of Dictaphone tape made February 18, 19—, from Dr. Julian Solo to his secretary, Melanie Graice.

Good morning, Melanie. I have a meeting with Dr. Humphries at 8:30 this morning, and lectures at the Teaching Hospital all afternoon, so please excuse the abruptness of my greeting on my first day back from the hospital.

I have attached a list of names and addresses to this tape. Please send all of these people brief notes on my letterhead thanking them for their cards, candy, or flowers (I've put which in parentheses after their names). The text should read something like: Dear Dr. So and So (or Dear John—I've underlined the salutation), thank you very much for making my hospital stay so much more pleasant with your thoughtful card or flowers or wind-up dancing bear—as appropriate. I am happy to report that my recovery is complete, that I am back at work, and that all is well with me. Hoping the same is true for you and your family, I remain . . .

When you have finished the letters, I want you to call up the New York Medical Institute Library on East Seventy-sixth Street. The phone number is on my Rolodex. Ask to speak to Miss Mary Beth O'Dowd in circulation, and tell her who you are. She'll warm up immediately. I want you to read Miss O'Dowd the list of books on my desk, and ask her which of them she has, and if she can get the others for me. Also ask her for any of the most recent books, articles, or studies on hypothermia, cryosurgery, and the hypothalamus. I want not only what has been written, but information on any research projects currently underway. Ask her when we can pick it all up, and then send a messenger with a car. After thanking Miss O'Dowd profusely, in a manner in which I am sure you will convey my deepest gratitude, *always keeping in mind, Melanie, that one is not permitted to remove books from the New York Medical Institute Library but that Miss Mary Beth O'Dowd so permits me, because she has a fancy for my beautiful blue eyes* . . . Where was I . . . Oh, yes. After proffering to Miss O'Dowd my undying gratitude, you will telephone the Turtle Bay Florist on East Forty-eighth Street and ask them what arrangement of flowers would most appeal to a seventy-one-year-old librarian, and then acting on his advice, send same to Miss O'Dowd at her home address, listed on my Rolodex under "S" for Sweet Old Thing.

Next, I would like you to do some research for me on video equipment. As this is an area about which I know nothing, I suggest that you telephone one of the major television networks and ask to speak to one of the engineers in the videotape department. If there is no such department, fumble and bluff persistently until you are put through to an expert. Then, if said expert is male, in an appropriately restrained yet flirtatious manner, see if you can separate from this gentleman his advice on what type of videotape equipment one would need if, on a rather small scale, he chose to record various medical experiences and experiments. The device in question must have an audio contraption so that I can describe the experiments as I film them. I should also like to know where I can get such equipment, and at what cost.

Then, of course, you will call up the other three or four or however many networks there are, and repeat the process with them, after which you will assess the various recommendations and proceed to your Yellow Pages, using which you will do some comparison shopping.

Type out a memo on your findings and leave it in the lab, as I may have a chance to look at it tonight.

When you are finished with that, type a letter to Dr. Eric Lilljigren in Norway, address also on my Rolodex. Dear Eric, as I am about to begin some elaborate experiments on hypothermia, I was delighted to read in last month's *Journal* that this has become your specialty. I am wondering if you might advise me as to any research material that has been printed in this field, as well as an update on your own findings, if they are currently available. I am particularly interested in the length of time, and at what body temperature, a human being can be "frozen" and yet revived without any organ damage. The object of these studies is medical; the purpose to slow down the body's vital functions to enable the performance of delicate operations without the haste and consequent risk that at present exists.

Of course, we shall talk about this in greater depth when I see you at the convention in San Francisco this July, but any direction you can provide me would be greatly appreciated.

Am I right in assuming that the hypothalamus can be manipulated to lengthen the stay of a body at a lower temperature, without adverse consequences? Have you had any luck doing this?

I appreciate your assistance in this matter, Eric, and under separate cover I am sending you the first edition of the Coulomb book that you so admired and with which I now intend to bribe you.

Do give Heidi and Veronika my love; and to whatever extent is humanly possible, my friend, make haste. The scent is upon me!

Best regards, et cetera.

The next letter is to the Song Writers' Museum in Times Square. Look up their address in the phone book, but call them first and find out who is the curator of early twentieth-century American music. Address this letter to him or her.

Dear So and So. I currently own an upright grand piano made in New York in 1919 by Heller & Sons, and inherited by me from my great uncle's estate. Shortly prior to his death, this same gentleman, Howard Craven Solo, informed me that he had purchased this piano from the great Moses Belasco in 19— as a memento of a follies in which he (my great uncle) had invested. The piano has been perfectly maintained, its sound is true; its original finish and patina have not been altered, and it is a real beauty.

Since I am at present negotiating to purchase a Steinway baby grand, I find I no longer have any need for this upright.

A dedication to my great uncle's memory and intentions prevents me from selling it, however, and, with your permission, I would like to donate this historic instrument to your museum.

I shall have it appraised prior to its delivery for the purposes of an income tax deduction, and I sincerely congratulate you on your new acquisition.

Very truly yours.

And just one last thing, Melanie. I want you to telephone a Mrs. Cynthia Wylie at the piano showroom on West Fifty-seventh Street. Make an appointment with her to show me pianos on either Thursday or Friday of the week after next, at her convenience. If she draws a blank on my name, remind her that her son was my friend at the hospital, and that it was he who suggested I call.

And now, my dear Melanie, when you have completed all of the assignments on this tape, please take the ten-dollar bill that I tucked at the bottom of your pencil cup, and go out and buy yourself a nice dinner, a Cadillac convertible, or a new wardrobe.

One in my position who so readily abuses his secretary with overwork must take care to temper his injustice with mercy.

Narrative by myself—Mathew Wylie.

At this point it would probably be advisable to introduce the third member of the Roosevelt Island Psychiatric Hospital triumvirate. This is Melanie Graice, twenty-six years old, graduate of the Kathleen Bowers Secretarial School in St. Louis, Missouri, ostensibly sweet, hard-working, virginal, and pure, and possessed of the kind of Southern Belle face and baby-bottom-soft complexion that you would expect to see in an advertisement for talcum powder or vitamin E no-chemicals-added night cream.

Melanie Graice was, of course, Julian Solo's secretary.

Even to this day I have mixed feelings about her, although nobody else does; as far as I can ascertain, she is universally hated. Perhaps I don't hate her, despite what she has done, because it was so obvious to me, from the first glimpse I had of her, that she was a dreadfully unhappy and probably pathologically repressed (I got that from Dr. Humphries) girl.

I suppose that Melanie is a woman and that it's condescending to refer to a twenty-six-year-old female as a girl, but she always seemed to go out of her way to underplay her maturity. Everything that she either did or wore was just this side of adolescent, and just that side of sexual, from her shirtwaist dresses to the cheap romantic novels that she sometimes read and left open to a rape scene on her desk at the office. Whether she did this intentionally, or even consciously, I cannot say. But she is a strange human being.

Her hair is the color of overripe dandelions. Her eyes are dark blue, a shade of blue that one never sees on anything other than another human being's eyes, or semiprecious stones backlighted in a display case at the Smithsonian. Melanie has a small, pert, pretty nose, and baby doll lips. Her lips are clearly defined in a girlish pout, and they project the type of provocative innocence that was the vogue of screen sirens in the early days of silent films.

Melanie isn't tall, nor is she fashionably thin. She has a delicious skin-fullness (that's the only way I can describe it) about her. Her skin, from the open neck of those ridiculous Peter Pan collar blouses she wears, to the wide expanse of leg line beneath her shapeless plaid skirts, is so incredibly *touchable* looking that one's mind reeled from the unending sensuality of it all.

Poor Melanie.

I know she doesn't hate me. Even when we appeared at her door and it became infinitely clear that I was equally responsible for that ultimate confrontation, her looks of hatred were reserved for the others. For Laffy. For Dr. Humphries. For my mother. For Nancy Lee. But not for me.

Maybe I was the exception in her life. The easy, breezy, unassuming, undemanding exception. The exclusion from passion for a woman who otherwise divides her emotions strictly into wild and devouring love, or wild and devouring hate.

I was the air pocket in this whirlwind of emotions that she could bother merely to *like*, because . . . who knows why, really? Perhaps because she looked upon me as the brother or pet Saint Bernard puppy she'd never had. Perhaps because she sensed that I was rhapsodically in love with her miles and miles of intoxicating skin, and she, who spent so many hours of her life loving, if you can call it that, enjoyed basking in the power of having been able to evoke love.

I don't know. I do know that aside from some mild and detached pity, I now feel nothing else for her. I do not place all of the blame for what has happened on her turbulent conscience. Oh, no.

He who had aspired to manipulate the life and death of his beloved without either her knowledge or her consent . . . it is he whom I blame for all of our misfortunes.

30

Entry in diary belonging to Melanie Graice, dated February 18, 19—.

Dearest Sweet Diary:

My Dr. Solo came back to the office today, and I missed seeing him. I know that he was back, though, because he left messages for me on the Dictaphone. He also left me a ten-dollar bill for supper money, but I won't spend it. I have wrapped it up carefully in cellophane and tucked it in my negligee drawer. I read somewhere once that paper money retains the skin oils of the last person who has touched it.

I have also brought home the Dictaphone tape that Dr. Solo made. I never told you this before, dear Diary, but I have been taking tapes home ever since the first week I worked for him. It is very simple for me to replace the ones that I have taken, and nobody knows what I have done. I don't take many. But sometimes, late at night, when I am lonesome, I play a tape of Dr. Solo's voice to keep me company.

I don't think I am doing anyone any harm. After all, Dr. Solo isn't married, and neither am I. I know that he isn't married because after he was hit by the automobile I worked late one night and sneaked into the personnel department to look at his file. I now know where he lives, and his home phone number.

Dr. Solo is forty-six years old, and divorced.

I wonder why he has never remarried.

I am consumed totally by love for this man. He is a god to me, Diary. I wish now that I could speak French, because French is supposed to be the language of love, and perhaps in French you would understand better how I feel.

You know, transcribing the tape today, when I got to the part about Mary Beth O'Dowd, the librarian, I was insane with jealousy until he told me that she is seventy-one years old.

I had never felt so angry, so enraged, so betrayed before.

Why can't he see how I adore him? Why can't he feel those waves and waves of love that I send his way? I sometimes do a little chant as I sit at my desk and type. While my fingers tap at the keyboard, my mind intones, "Love me, love me, love me."

It is now late, and tomorrow I shall see Dr. Solo for the first time since his accident.

I will wear my white, sheer nylon blouse with the lace camisole.

I must get my beauty sleep, dear Diary. Good night.

Memorandum from Dr. T. Gideon Humphries to Dr. Julian Solo, dated February 26, 19—.

And so, my friend, as soon as the doctors have finished gluing and safety-pinning you together, you are endeavoring to unhook the whole kit and caboodle from overzealous work?

The body cannot withstand such a commotion in so short a time. Recovery is not enough to sustain health. You should give also to your physique a little rest and recompensation. Maybe here a little nap. There a walk by the promenade in the sunshine with, on the horizon, a view of the Queensboro Bridge, a skyline, some birds, a nurse with long legs, a hot-dog stand, or a cup of hot cocoa.

So? Why the long hours?

My spies are reporting that the light is still on in your office when they go home. Do you think this is a nice thing to do, Julian? Putting in longer hours than Miss Bengelsdorf in accounting and Mrs. Slotten in radiography, my two chief busybodies and informants? Soon, who knows, they'll be asking to work overtime, just to keep up with you.

And so what are you doing, Julian, so late into the night? Is this perhaps a new paper you are writing on the neurobiology of the brain?

Have you again become inspired to trek through the cerebellum to the thalamus, seeking inspiration from the limbic system, and plunging, with boundless enthusiasm, into the brain stem itself?

You are at it again, Julian, aren't you? Seeking out the secret of life somewhere between a neutron and a conditioned reflex. And how many times have I told you that all you will find in the brain itself are *processes*?

Secrets, my friend, unravel and are beheld *in the synthesis of all of the processes*. In the integration of all of the systems — neurologic, biological, respiratory, circulatory, digestive, reflective, demonstrative, remonstrative, genetic, poetic, and prophetic.

I do not scorn the microscope in the search for the components of life. But for the *secret* of life, you must look first to the total, unified man, then to the universe, and then, of course, back to man again.

It is in how all of these variables interact that man's purpose and his nature will be revealed.

Remember, Julian, as you probe your medullas and pinch your corpus callosum, that philosophy is the key to "what," just as metaphysics is the key to "why and how."

And so.

What are you doing?

Why are you doing it so much and so late at night?

How do I get you to take it less strenuously so that poor Miss Bengelsdorf in accounting and Mrs. Slotten in radiography shouldn't worry?

Memorandum from Dr. Julian Solo to Dr. T. Gideon Humphries, dated February 27, 19—.

Gideon:

I am in receipt of your memo dated yesterday.

What can I say to one who so generously offers to probe into the mystery of my purpose? How can I satisfy the never-ending curiosities of the Bengelsdorfs and Slottens of the world, to say nothing of the T. Gideon Humphrieses?

Late at night, when all bland and sociable folk are huddled around their dinner tables, doing that which mere mortals do, I do indeed plunge deep into the brain, and thereby, up into the stars.

I soar with exhilaration over my studies, for, although I may not find the secret of life "between a conditioned reflex and a neutron," as you say, *you* are less likely to find it between a syllogism and a poem.

I may in fact be on the track of at least one secret of life, if not the whole "kit and caboodle." The secret in question is that of how to *sustain* life by preventing the breakdown of tissue when metabolism itself has stopped.

What do you think, Gideon? May we meet tomorrow for breakfast to discuss my project? I am particularly concerned with the hypothalamus, and I respectfully request that for the duration of our little breakfast conference you refrain from imparting any of your homey-folksy wisdom, and just give me the benefit of your clear, lucid, and overeducated brain.

How about 7 A.M. in the Edwardian Room at the Plaza? Let's get off this wretched island for a change. My treat.

Memorandum from Dr. T. Gideon Humphries to Dr. Julian Solo, dated February 27, 19—.

My friend, Julian.

One minute you are knee deep in cerebellum, and the next minute you are up into the stars. No wonder why to Miss Bengelsdorf your activities are so confusing.

Perhaps, when I meet you tomorrow for breakfast, you will have taken a wrong turn, and land up on the moon?

Seven A.M. is far too early, but I indulge your reckless youth and will meet you.

So, when did you stop liking my homey-folksy wisdom? I never stopped liking your hypothalamus.

Dear Julian:

Enclosed please find my paper entitled "Reaksjon på Varme og Kuld," which is scheduled to appear in the spring issue of *Norsk Medisinsk Vitenskap*. I am most regretful that I was unable to translate this for you, however, your letter expressed a need for haste, and I could not thus spare the time.

Also, here is a list that my secretary has prepared on the most recent studies on hypothermia. Movement in this field goes slowly (no pun intended). I am in hopes that perhaps you will enlighten me of your studies, as well.

In April I begin work on cryosurgery as a method of containing cancerous cells. I should be most happy to provide you with reports on my findings if you would be willing to part with the Havighurst book on biomutants, which I perceived on the top shelf of the bookcase on the left of your dictating machine, in your outer office.

Although I will provide you with this information without receipt of the Havighurst book, I will leave out all punctuation marks, paragraphing, and capital letters, and I will remove the page numbers and shuffle the pages.

Don't you think this free and open exchange of scientific knowledge has gone too far?

Heidi and Veronika are fine. Heidi wants to know when you are coming here, as her sister is recently divorced and would like to meet a rich American.

Fondest regards.

Letter from Julian Solo to Dr. Eric Lilljigren in
Norway, dated April 5, 19—.

Dear Eric:

I have received your paper on hypothermia, have had same translated, and must convey to you my gratitude and admiration. You are doing splendid things in this field, and the idea of clinically lowered body temperature having a positive effect on hysterical schizophrenia is both novel and intriguing.

I realize, though, as I study your works, that we seem to be traveling along different routes of inquiry, and I might add, you seem to be moving at a steady gallop, while I stumble along with less agility than determination.

Do you mind, Eric, if I toss off a few of my ideas for your evaluation and response? Perhaps in the course of verbalizing my goals to you, a heretofore undiscovered connection will suddenly reveal itself to me . . . or to you, as I am not averse to negotiating away my entire library of first editions in the cause of this particular area of research.

My goal, with regard to this specific series of experiments, is to find a means of manipulating the hypothalamus in order to put the body on physiological "hold" so that it ceases all bodily functions but does not decompose.

Or, to rephrase it, without freezing the body or lowering its *actual* body temperature, I want to manufacture a chemical catalyst that I can inject into the hypothalamus, which will cause the body to react as though frozen, without the imposition of external cold.

This is my line of thinking.

The hypothalamus is the body's regulator of temperature. It responds to heat and cold, regulates blood pressure, breathing, shivering, etc.

Cold is the slowing of molecular movement.

Cold has been used medically in the past to decelerate the body's rate of metabolism for the purposes of cardiac operations, brain surgery, microsurgery, and so on. On several occasions, individuals have had their body temperatures lowered to 48.2°F, at which level their hearts and respiration were stopped for over forty-five minutes; yet, after their bodies were returned to normal, they regained consciousness with absolutely no indication of brain damage.

We know that despite the threat of ventricular fibrillation at these low body temperatures, individuals who have been discovered frozen solid, and, for all practical purposes, *frozen to death*, have been placed in water at temperatures of 115° to 120°F, and have recovered completely. We know that every time someone has placed a limitation on the human capacity to survive cold, he has been proven wrong.

We know that just as absolute cold is the moment at which *all* molecular activity stops, death is the moment at which all metabolism in living things stops.

Now, my purpose is to correlate "death" with "cold," so that via manipulation of the hypothalamus into the appropriate set of responses for extremely cold temperatures, the body will arrest function completely, but not die.

Because, in this instance, the hypothalamus will respond to cold, the cessation of activity therein achieved would not be followed by the molecular breakdown and decomposition that is normally associated with death.

This means that if I injected my cryogenic catalystic serum into Joe Doaks, his bodily functions would become slower and slower until they appeared to cease altogether.

However, because his body was responding *as if to cold*, Mr. Doaks could be lying in this state for days—perhaps even months or years—without any decomposition processes setting in. He could be lying in a room heated at 40°F or a room sweltering with tropical heat, and the *external* temperature of his surroundings would not affect his body, because it would be constantly attuned to the messages being sent to it by the hypothalamus, which, in turn, is constantly attuned to the cryogenic catalystic serum that had been injected for the purpose of initiating this process.

Now, you are asking, why does not decomposition begin? Why is there no brain damage should Mr. Doaks revive? Why is this body sustained as if frozen, in a state of literal suspended animation, when we know that *process* is inevitable; that one heartbeat must follow another in the *process* called life; or that one heartbeat *not* followed by another begins the *process* of decomposition called death.

My answer to the "whys," Eric, is contained in what I call the "Other Shoe Principle."

Remember the cartoon of a man in bed on the sixth floor of a hotel who hears his neighbor, above, drop one shoe onto the floor, and cannot fall asleep until he hears the other shoe drop? This man cannot go to sleep because programmed irreversibly into his psychological makeup is the logical sequence of the "going to bed" process, i.e., there are *two* shoes that have to be removed, and until *both* shoes have been removed, the process is uncompleted.

Our restless friend is unable to go to sleep himself because he knows that somewhere, something is wrong. He lies in bed, exhausted but awake and alert; poised as if on the edge of something hour after hour, perhaps until, at long last, from upstairs, he hears that other shoe drop, and he realizes that the process is complete, and he can finally go to sleep.

I propose, with my Cryogenic Catalystic Serum (CCS), to do the same thing. To drop one shoe, as it were, within "hearing range" of the hypothalamus, as well as the completed program of reanimation, which is the other shoe for which the hypothalamus must wait until it can go to sleep.

Is any of this clear to you, Eric? Do you understand how I intend to prevent decomposition and ensure revitalization by instilling within this vital gland the biochemical "knowledge" that its process is not yet completed until a reawakening has occurred? How, despite the outward appearance of death and the apparent lack of all circulation, the body is, in actuality, merely arrested *between* heartbeats?

Can you see, indeed, how thrilling it is for me to be on the edge of this new discovery? How great such a breakthrough would be in the advancement of medical science?

Why, as I sit here now, dozens of potential benefits occur to me.

Cryogenic "death" can be induced to forestall aging. Instead of going to sleep at night, one can simply cease both to metabolize and to age for an eight-hour stretch. Add year after year of eight-hour segments together and you will see how one can increase his life span by at least one third. Truly a fountain of youth to those who seek it.

Or, these mini-"deaths" could be used to improve the chance of a critically ill patient to survive difficult and lengthy surgical operations. What a blessing to a surgeon or an anesthesiologist no longer to have to worry about the rate of respiration, the pulse, the heartbeat during surgery, for all bodily functions will have ceased during the course of the operation, and, as if magically they will resume only after the clamps have been removed and the stitches are in place.

And disease, Eric. Why, those who are afflicted with currently incurable illnesses can now submit to large doses of the cryogenic catalystic serum in order to "freeze" themselves in this deathlike state until science is able to come up with a cure.

Fantastic, isn't it? I marvel at my own genius in being able to conceive of such wonders.

But despite the delight I take in what I have already managed to achieve, I can assure you that I maintain a healthy humility about what is left to be done.

For I do not yet know:

How can my serum be regulated to achieve the appropriate time lengths of deanimation?

How can the serum be delivered to the hypothalamus so that it can go to work directly and only on that gland?

What will be the medical effects of deanimation on the molecular structure of the cells? On the brain? On the consciousness?

How will deanimation affect such normal bodily functions as growth, puberty, maturation, pregnancy, and aging?

Alas, there is much left to do.

If, indeed, it can be done.

I have thus far been able to lower Penelope's (my lab mouse's) heartbeat to three times per minute, and her oxygen intake to 1/50th the norm, as well as her body temperature to barely a degree above freezing, so that ice crystals do not form and distort the molecular structure of the cells. This bodes well, for when revived, Penelope, although momentarily a bit testy, invariably reassumes her usual more or less nonspectacular personality. We are as yet, however, to achieve a *zero* heartbeat.

Can it be done? Of course it can be done. I, in fact, have done it, although inadvertently, when after an automobile accident on January 15 of this year, I "died."

And am I not now as alive, as alert, and as intelligent as ever I was?

On this note, I close, earnestly imploring you *not* to reply with *too* many derogatory shots at my (1) aliveness, (2) alertness, and (3) intelligence.

Answer this letter soon, Eric, for I want to know how you react to my ideas on chemically induced hypothermia.

Warmest regards to all, and do respond quickly. The first shoe, as it were, has already dropped.

Entry into Experimental Log of Julian Solo, dated April 6, 19—.

Injected lab mouse Penelope with .10 ml of cryogenic catalystic serum at 0800 hours. Slowly brought heartbeat down to 2 per minute. Oxygen intake down to 1/75th of norm. Body temperature remains constant.

Maintained state of Artificially Induced Hypothermic Response for six hours. Injected Penelope at 1400 hours with CCS antidote, and noted slow increase in oxygen intake and heartbeat at rates of 1/15th for oxygen and 2.5 beats per second respectively.

At 1433 hours, Penelope's heartbeat and oxygen intake normal, and I put her in the same cage as Odysseus, her mate. She initially manifested antisocial behavior of sulking in the corner of the cage and then baring her teeth at Odysseus when he came over to eat from her dish.

Antisocial episode lasted only three minutes, and at 1436, Penelope and Odysseus reunited in connubial bliss.

Log entry, dated April 7, 19—.

At 0830 hours, Penelope displaying symptoms of irritability, uncooperativeness, and general discontent. At 0900 hours, Dr. Humphries stopped by to pick up video disk and at my request examined Odysseus's irritable companion. Dr. Humphries has informed us that congratulations are in order. The reason for Penelope's discontent is pregnancy.

This is splendid for my research. If I can achieve zero heartbeat in Odysseus, will then test proper dose of CCS on Penelope to prolong pregnancy, and observe if any negative effects.

Log entry, dated April 8, 19—.

Have decided that most efficient means of delivering CCS directly to hypothalamus is an adaptation of the Senyei-Widder technique. Shall enclose serum with minute particles of the magnetic mineral magnetite inside protein packets that are approximately 1/5th the size of a red blood corpuscle. I can inject these microspheres into the bloodstream and then direct them through the veins by passing a magnet over the surface of the subject's body, thereby delivering the serum directly to the area of the hypothalamus.

Odysseus is being prepared for injection tomorrow. CCS will be delivered to hypothalamus as above, in amount adequate to induce state of total cryogenic death.

I shall sustain this deanimated state for a period of fifteen minutes before injecting CCS antidote.

Penelope still cranky. Gained ¼ ounce.

Log entry, dated April 9, 19—.

7000 hours: Injected Odysseus with .10 ml of CCS in protein microsphere.

7002 hours: Odysseus heartbeat 30 per minute.

7004 hours: Odysseus heartbeat 12 per minute.

7007 hours: Odysseus heartbeat 5 per minute. Oxygen intake 1/90th normal.

7010 hours: All bodily functions ceased.

7025 hours: Antidote for CCS introduced in bloodstream.

7026 hours: No pulse or respiration.

7027 hours: No pulse or respiration.

7028 hours: No pulse or respiration.

7029 hours: Increased dosage of CCS antidote.

7030 hours: No pulse or respiration.

7031 hours: Inserted electrode into Odysseus's heart. Activated.

8030 hours: Limbs stiffening; internal body temperature dropping.

9000 hours: Odysseus pronounced dead.

Log entry, dated April 10, 19—.

Autopsy performed on experimental mouse Odysseus revealed that death was caused by cardiac arrest.

In future experiments shall decrease dosage of CCS and sustain deanimated state for only five-minute segment.

If zero heartbeat sustainable for proscribed time, and with subsequent successful reanimation achieved, I will then increase length of cryogenic death state by one-minute increments each day until enough data are obtained from which I can analyze long- and short-range effects.

Experimental mouse Penelope is still pregnant and growing. Disposition greatly improved. Weight up ⅛ ounce. Odysseus's death doesn't seem to have affected her markedly, and she was observed today engaged in boldly flirtatious behavior with Horatius. Let us hope that the mouse Horatius will prove to deserve the benefits of her charms.

Log entry, dated April 25, 19—.

Total satisfaction with Horatius. As of 1100 hours, he successfully reanimated from a five-hour state of absolute cryogenic death.

After weeks of slowly increasing the time lengths of Horatius's deanimated state, today marks a day of resounding triumph. Horatius has survived over two hundred times the death state to which I, myself, was inadvertently subjected.

I stand in awe of the possibilities this endurance capability presents. For if life can be manipulated to simulate death for the purpose of overcoming death, what then can man not achieve?

To my mind now come the words of Shelley's poem: Hail to thee, blithe Spirit! But what I feel is: Hail to *me*, blithe Spirit! That from Heaven, or near it, Pourest thy full heart/ In profuse strains of unpremeditated art.

Why are such words wasted on a bird, when there are none to express the splendor of having a mind that is set loose by virtue of one's birth into a world accessible to one's reason, with limitless variables to perceive, categorize, and arrange in an infinite number of combinations with which one can improve the quality of life?

My inquiries proceed superbly; our first series of experiments ends on this positive note. All work to cease temporarily. When resumed Horatius will retire, and Penelope will continue as our in-laboratory star.

Narrative by myself—Mathew Wylie.

I have learned a lot about philosophy since I met Dr. Humphries. After my arrest, he brought me a book by Aristotle. About a week later, he came by again and wanted to know if I had read it yet.

"Yes."

"So, what do you think, my little student. Are you not overwhelmed by the magnificence of this great thinker?"

"Uhm . . ."

"Are you not fraught with admiration for the clarity and simplicity of his mind?"

"Well . . ."

"And to think that before him, men looked for understanding from sun gods and centaurs. From Zeus, Athena, Prometheus, and even the delightful demigod Pan, but never did it occur to any of them to look beyond the gods for their comprehension, and to study the most obvious thing of them all."

"Which is what?"

"Which is reality itself, my friend. For reality is all that we have. Ah, if only the great poet Alexander Pope had thought to write a sequel to his poem, adding that if indeed the proper study of mankind is man, then what could possibly be a more appropriate study of reality than reality itself?"

"Are you asking me a question?" I asked Dr. Humphries sophomorically. "Or are you merely being rhetorical?"

"Young man," Dr. Humphries exploded, "I am not being either. I am trying to drive home to you a point upon which your salvation may depend. Pay heed, because this reality of which I speak is not only your best defense, it is also your *only* recourse. Before you discuss this case with anybody, you had best resource yourself of your memory; review the contents of your immediate past and find in it the meaning of all that which has transpired."

The direction and emphasis of all of my talks with Dr. Humphries from that point on were the same: my only way out of the mess that I was in was to rehash the specifics of what had happened; to put these specific incidents into proper sequence; and then to determine what the significance of those incidents can have been.

How much easier this would all have been on me if, instead of being saddled with an Aristotelian like Dr. Humphries, I had had the luck to come under the far less exhausting auspices of a determinist or a Marxist or even a behavioralist. For a determinist would have happily permitted me to believe that what had happened had been completely outside the arena of my control; that nothing I had done or said could or would have prevented that billiard ball named Julian Solo from bumping into the far more delicate billiard ball named Cynthia Wylie. Oh, how morally absolving it would be just to accept a viewpoint in which one exists without responsibility, without guilt, without innocence. Clunk. Hello, Mrs. Wylie. Clunk. Hello, Dr. Solo. Clunk. Screwball in the right pocket. Good night.

Or, being a Marxist. How easy that would be on the anemic and ailing conscience, for whatever one has not (money, property, ethics, talent, conscience), one can blame on those who have; and all activity as well as all responsibility for said activity is reduced to one all-absolving conflict—the class struggle. Why did you send Dr. Solo, a "have," to buy a piano from your mother, a "have not"? Why did Dr. Solo walk into that showroom and look at that woman the way he did? Why did Cynthia Wylie agree to see him again? The class struggle. That is why. Why is that why? Well, why not? Don't bother

45

me. Oh, how lovely and easy and uncerebral it would be to be a Marxist.

Or to be a behavioralist. Here is little Mathew Wylie. He is four years old. His father has just disappeared. He is sorry. He wants a new daddy. Here is older Mathew Wylie. He loves his mother just enough, but not too much. And he still wants a father, because society has taught him that all little boys should have fathers. So, here is Mathew Wylie acting on the compulsions and conditionings that society has imposed on him, introducing Dr. Solo to his mother, because seventeen years before, a mixed-up veteran deserted his wife and son. Wouldn't that all be nice, for then Mathew Wylie would not be responsible for what he has done, because the meeting between his friend and his mother was nothing more than two molecules colliding in the sky, or an extension of a Marxist theory on dialectical materialism, or an "acting out" of behavioral patterns for which we bear no responsibility and over which we have no control.

Yes, wouldn't such an alternative — any alternative in fact — be easier to look at and assess than the reality on which Dr. T. Gideon Humphries, the Aristotelian, unceasingly expounds?

"Before one can understand 'why' something has occurred, he must first with scrutiny comprehend 'what' has occurred. Then and only then can one begin to ascribe responsibility for a given action, if there is indeed any human agency responsible at all."

And so, on Dr. Humphries's advice, I do not herein assume any guilt for bringing Dr. Solo to the piano showroom on Fifty-seventh Street that clear and crystal morning of March 5. I do not deny responsibility, either. I do not analyze. I shall leave that to my friends, my attorney, and my family, if ever again I shall have one. It is for me merely to describe, as Dr. Humphries says, "that which has transpired."

I had left my apartment just after the morning rush hour, and was walking down Central Park West to Fifty-seventh

46

Street. It was the kind of a day that sends a special, urgent message to those who live in five-flight walk-ups, or down the hall from the elevator in expensive catacomb condominiums on the sixtieth floor. A day in which an apartment dweller instinctively knows that winter is about to drop her thick and woolly trousers to reveal the intoxicating aroma of bare-skinned spring.

Spring. It is a call of the wild to a New Yorker. A heady, sunlit drink with a twist of aphrodisiac, no ice, and pardon me, but are you taken for this dance? Strangers not only smile at one another on such a day, but their eyes grope the air to make contact with any other human being, who, with a background of fresh breezes sterilized by bright yellow sunlight, is assumed to be a lady or gentleman of great innocence and unending good will.

Such a day makes one long to have lived a century before, when men could tip their hats to ladies; and then suddenly, it doesn't matter which century this is, because it is March 5, and you are a gentleman, and all of the ladies in the world love you, and the crocuses are pushing their little pointed heads up through the lush, plush, delicious dark earth, and before you know it, you have walked twenty-five blocks, turned, and entered the opulent and austere premises where royalty buys and Cynthia Wylie sells the most expensive pianos in the world.

Now, I shall find it difficult to describe this incredible showroom, this place of business that puts one more to mind of a place of worship for those who stand on the altars of both unselfconscious elegance and music. Music. Music. Music. How shall I convey the look and feel of the pale gold brocade curtains, and the soft, worn, needlepoint floral sofa cushions; the Oriental carpets; the artfully scattered vases; the ornate, gilt-framed oil paintings with diverse styles and by different artists, but all with the same either musical and/or pastoral motifs? What words should I use to convey the overpowering sense of elegance and space with which these rooms surround you, a sense that propels you from chamber to chamber, always to the accompaniment of music? Music. Music, as you open one set of French doors and see before you a tall, slender, elderly gentleman in a dark suit, whose fingers are lightly eliciting rhapsodies from an ebony concert grand. He barely nods an acknowledgment of your presence, and you move on through more French doors, which lead to more carpeted rooms, to more magnificent pianos and paintings and brocades and vases and melodies. Here is Mr. Hazard who used to play with the Chicago Symphony Orchestra, and who has been working at the showroom for more than thirty years. Mr. Hazard is eighty-three years old and his hair is white, but his heart loves Chopin, and his fingers are barely twenty-one. Here is Clarence Fullerton-Peabody, whose father worked in these very same quarters in 1932, and whose grandfather built pianos to be sold here in 1897, and whose great-great-great grandfather designed harpsichords sometime not too long after our Founding Fathers declared this nation to be free.

Here are rooms through which I have often wandered in a dreamy haze, my brain less attuned to the salons through which I was walking than to whatever secret or mystery or romance might be waiting for me just beyond the bend.

It was in these chambers that my mother, Cynthia Wylie, worked eight to ten hours a day, five days a week. It was to these chambers that I had sent Julian Solo when, as my patient, he had mentioned that he was in the market to purchase a piano.

I do not know why, when I so eagerly communicated to Dr. Solo the nature of my mother's profession, it did not occur to me what would have to happen, given the natures of both of them, but when I pushed open the doors leading to the blue brocade parlor off the white marble corridor at the end of the hall, I saw at once the logical consequence of what their meeting would be.

Julian Solo, tall, handsome in that square-jawed, competent, purely American way, seated on a teal blue brocade piano bench, his fingers traveling deftly up and down the keyboard of a baby grand, his mouth almost quivering back a smile that seems ready to illuminate his face with joy. Pure joy. Radiant joy. Manly. Passionate. Powerful. Surging joy. As his blue eyes, larger, clearer, and lighter than ever before, looked up and over to Cynthia Wylie.

I say Cynthia Wylie, because at that moment, and for the first time in my life, I saw her not as my mother, but as a woman. Perhaps, too, for the first time, I realized that she was a beautiful woman. I know for a fact that this was the first time that I ever perceived her as being small, or that I ever perceived her as being feminine.

I suppose it is not unusual for a child who was raised by a single parent to perceive that parent as strong beyond strength, wise beyond knowledge, and all-knowing, all-controlling, all-powerful. Some children with strong fathers perceive God to be something like Daddy, with a faint aroma of after-shave lotion beneath his white beard, and golf bags stored behind the nearest cloud.

I think that if, before I stopped believing in God, I had been asked to describe him, his soul would have looked exactly like my mother's. I do not mean this to sound like feminist propaganda, for I envisioned God as a distinctly masculine being. I realized, however, as I saw my mother gazing down at Julian Solo, that until coming upon them here, in this room, I had also envisioned my mother as a distinctly masculine being. Of course, I had always seen her in relationship to myself. The rule-maker, the bread-winner, the authority, the support system, the all-seeing, all-knowing "mom."

Although some time after my sixteenth birthday, I shot up to half a foot taller than her, my mother's *metaphysical* height prevented me from ever recognizing that a change had taken place. And there is the possibility that if she had not met Julian Solo, if I had not walked in on this intimate scene, I might have lived my whole life believing that my mother was an amazon with a soul that was half merry-go-round and half Mack truck.

But seeing her with Julian Solo changed all that. Or, perhaps, seeing the softness in her eyes as she looked at Julian

Solo is what made the change. Seeing the way her body seemed to lose all of its tension . . . seeing her spine develop a look of pliancy, as if for the first time in her life she did not have to be in absolute control, as if she suddenly realized that she could rely on instead of being relied on . . . as if she could relax. All of these subtle yet to me so obvious reactions to the man whose long, competent fingers traveled up and down the piano as his eyes stared across at her . . . all changed my mother forever for me, and I immediately realized that if she was no longer the man on whom myself, the boy, depended, then I must no longer be the boy, but have become a man.

For I had no doubt, as Julian played . . . what was it that Julian Solo was playing? The eighteenth variation on a theme of Paganini by Rachmaninoff . . . I had no doubt about what was going on. The air was tactile. Electric. Invisible currents were passing from Julian's soul to his fingers to the keys of the piano, to Cynthia Wylie. When I approached them, both of their eyes moved over to greet me. Hello, their eyes said. Aren't we lovely? Isn't life impeccable? Did you really believe the cynics when they told you that there was no such thing as love at first sight? Hear the beautiful music. See the beautiful woman. Oh, was she your mother? Thank you for having kept her safe for me until I came along, but we won't need you here any longer, because, of course, she loves me, and I am the man for whom she has been waiting her entire life, and I shall cherish her and worship her and keep her safe and hold her and love her.

Music. Music. Music.

My mother, Cynthia Wylie, looked like a long, slim column of silver metallic fire as she stood there at Julian Solo's side. She was luminescent with so great a joy that one would have been afraid to touch her, lest he be consumed by her radiance. I did not touch her. She reached out for my arm, though, and pulled me to her side. Then she put her arm through my arm, dropped her head to my shoulder, and smiled down at the man at the piano. His answering smile was an acceptance, a benediction, a blessing, and a bond.

At the age of fifteen, Cynthia Christianson left her home in Plattsburgh, New York, and came to live with her aunt Lotte Miller on Avenue X in Brooklyn. Cynthia's ambition and drive were too big for the small town from which she came, and her musical talent needed to be nurtured, channeled, disciplined, and challenged by the grade of professional that could be found only in a city as big and as conceited as New York.

At the age of seventeen, Cynthia began to believe something she had been told her whole life — that she was beautiful. And it was Miss Rappaport, Cynthia's music theory teacher, who suggested that if my mother wanted to supplement her small scholarship, she might take a portfolio of photographs around town to some of the top model agencies and see if any would take her on.

An agency composite of her taken about twenty-one years ago shows a slim, unsmiling woman with long white-blond hair and a Slavic, sunken-cheeked bone structure. Her forehead was high and her hair was worn pulled back, increasing the serious and severe look on her face. Cynthia's eyes were green, large and catlike, and her naturally dark eyebrows and eyelashes were such a startling contrast to her otherwise all-pervading blondness, that, as Lodi Quay-Stapleton, the president of Lodi Models, once said, "Our clients don't know if they're supposed to think that you are some sort of a mutant, or the most beautiful woman that they've ever seen."

As a model, my mother was only a moderate success, for she was coming of age in an era that venerated the cherub, the pert-nosed, freckle-faced cheerleader . . . the squeaky-clean virgin who, if she ever did condescend to do "it," would do "it" only wearing a madras skirt and a circle pin, with her parents listening at the door in the next room.

Cynthia Christianson was an alien being in a world that preferred the perennial girl to the eternal woman. She belonged in an era of jade cigarette holders, gold lamé gowns, transatlantic cruises, and champagne cocktails; but she lived in an age of bobby sox, jitterbugs, and pom-poms.

51

The successes that she had as a model were almost always for eye, hand, or leg products, and when Cynthia modeled mascara or eyeliner, she was inevitably told to wear a brunette wig, as her hair was far too fair to appear real.

These modeling jobs, few though they were, were enough to pay both for the balance of Cynthia's tuition at the Manhattan School of Music and for the small apartment into which she moved on East Twenty-seventh Street.

June 17, 19—, The New York Tribune. Music Critic, Gerald Blume.

Yesterday, at Carnegie Hall, I had what is perhaps the most perplexing musical experience of my life, for in observing pianist Cynthia Christianson play Chopin's Fantasie-Impromptu in C-Sharp Minor, Opus 66, I found myself unable to shake the feeling that I was watching either a melodramatic film presentation, or a high-priced, high-fashion, dress-designer extravaganza. Undoubtedly, this is because Miss Christianson is such an astonishing-looking creature, and as one perceived her, gowned in black silk, her pale gold hair barely touching a pair of ivory shoulders of a purer and more irresistible white than the keys of the piano . . . as one observed her at stage center with her beautifully shaped arms and slender body perched before the Steinway Concert Grand, one questioned if one was, indeed, at Carnegie Hall, listening to mere music, or if one was, instead, watching the unraveling of an episode from *The Phantom of the Opera*, with the delectable morsel on stage having been provided to us as the talented bait intended to lure an unfortunate monster to a terrible fate.

Indeed, it is even possible that I, myself, am the Phantom Monster whom I have perceived in this drama, for of Miss Christianson's performance, I must darken the horizon with my pronouncement that her beauty will be her undoing, for only a great, great pianist could compete musically with the visual excitement that she brings to the stage. I fear that, although Miss Christianson's playing far exceeds mediocre, as her beauty far exceeds her playing, her talent is not great enough to outweigh the distraction of her looks.

A lesser talent of lesser beauty will go much farther in her career than Miss Christianson. Perhaps there is a moral to Miss Christianson's misfortune that would educate us all, but being unable to perceive it, I state, simply, and for Miss Christianson's benefit, that nobody ever said that life was fair.

My mother, although an accomplished pianist, was never a driven or compulsive person. Had her first concert performance been an outstanding success, she would have proceeded to make a career for herself on the stage. Since she agreed that her talents fell just short of greatness, she continued with her modeling and her musical studies, knowing that she would always be able to do nonsoloist concert playing, teach, or accompany nightclub acts.

The adaptability she had to life's blessings and blows gave Cynthia Christianson's youth a sweet and lackadaisical quality, and when I was growing up she often told me stories about her early years with an air of affectionate humor; I know now that most women in her place would have related these same experiences in tones of martyred self-pity.

I am certain that it was because of her ability to thoroughly enjoy the pleasures she'd experienced that the ordeals my mother suffered so quickly and completely receded to levels of unimportance in my mind. This is why, unlike most children whose fathers abandoned them, I look at my father's disappearance with a detached affection that has extraneous elements of curiosity and sympathy mixed in. I adapted this attitude, in part, from my mother's own attitude toward her errant husband.

As my mother tells the story, she met Martin Wylie just before her nineteenth birthday, in the week between Christmas and New Year's, on the promenade overlooking the

Rockefeller Center ice skating rink. When Cynthia describes the way that Martin was then, her eyes sparkle and dance, and her voice takes on an ebullience, and there is joy in her heart, and love there, too, for the remembered man and the remembered laughter. "I don't think any girl was ever as young . . . as sweetly and ridiculously and romantically young as I was when I met your father. My heart was so happy and so light . . . you know, I was wearing white angora mittens with little roses sewn on them when your father came up to me. And he was so big and strong and handsome, and so funny and gay. Like a character out of a musical comedy, except not so graceful . . . in fact, clumsy, but not clumsy with his mind or his tongue. Oh, dear, it is a fact, Mathew" — and here, my mother would sometimes clap her hands in childish glee — "that your father could talk. Oh, could he talk! He romanced me with words, dazzled me with speeches . . . letters . . . poems . . . even songs. That's right, songs. And before he went to the Far East with his outfit — and he was ever so handsome in his uniform — he sang to me. Yes, he did, and I don't care if everyone in the world tells you that people don't really sing love songs to each other, because when they are young enough, and when their hearts are big and bold and boisterous enough, and when they are in love enough, they can sing to each other all of the time."

Apparently, my father stopped singing long enough to propose, and Cynthia Christianson became Cynthia Wylie on New Year's Eve, 19 — . I know it sounds like a bad joke, but I was born exactly nine months later. And by then, my father was sloshing about in rice paddies, dodging all manner of perils, from low-flying enemy helicopters to fire bombs to babies with hand grenades stuffed into their diapers.

After their marriage, Cynthia and Martin Wylie spent only four days together before he was shipped overseas. "But the words didn't stop when he left," my mother explained, and at this point in the story her voice would lower, and the sparkle in her eyes would mute itself into a tearful sheen. "The letters he wrote, Mathew, why, the quantity of them alone was astounding. Where did he have the time, the space, the sheer and glorious brave determination to write those pages and pages of love?"

I was never permitted to read any of these letters, and despite my halfhearted endeavors, I've yet to turn them up among her things. But she did save for me the delightful notes that he sent me from such remote places as Malacca, Nagasaki, Halmahera, and Chittagong.

"My Dear Boy," the letters would invariably begin, and thereafter would follow little poems that he had composed: "I miss you as much as the starlight is high; I love you as big as a Midwestern sky; I think of you only as much as a lot; my little loved baby, my faraway tot."

My mother said that my father's soul was the stuff of which musical comedies are made, and that when life handed him the sheet music for grand opera, he couldn't take the pressure, and ran . . . or cracked . . . or crumbled.

Martin Wylie was discharged from the Army and returned to us when I was three years old. Mother said that during that year when he lived with us, he was as romantic and lyrical and charming as ever, "but I have no doubt that he was also crazy. Wonderful, attractive, and loving, but crazy. Lunatic. Out."

"Out where?"

And mother would shake her head. "Before he disappeared, he still occasionally would take out a book of Noel Coward's lyrics and make me laugh at the antics of putting Mrs. Worthington's daughter on the stage, or make me tremble at his frailty when he sang to me, 'Someday I'll find you. . . .' My heart would laugh and cry with and for him, because I knew that although this man whom I had married and known and loved was a poet and a lover in the deepest and sweetest and saddest sense of the words, he was also damaged, somehow, and the damage went beyond what he had suffered in the war, to some deep, inner flaw . . . some weakness and sensitivity too great to be able to look out upon life's cruelties without screaming and turning inward and running and hiding in some far-off crevice of his own mind."

It was not long after the love songs and poetry stopped that they were almost completely replaced by complaints about mysterious afflictions that he had acquired overseas. These included cancer in his right (and sometimes left) arm; a metal plate that had been inserted over his skull after a plane crash in Guam and that now caused him discomfort (he had never been in a plane crash, or in Guam); and, among other things, petit mal epilepsy, muscular dystrophy, and heart disease.

At this same time, my father also began to have difficulty holding down a job or finishing anything. He started and dropped out of three colleges. He got jobs at an airline terminal, a department store, and an accounting firm, and quit or just drifted away from them all; and he began to drink, although even as a drunk he never seemed to be able to summon up the follow-through for liquor to have become that thing which was *his* problem.

What *was* his problem?

Everything, according to my mother. Life itself. It was just too vivid and demanding for Martin Wylie. He began to lock himself in the bathroom for hours at a time, ranting about conspiracies in which he was involved and for which he'd been commissioned to kill an enemy agent. Other times, he'd whisper to my mother long, involved confidences about other enemy agents whom he had already killed on missions that he had performed for agencies far too secret to be uttered aloud.

At about the time he began to speak of these conspiracies, my father also started to refer to himself in the third person, often going up to my mother and saying such things as "Martin knows that you don't love him as much as you used to," or "Martin can take it. Don't you ever underestimate Old Martin in the endurance department."

And old Martin *did* take it, whatever "it" was. Week after week after week, until one day, when he had been baby-sitting for me, after he had decided to vacuum and dust our home as a surprise for my mother.

That evening when Cynthia came home from work, Martin was devastated that she did not immediately notice the effort that he had put into cleaning the apartment. But, after he drew the sparkling furniture and newly fluffed-up carpet to her attention, nothing that she could do or say would make up for the initial and inadvertent slight. Hadn't he cleaned all day? And hadn't she, his wife, the mother of his child, failed to notice?

As my mother described it, intermixed with her sorrow about and pity for my father was an almost amused objectivity about the comical nature of his complaint.

"Poor Martin," I once heard her say to my aunt Nancy Lee, "if only his lunacy had achieved a certain measure of stature."

In any event, the night after the incident of the unappreciated housekeeping, Martin walked out on us, never to reappear or return, and other than her calling the police to report him missing, I remember only one occasion on which she discussed him with anyone other than myself.

This was when I was about four years old, and I remember it distinctly. My mother and I were walking down Forty-seventh Street, and we saw a large red-headed man standing about half a block away. As soon as my mother saw him, she began to wave and call out frantically, "Andy! Andy!" She dropped my hand, ran up the block, and jumped into this other man's arms. As I ran after her, he lifted her up and twirled her around, and my mother threw back her head and exulted, "Oh, Andy, Martin has left me. Poor, weak, sad, sweet, and ineffectual Martin has left me. I'm so happy, I could cry." And she did.

Whoever Andy was, an old friend from her school days, a photographer, a musician . . . it didn't matter. What mattered was that here was my mother, at twenty-three years of age, saddled with a child, abandoned by a husband, and her response was joy. Pure, unadulterated, undiluted, albeit tearful, exhilaration. Why? Because she was free.

Of course, as I mentioned before, she did report Martin's departure to the Missing Persons Bureau, and, as a logical consequence, his disappearance was advertised and investigated by the police, but psychologically, my mother was through with Martin Wylie the minute he walked out the door.

His disappearance, although it deprived me of a father, did provide me with another male, in the person of the police officer who did the initial investigation for Missing Persons.

This police officer was and is Michael Patrick Laffy. Mike Laffy to me.

Now, I make fun of Mike Laffy a lot, but the fact is that I love the guy, and other than my mother, he is the most important person to me in the world. He was, I finally figured out after an intense discussion one Sunday with Nancy Lee, my "male role model."

As she explained it to me, back in the era when I was born, neither unwed motherhood nor single-parent families was considered to be productive or healthy for a child. If, in those days, a father suddenly found himself widowed, he would immediately, if possible, hire a female housekeeper or bring his mother or sister or some other lady into the household to provide "a woman's touch."

Equally, of course, widowed or abandoned mothers, although they did not hire male housekeepers, usually sought out a "male role model" as an influence for the child. Particularly if it was a male child, Nancy stressed. Because it was assumed that there were subtle innuendos of speech, manner, attitude, and behavior which, no matter how hard she tried, a woman could not teach a boy, that he had to learn by imitation.

Contrary to the attitudes so prevalent today, there was, when I was growing up, a certain mysterious respect that the sexes had for each other, and a pleasant deference, too. I am also beginning to suspect that despite the modern cynicism and reference to the "good old days" as a time of innocence and naïveté, people thirty years ago knew a great deal *more* about the perils and pitfalls and problems of raising healthy children than they do now. Certainly, Cynthia Wylie did.

She adhered completely to the philosophy that men and women are psychologically as well as physically different from each other, and she knew from the second that her husband left that she needed an immediate replacement as a masculine influence for me, if not for herself. That was where Laffy came in.

Mike Laffy was a third-grade detective with the New York City Police Department when he came to our apartment to investigate my father's disappearance. He looked then very much the same as he looks now, although his hair is sparer and grayer, and, over the years, his posture seems to have improved.

Laffy is medium height, medium build, and you realize he is Irish only after he opens his mouth and the romantic in him begins to spill out. He has grayish-blue eyes, a fat stubby nose, and nice, comfortable, worn, man's hands. My mother once said that "if the rest of Laffy were like his hands, I would have lured him away from his wife and children and married him long ago."

Laffy was about thirty-eight years old when he met my mother, and is around fifty-five now. Then, as now, he had a short, fat, dark-haired, mustached wife who went to church every morning, hated Mike, and brought up their five daughters to do the same.

Before Laffy had transferred to Missing Persons, when he left home every night for his duty on uniformed patrol, his wife would call out after him, "I hope you get into a street fight and they kill you."

His daughters treated him with all of the contempt that they felt he was owed, recognized that he was the vilest of all of God's beings, i.e., a man, a working male, and a basically sweet and inoffensive guy.

One day I overheard Laffy telling my mother that he was certain that if he suddenly took to beating Rosemary, his wife, she would immediately respect him, and that the only problem with using that route to domestic bliss was that if he beat up anybody, he would lose all self-respect.

Mike Laffy did and does respect himself, and with good reason. He is a moral, decent, manly man who deserved so much better than the bovine creatures that he both married and sired. Recognizing how enormously much this man gave me, I can just hope that the love and affection that he got through his attachment to us compensated for the abuse that he continually received at home; as I look back, I am sure that if Laffy hadn't met my mother, he would have left Rosemary and the girls many, many years ago. But my mother's presence managed to make his life so utterly palatable that his times with us more than made up for the suffering that he endured in the minimum amount of time that he spent at home.

But I've gone far afield from that day, seventeen years ago, when Cynthia Wylie and Detective Michael Patrick Laffy met.

She let him in; he asked dozens of police-type questions; she made him a cup of coffee; she introduced him to me; I crawled up onto his lap, put my arms around his neck, and fell asleep.

Poor Laffy never had a chance from that moment on, and if he ever did attempt to find my father, I am certain that the attempt to do so was halfhearted, at best.

That Laffy adored me goes without saying. I gave him the one thing he had never had from another human being—admiration. I idolized him. I respected him. He was my hero. My Lone Ranger, Superman, and Sherlock Holmes all rolled into one. He was that great big godlike presence in my life who taught me how to pick locks, took me to crime labs, and sat me down in courtrooms during jury trials "to learn," as he put it, "about life."

Aside from the affection that Laffy got from me, I suspect the reason that he really stayed around was Mother. I have no doubt that Michael Laffy was in love with my mother.

He worshiped her. He revered her. He loved her with such humility and awe that I always expected him to do something dramatic when she came into the room: like kneel and kiss the hem of her skirt, or bow and kiss her hand, or stand as if frozen and simply stare at her for hour after hour, or cry.

But he never did any of the above. He just gazed upon her, day in and year out, with the earnest look of an obedient dog, and he occasionally brought her a bouquet of flowers or a book that he knew she wanted to read, but she would not let him spend very much money on her, nor, and I realize this now after seeing her in the same room with Julian Solo, would she ever let his love for her become intrusive enough to require acknowledgment.

I have come to realize that the difference in the way that the two men loved Cynthia Wylie was, at the same time that it was subtle, also very pronounced.

In both of their eyes as they looked at her one could see worship. But whereas Laffy seemed to worship her tremulously, as a supplicant, Julian Solo worshiped her forcefully, as a man. Laffy would kiss the ground that she had walked on; but Julian Solo would scoop her up off the ground into his arms and kiss *her*.

One of the reasons I was so glad that I had walked in on that intimate scene in the piano showroom was that it dispelled once and for all the pity I had felt for Laffy over all those years.

Nancy Lee had tried time and time again to convince me of that which suddenly became obvious the minute I saw Mother and Julian together. And that is that Mike Laffy never really wanted Mother to love him as a woman loves a man. Nancy Lee had said once, laughing, that "if Cynthia ever lowered her guard for a minute or softened, or behaved seductively or as if she craved to expose him to her vulnerability, I swear Laffy would croak on the spot."

Now I believe this to be true. Michael Laffy did love my mother, but as a dream woman, as one who was unattainable.

And unattainable is exactly how he had always wanted her to remain.

Me, though, he loved and loves as a man loves a son. And just as my mother gave him to me, so did she give me to Laffy, and on weekends and on holidays, the three of us, and later, including Nancy Lee, the four, became a make-believe family, with more real love and laughter and sharing and affection going back and forth than most families with blood ties even begin to achieve.

Nancy Lee, the latecomer to our trio, lived diagonally across from us, in a large studio apartment on the top floor of our building. When we met her, she was a borderline starving young artist in the best tradition, and like my mother, she was filled with verve and grit and joy and determination. She was, however, more outspoken and fiery than Mom, and part of this overt behavior may have come as a result of an essentially proud, private, and self-motivated individual coming of age in an era of bra-burning lip service to brotherhood. Nancy Lee, although racially Negro, has always taken the posture that she is nobody's damn brother or sister unless her mother or father can *prove* it.

Mom and Nancy Lee loved each other because both essentially loved and had complete confidence in themselves. They were two women who were wildly enthralled with life, surrounded by a humanity that first built and then beat its head against easily circumnavigable walls. Personalitywise, however, Nancy Lee and my mother couldn't have been more different. Just as Cynthia Wylie looked like her soul, with her generally calm and gentlewomanly way of getting things done, Nancy Lee looked and acted like an explosion. Nancy Lee was petite, with a mass of curly, reddish-brown hair, cupid lips, black eyes, silky brown skin, a valentine-shaped face, and a joie de vivre so immediate that one always expected her to be laughing instead of smiling, shouting instead of talking, and painting in only primary colors instead of pastels. That she does laugh, shout, and use bright reds and yellows a lot seems to matter considerably less than that *it has to be so.*

This, then, was our family at the time. Cynthia Wylie, musician, model, and mother; Mathew Wylie, son; Michael Laffy, police officer and surrogate father; Nancy Lee, artist and surrogate aunt.

Amazingly, this tight little group stayed together for many years, carrying me all the way through my childhood, my puberty, and my teens. It began to come apart only two years ago, when Nancy Lee married David Meyers and moved to the West Coast. But it was the second marriage, that of my mother to Julian Solo, that really finished us off.

For there was no viable way for Cynthia and Julian Solo to integrate Patrick Laffy into their lives, and I was too old, by the time they got married, to be anything more than the "occasional child" that all children become after they have left the nest.

So with Mother and Julian living in the big, forbidding gingerbread house overlooking the Verrazano Narrows, and with Nancy Lee suddenly married, maternalized, and relocated to California, that left only Laffy and me.

As I write this now, I fear there is still only Laffy and me. And perhaps, if my attorney doesn't discover something in these notes and journals to redeem me, there will soon be only Laffy.

Memo from Dr. T. Gideon Humphries to Julian Solo, dated April 26, 19—.

Friend, Julian:

My spies have observed pockets under your eyes and electric lights under your doors at hours unbefitting a tenured scholar.

So, what's wrong? You still can't turn into a lazy bum like all of the rest of them? You can't comb through other people's theses for a bit here, a piece there to make a grand and irrelevant paper of your own for a publication no one reads, which will increase your academic stature and lower the hospital's electric bill?

Instead, you have to do independent research late at night?

Julian. Julian. Julian. How can you do such a thing to me, an old man, at an age when nothing exciting should apoplex me.

All my life, I hire research scientists, and I make a little prayer that maybe this one has a mind. Like clockwork, all of them run out of steam before any independent study is done. After years go by of this, a man has the right to a few of his expectations.

So, he hires a research scholar, and the scholar doesn't do research. That's the way it gets to be. Not flashy, maybe, but reliable. And after a while, ten or twelve years, a person like me gets used to being disappointed. At Christmastime each year, does he look into the bottom of his socks to find a movie star in a low-cut dress? No. What does he expect to find there? Coal.

Like always.

So, what are you doing at the bottom of my sock?

My heart, Julian. How could you do this to me?

After all these years, do you think that it's fair not to disappoint me?

At two o'clock today, brace yourself. I come to introspect and observe your findings.

So, maybe you'll even be a little bit glad to see me?

Transcript of Dictaphone tape from Julian Solo to his secretary, Melanie Graice, dated April 26, 19—.

Melanie, head this memo Notes to Myself, and file it under Cryogenic Catalystic Serum. It requires no signature.

Today at 2:00 P.M., Dr. Humphries came by my laboratory to review my findings and discuss my progress. As always in our discussions about the anatomy of the brain or the life span of a molecule, we seem to have drifted (been pushed) away from biochemistry and into the ever-welcoming and unavoidable arms of philosophy. Unavoidable, that is, in any discussion with Dr. Humphries.

Although Gideon had nothing but praise for my work on both the Artificially Induced Hypothermic Response, and deanimation in general, he did raise several interesting points about the practical application of my results, should I achieve the success that now appears to be inevitable.

Of course, his concern was that in the manufacture, marketing, and implementation of this cryogenic procedure, an impeccable standard of ethics be strictly adhered to in order to prevent any usage for immoral purposes, or, as he put it, "to make sure a man with such a good head like yourself doesn't get corrupt from so much power."

I tried to explain that Gideon's concern was both unwarranted and premature. Unwarranted because I believe that I have always maintained the utmost integrity in my dealings with the scientific community, and premature because the global, cosmic, and metaphysical applications of my experiments on a few mice are hardly apparent to me or, as yet, to anybody else.

Although I believe it is wise to make oneself aware of the dangers that result from too much zeal, I also believe that the longevity of Penelope and Horatius are a far cry from a mad scientist in a concentration camp or a "respectable" scientist at an Ivy League university performing merciless experiments on helpless students.

My belief is that as long as one does not experiment on a fellow human being; as long as one does not cause gratuitous pain to any living creature, be it mosquito or mouse, one's avenues of inquiry remain as morally pure as the "pure" scientific research in which one is engaged.

That my work may eventually benefit mankind is as irrelevant to me at this stage as would be the information that at some remote time in the future, a sophisticated band of manipulators learns to misuse my technique of deanimation as a means for faking death and submitting false life insurance claims.

I believe that the morality and integrity of the Louis Pasteurs and Jonas Salks of this world are in no way affected because the vaccines and medications that they invented were used to prolong the lives of madmen who may have then gone on to assassinate innocent victims.

Of course, if I am given the opportunity, I wil keep my formulas and serums far from the grasp of lunatics and madmen everywhere, but in reality, I can be responsible only for that which is under my control.

I do, however, intend to maintain tight, exclusive, and, indeed, peremptory control over all of my work in the field of Artificially Induced Hypothermic Response, deanimation, and cryogenic death.

And, on that note, it is time to put away all thoughts of responsibility, integrity, morality, ethics, and death. For the first phases of my work have been completed; my experiments can be designated an unequivocal success. And I happen to be hungry.

Melanie, delete the last two sentences from this memorandum, and grab your coat. A celebration is in order, and the boss is taking you to lunch.

Diary entry of Melanie Graice, dated April 26, 19—.

It has happened.

Finally, it has happened. But it *had* to happen. I wished so hard and so long for it, and when he was in his office at his desk, I'd close my eyes and pray and send messages to him through the air for him to please pay some attention to me. And now, at long last, he has.

I don't know if it's just that he suddenly realized that I was there, or if the power of the suggestions that I sent to him have awakened him to my love, but finally, finally, he has noticed me. As a woman.

At one minute after one o'clock this afternoon, Dr. Solo threw my coat at me, grabbed me by the arm, and pulled me down the hall, saying (I thought a little bit too loudly), "Celebrate we must, and celebrate we shall."

The place he took me to was one of those French restaurants on Third Avenue that you always read about celebrities going to, and there were no prices on the menu, and I don't even know what he ordered or what (or if) I ate, because all I remember is that he made me laugh from the minute we sat down until after lunch, when he put me in a cab and told me to take the rest of the day off.

The whole time through lunch, he called me Nurse Ames, and I didn't understand why, until he explained that a generation ago, a series of books came out in which a character named Nurse Ames, assisting the dedicated elderly physician, always stood by her doctor during a crisis, and through her loyalty, competence, and consideration, consistently managed to save the day.

Although I protested that, first, I was not a nurse, and second, I had hardly done anything noble enough to warrant such a comparison, he laughingly told me that by today's standards, a nurse, secretary, or assistant who was able to get a telephone message straight, type a letter, or serve coffee without spilling it was enough of a miracle to merit an enormous amount of exuberance.

Dr. Solo ordered expensive champagne, and when we clicked glasses, he toasted something to do with some gland, which wasn't in the least bit romantic, but after my first glass of champagne I became giddy and didn't care, and he was so gentlemanly and interested, and several times during the meal, said, "Nurse Ames, tell me why a little midwestern farm girl came to seek her fame and fortune in the big city," or "Nurse Ames, what is a charming child like yourself doing

67

working in a depressing hospital like ours?," and when I tried to explain that I wasn't from the Midwest, wasn't a farm girl, and that I thought the hospital was exciting, not depressing, he just poured me another glass of champagne and talked on and on about the laboratory mice and metabolism and body temperatures and heartbeats, so that my head spun. And his eyes were so light blue and transparent that when he looked at me I didn't know if he was looking through me, or if I was looking through him, and my heart was pounding against my rib cage as though it were trying to escape, and at last, at long last, he has noticed me, and it is all right for me to be in love.

Diary entry of Melanie Graice, dated April 27, 19—.

This is the worst day of my life.

I hate everybody. I hate him, or at least I would hate him if my love for him hadn't thrust me into such uncontrollable pain. So that leaves her to hate, and I do hate her with such a passion that my teeth are hurting from the way that I am clenching my jaw, and I am almost blinded from seeing what I am writing through a haze of rage that seems to be standing in front of my eyes like mist or smoke or steam from the fire and brimstone that is seething in my heart.

Hatred and mortification.

I have nothing left. Of the girl who floated into the office this morning on gossamer wings with joy in her heart for the man that she loved, there is nothing left.

Slain, like my wishes and hopes and dreams.

My heart, this morning, was a Christmas present all eager to be unwrapped. My body was light, like a child's prayer. My step was lively, like a merry melody. I knocked on Dr. Solo's door, and waltzed in before waiting for a response.

Julian, I said, and ran across the room to his desk.

Julian, I am so happy that I could cry.

I reached out my arms for him.

Julian, let us get together tonight. I live here, on Roosevelt Island, only ten minutes from the hospital. Tonight, let *me* entertain you for dinner, and again we will have champagne and celebrate, but on this occasion, we will not celebrate a molecule or a microscope or a corpuscle, for tonight, and throughout the night, we shall celebrate ourselves.

And I stood there, with sparkles in my eyes and elation in my heart, with my arms wide open and my soul completely exposed. Dr. Solo did not move, but his transparent light blue eyes stared at me without blinking, and his palms fell open and helpless against the desk, and he whispered, "Ourselves?" almost as though in a state of terror or in shock.

And then I knew. I knew that I had been wrong. Wrong. Wrong from the moment he threw me my coat and dragged me out to lunch. Wrong when he toasted a microbe instead of toasting me. Wrong when he asked me to tell him all about myself, but had neither the patience nor the interest in me to listen to anything that I might have had to say. Wrong to interpret his desire to share his professional success with his secretary as anything more than a crumb tossed from a god to a serviceable pigeon that just happened to be waiting humbly at his feet in the right place and at the right time.

I knew, even before he opened his mouth to explain, how grave and mortifying my error had been, and though I could not keep the hot tears from filling up my eyes, I did shake my head back and forth doggedly, murmuring, "No, no, please don't talk like that. No, no," as he stumbled out stupid and irrelevant words to me about a woman named Cynthia, an engagement, a marriage, and an apology if I had misunderstood.

But, "No, no," I continued to cry, and shame myself in front of this man. And other than the shame and humiliation, the only thing I remember about that day is that Dr. Humphries's secretary helped me get on the bus, and took me home, and that when we got in the front door of my apartment, I fainted.

Oh, how shall I face him at work on Monday? I wish that I could die.

Diary entry of Melanie Graice, dated April 30, 19—.

I lived through today, and nothing else that I will do in my entire life can ever be as heart-wrenching. I knew that it was going to be a terrible day. I tried to prepare myself for it, and I wore my brown and beige suit, no makeup or jewelry, so that I would appear to be professional, unhysterical, and businesslike to face what I knew I would have to face.

"Good morning, Dr. Solo," I said to him when he walked into the office. Not too friendly, but not hard or cold, either. The way Mrs. Delahaney had taught us to talk to customers back at the secretarial school.

"Good morning, Melanie," he said back to me, and then he added, "Won't you come into my office for a moment, please."

And I picked up my ballpoint pen and my steno pad, but he said, "You can leave those behind."

I sat down opposite his desk, and my heart was pounding again, the way it had the previous week at lunch, but I didn't allow anything to show on my face as I sat there, and I kept my knees clenched together, folded my hands on my lap, and wouldn't look up into his eyes when he said, "Melanie, I realize that my blundering behavior may have made it uncomfortable for you to continue to work as my secretary. Therefore, I am giving you the option, if you choose to accept it, of transferring out of this department, and working for either Dr. Engelhardt in psychosurgery, or Mrs. Popper in administration, both of whom have openings at the same salary level that you are at present receiving."

I don't know how or why I was able to listen to these words without panicking, but I managed to keep my composure despite the frenzy that I suddenly felt in my heart, and I said, "Dr. Solo, it is not you who should apologize, but I, for my behavior last week was the result of both influenza and exhaustion, and I stupidly came into the office even though I was sick, and the unfortunate result of my combined illnesses and weakened condition was the delirium that I exhibited and seemed unable to prevent. I have rested, however, all weekend, I no longer have a fever, and if you will forgive me for that ridiculous display, I would be very happy to continue as—"

And here I stopped, unfolded my hands, looked up to him, smiled, and said, "—as your Nurse Ames."

I could not have asked for a better reaction. Dr. Solo stood up from behind his desk, slapped his hands together, grinned, and said, "Why, Melanie, that's just dandy."

We spent the rest of the morning in dictation, and I managed to project myself as though I were in a good mood. But inwardly I was screaming, for I knew as our day went forward in pleasant conversation and clever repartee, that were it not for her, for Cynthia, for this white-faced, skinny, bloodless fiancée, he would *long* ago have let his heart reach out to mine.

Dr. Solo has put away his work on the serum until after the wedding. They are getting married in six weeks.

I wish that she were dead.

Engraved wedding invitation from Julian Solo,
mailed May 10, 19—.

On Saturday, the fifteenth of June
at four o'clock
Cynthia Wylie
will honour me by becoming my wife

We would be pleased to have you
share in our happiness
by attending both the wedding service
and the reception which will follow

At the Gingerbread House
on Shore Road overlooking the Verrazano Narrows

R.s.v.p.

R.S.V.P. from Nancy Lee Meyers to Cynthia Wylie,
dated May 14, 19—.

Dear Little Cockatoo:

My heart sings out, Profidia! Profidia! For before you are too long in the tooth, you have decided to make your little niece (alas, how she has wept for you in your spinster state) legitimate at last.

I thought your wedding invitations were nifty, and in lieu of a pair of convenient parents to announce and invite for you, I consider the job you did on yourselves exemplary, at worst.

Now, brace yourself. Are you sitting down? O.K. . . . grab the arm of your chair, because this is going to blow you out of the water.

Instructions: Read the following sentence as fast as the speed of light so that your disappointment is tempered with joy on my behalf.

Ready. Set. Go.

I can't come to the wedding (bad news), because I have finally, after twenty years of excruciating and unrewarded labor (good news) gotten my first one-man show at the Mediterranean (don't ask me why) Gallery on Rodeo Drive in BEVERLY HILLS, can you believe it? And the date of the opening, on which my entire and undivided soul, spirit, youth, vigor, fame, flame, and happiness depend, is June 15, the self-same June 15 on which my very best friend in the whole wide world as well as the aunt of my child and mother of my more-or-less nephew is getting married.

How's that for bad timing?

Of course, when I got your invitation I didn't hesitate for a second to reject my devotion, love, and loyalty to you in favor of my career.

I figured that if you picked a loser, why go to a beautiful wedding the memory of which will just break my heart when three weeks later it is discovered that your handsome prince has another wife in the Ozarks, and three children by Madam Zircon, the infamous reader of palms, tea leaves, and Arabic telephone directories?

On the other hand, if the marriage lasts, and I expect it will, I can always visit you two on Thanksgivings and Christmases for the rest of our lives, and you and Julian can stop up and visit me (make an appointment first with my engagement secretary) in my penthouse studio gallery in downtown-uptown Beverly Hills, and so it won't matter if I miss the wedding. Right?

Oh, I'm mad with joy.

David has gone ecstatic on me, and worked up a humongous telephone bill calling everyone we know, love, hate, and owe money to about the opening. And, of course, little Judy is exhilarated with her mother's success, and yesterday gnawed on three paint tubes (cerise, viridian, and cerulean) in an attempt to let me know either that she wants to follow in my footsteps, or that in my exuberance I forgot to feed the little monster.

And speaking of monsters, how is that son of yours? Is he giving you away at the altar?

I think that's wonderful, and I think he's wonderful, and I'm wildly happy that you've finally found somebody good enough to drag you out of that petrified piano showroom into the LIGHT OF DAY.

What's he like? Is he handsome? Virile? Intelligent? Sophisticated? Funny? Does he have hobbit ears with little tufts of hair growing out of them? Are his hands beautiful? Do the veins in his forearms stand out like Michelangelo's David? If they don't, you absolutely *can't* marry him. What color are his eyes? Blue, I bet. What does he smell like? Sweat? After-shave? Formaldehyde?

Oh, Cyn, I do love you. I am so happy for you that I could cry. I *am* crying. See this discoloration here → ←. That's a tear. *My* tear, shed for your happiness. Isn't that DRAMATIC?

Now, after the bad news of my not coming to the wedding, followed by the good news of my having my first show, I have more good news for you and for Julian (unless he's a twerp).

I'm coming for an all-expense-paid visit to New York *before* the wedding. I'm supposed to go to the Mezzanine Showroom on East Fifty-seventh Street on Saturday to sign five hundred copies of my Central Park lithograph. So I will be able to check out your betrothed and either give you my blessings or have them impounded on your behalf until further notice.

I'm arriving Friday night, 6:30 P.M. at LaGuardia, flight #406A. Can you pick me up? Can I stay with you? Can you get Julian to spend some time with us so that I can take his psychic temperature (as it were)?

Anyway, I have a present for you both, so consider this by way of being a bribe. And an expensive one. I want to see

74

Julian, where you're going to live (what the hell is a "ginger-bread house overlooking the Verrazano Narrows"?), where he works, what his secretary looks like, and how his eyes look when he looks at you.

I want to squeeze Mathew to pieces, so he'd better be there in all of his newly sophisticated splendor. And I want to see Mathew's apartment, as I have a present for him, too.

I want to see old Laffy, and give him a big kiss and a gossip. David is dying to meet him, as my inamorato is definitely a cop-buff, and I've been instructed to invite Laffy to come for a visit to L.A. so that he can teach David and Judy how to pick locks.

And that's all. Phew!

Except. What are you going to wear? Lace? Silk? White? Ivory? Blue?

Oh, I can't wait to see you. Do take care of yourself, and tell Matt and Laffy I'm coming. I love and miss you all so.

Being married to David is wonderful, but one does miss the wild, rambunctious, capricious, and electrifying elements of one's Raw Youth, i.e., you guys.

So, 'til Friday.

Love a trillion times over.

Narrative by myself—Mathew Wylie.

Nancy Lee did come to visit us on that weekend, and my memories of her stay are like those of a childhood birthday party, with merriment and laughter and the constant cheerful explosions of multicolored balloons popping red-ly, green-ly, and yellow-ly all throughout the day.

Thinking back on that time, I cannot help but stand in awe of that tiny woman and her vast quantities of energy, talent, loyalty, and ferocity. Up until my arrest, if anyone had asked me to describe Nancy Lee's soul, I would have done so just as I described above. Joyful. Festive. Abrupt. Explosive. Colorful and cheerfully autocratic.

If asked now, however, I would insist on adding these qualities. She is fiercely protective. Fearlessly loyal. Objective. Keenly intelligent. Ruthlessly organized. It was Nancy Lee who literally punched three reporters out of our way when we were en route to the police department after I was put under arrest; and it was Nancy Lee who has insisted on retaining my attorney, Mr. D'Amato, and guaranteeing his legal fees in the event that the confusion surrounding my parents' wills is never resolved. (If I murdered my stepfather, I cannot benefit from my crime by inheriting his fortune; and if my mother is not really dead, and only time will tell us that, then I cannot inherit my stepfather's fortune from her, because . . . well, it's obvious why I can't inherit.) In any event, it was also Nancy Lee who helped Laffy to ransack Julian Solo's office for his files, contacted Eric Lilljigren in Norway and Dr. Humphries across the hall to get them involved in the case, and who has ceaselessly maintained my innocence in press conferences and interviews throughout the country.

I love Nancy Lee. She is my friend and protectress. If I had had my way years ago, Laffy would have been in love with her instead of with my mother, and would have married her and lived happily ever after. And here in New York, where she belongs. Instead of all of the way across the country, west of the San Andreas fault.

Nancy Lee is an explosion, and Nancy Lee *was* an explosion on that blissfully innocent and ignorant weekend, a little bit over nine months ago, when she flew down the exit ramp and into our arms.

First she hugged and kissed my mother, then me. And then she walked over to Julian, cocked her head up at him like a suspicious puppy, met his eyes, made some sort of a noncommittal clicking noise with her tongue, clasped her hands behind her back, and, still holding Julian's eyes, circled him.

Julian Solo followed her progress with a look of amused attention, and when Nancy Lee stopped walking around him, he stopped turning to keep track of her movements. Then, all of a sudden, as though her scrutiny had been satisfactorily completed, Nancy Lee threw out her arms, broke into a wide, welcoming, truly joyful grin, and announced, "You'll do, Julian Solo. You'll do."

She grabbed him around the midsection, gave him a powerful hug, thrust one arm through my mother's arm and another arm through Julian's (who was now laughing), and turned back to me. She said, "Come on, Junior. Come on. We haven't got all day," and led us merrily on our way.

After we settled in that night, Nancy Lee did, indeed, proceed to see and comment on absolutely everything, as she had promised she would. My apartment was assessed as "having all of the decorating possibilities of an underground crypt," and on Saturday morning, before she was to sign her lithographs, Nancy Lee woke me up with bagels and curtain fabric, infused me with enthusiasm, and then told me what to buy and where to paint so that we could redecorate my living-and-only-room into what she would later describe as "a really snug and attractive little sensory deprivation chamber."

We painted the walls and ceilings white and the trim dark blue. We put up turquoise, beige, and aquamarine diagonally striped drapes, bought an inexpensive straw mat for the floor, and covered my bedspread and chair cushions with the same fabric as the drapes. On the only wall space I had in the room, Nancy Lee hung the present she had made for me: a bright, cheerful, whimsical painting of a small-town street on which six rose-covered, picket-fenced cottages were surrounding (three on each side) a tall, elegant, smart-looking skyscraper. On the top floor of the skyscraper was a large blue flower, giving the building the look of a dapper gentleman in a tailored business suit with a gay boutonniere in his lapel, who has inadvertently stumbled into an early morning coffee klatch.

I loved the painting and what Nancy Lee had done for my living space. I loved her visiting me and the endless chirrup of her conversation as we worked together, and as she bossed me around and told me what to do.

On the Saturday night after she signed her pictures, Julian deliberately stayed at home, thereby graciously allowing the four of us the luxury of a small reunion in my mother's apartment. There were just Mother, me, Nancy Lee, Laffy, and all of our memories of so much interdependency, good times, hard times, laughter, and growth.

I don't know why there was a tearful quality to that little party. Unlike Nancy Lee's going-away party, which despite its riotous laughter also had its share of air-gulping tears, but which, despite the tears, made us all feel as though we were embarking upon a new *beginning*, that impromptu Saturday-night gathering had very much the feeling about it of an ending. The end of an era. The end of the era in which my mother's wise, serene, judicial, elegant, and cheerful counsel somehow touched all of our acts, thoughts, and lives like calming feathers of snow, which beautify all into a gentle but mandatory calm.

The end of an era in which that "something exciting" or rather "someone exciting" was still lurking around the corner and waiting for the two dominant members of our group, and charging us all up with their own breathless anticipation; for I am as sure of this as I am of my own name that during all of those years when I was growing up, both Nancy Lee and my mother were projecting or containing that wild, impulsive, and electric "something" that hovers over one like a magnetic field, and the purpose of which is to detect, engage, and retain the member of the opposite sex with whom one will eventually share his or her destiny.

As best as we could identify it, the "current" has something to do with the unknown . . . with the energy that an unspoken-for male or female inadvertently expends on that mysterious aspect of one's life that is concerned with "what is going to happen next," which, translated, always means "*who* is going to happen next." Will *he* be the right man? The one with whom she'll fall in love? When she goes on this interview with that editor of these magazines, will the subject of the interview make her heart beat faster? Will she be drawn to him? Will he look into her eyes and will she feel a current of sexual excitement that will paralyze her with the realization that "this man is the one man for whom she has been waiting her entire life"?

I am convinced that both Nancy Lee and my mother subconsciously and constantly projected this almost animal magnetism and energy, and that the minute Nancy Lee met David, her magnetism went off to the rest of us, but we didn't really notice its absence because as soon as Nancy Lee was "taken," she just hopped onto my mother's electromagnetic bandwagon, as it were, and began to anticipate on my mother's behalf.

When Cynthia Wylie met Julian Solo, however, and when that for which she had been seeking, and he whom she had been anticipating actually became a fait accompli, all of the extraneous energy that either or both women had been emanating was finally turned off completely and forever to all of us.

And that, perhaps, is the main reason why our little party was such a sweet, melancholy affair. I remember that at one point, Laffy, propelled by who knows what impulse, put on a record of Christmas carols, and despite the beautiful spring breeze coming through the window, we all put our arms around one another and began to sing. Later on, Mother sat down at the piano and played some light Liszt melodies, and throughout the evening we sang a good deal, and looked at one another a lot, but hardly spoke at all, and by the time the three of us left, none of us had mentioned either Nancy Lee's husband or my mother's fiancé, but all of us knew that something which had been was no longer, and that the tight unit into which the four of us had been bound had been dispersed, at last.

Laffy and I put Nancy Lee into a taxicab, and then he and I went for a long, lonely, companionable walk. We walked because, for us, that magical something that is going to happen around the corner, and at which we can direct all of our excess energy and electricity, had not yet happened.

We walked until exhaustion took the place of melancholy. Then we went home.

The following morning was a new awakening, in every sense of the word. The sun shone white and warm in a clear blue sky, and the buildings in the city were sharp-edged and sparkling. As Nancy Lee and I rode downtown to Fifty-ninth Street on the bus, our heads hanging out the windows like children too excited to obey safety rules, we saw a thousand suns reflected in the thousands of sheer glass windowpanes of the buildings lining Fifth Avenue, and each sun seemed to be a new promise about a new option that life held in store for us on that glorious day.

The tram ride over the East River to Roosevelt Island became an adventure far out of proportion to the five hundred or so feet of river that the cable car actually traveled; and looking at Roosevelt Island with Nancy Lee's cheerful, humorous, and slightly bizarre editorial patter made even that terrible place on which Julian worked seem to be more farcical than threatening.

Letter from Nancy Lee to her husband, David Meyers, dated May 18, 19—.

Dear Lonely Old Husband:

I hope you miss me wildly and extravagantly, and that every corpuscle and cell in your body, down to the toenails of your funny-looking feet, are crying out, "Where's my wife?"

Well, youngster, I'll tell you where your wife has been, and YOU WON'T BELIEVE IT.

Remember Roosevelt Island, which used to be Welfare Island, which used to be Blackwell Island, and which . . . God knows what it was before that. Well, Cynthia's True Love, whom I met and who is not only a gorgeous hunk of male animal, but who is piss elegant in the exact same way that Cynthia is, and who, if Cynthia were a bookend, would make a perfect matched set with her for anybody's expensively furnished mantelpiece . . . anyway, where was I. Let me just stop a second here to reread. O.K., now I've got it. Julian Solo, Cynthia's aforementioned affianced, is a doctor of psychobiology (this doesn't mean that he psychoanalyzes amoebae, despite how it sounds), and he works for the Roosevelt Island Psychiatric Hospital, where he is the chairman or dean or whatever of the Psychobiology Department, and when he is not teaching, *he has to go to this terrible island every day* to work and do experiments and things, because he is wildly in love with the King Honcho here, a little grape-nut flake of a man named T. Gideon (can you believe it) Humphries, who is so damn cute that even I'd get on that idiotic cable car and come to this godforsaken place to work for him.

You *do* remember Roosevelt Island, don't you? It's sitting, lóngish and narrow, plop in the middle of the East River, and it extends north to about the equivalent of 115th Street in Manhattan, and south to about where the United Nations complex begins.

I *know* that you are not now nor have you ever been a card-carrying New Yorker, but I specifically remember pointing out Roosevelt Island to you every night we used to take those late, snug, and cuddly walks on the promenade by Carl Schurz Park. Remember how we used to bundle up together on the park bench, looking down at the river and up across the river at that beautiful line of buildings on the island, which seemed to climb gracefully in a series of cube upon cube, to create a diamond-lighted fairyland effect? Remember how I used to call that magical complex in the middle of the river "Oz"? Remember how I always used to say that someday I wanted to *go* there?

Well, ick, feh, gross, yuk. I *was* there, and believe me, it's an awful, terrible, horrible place, even if that cute little Gideon Humphries and that handsome hunk of Julian Solo *do* work there.

Roosevelt Island is absolutely *ominous*.

The ride over on the tram, of course, is a lot of fun. It runs right alongside the Queensboro Bridge, and starts at Second Avenue, so as the car is climbing up the cables for its trip across the East River, it passes lots of rooftops and apartment-building windows, and that, in itself, is a *great* voyeuristic experience.

When the little tram car is over the middle of the river, you get a terrific view up and down Manhattan, and of both tips of Roosevelt Island. So even before you land, you sense that you're going to be going someplace spooky.

For starters, I mean *just for starters*, at the northern end of the island is an abandoned lighthouse; and at the southern end are (get this!) an abandoned insane asylum, an abandoned morgue (yes, morgue; can you believe it?), and an abandoned, falling-down castle. With turrets, ghosts, and all.

The Roosevelt Island Psychiatric Hospital, where Julian Solo works, looks abandoned, but isn't; however, it is grossly underpopulated. And just north of the tramway station, where you get off of the cable car and begin to walk into that part of Roosevelt Island which from Carl Schurz Park looked like Oz, are *two more* gigantic, abandoned buildings. One a quarantine hospital, where the city used to ship its cases of communicable diseases like tuberculosis and the plague; and the other, an almost brand-new, spit and shiny factory, which, aside from the broken windows, looks as if it could be put back into business in less than a day.

These are the buildings we passed (I was walking with Laffy and Matt—Cynthia had gone on ahead and was going to meet us later with Julian for lunch) on our way to The New Roosevelt Island.

Oh, David, it is so creepy. There are no cars on the streets, because cars make noise and pollution, and some genius decided that noise and pollution don't belong in an Environmentally Perfect Place, which Roosevelt Island is supposed to be. All of the buildings there are the same ugly beige, with the same ugly cement beams and facades, overhanging the same ugly, empty, clean beige brick sidewalks, which are in front of the same ugly beige and glass storefronts.

All the stores on the island, except for one stationery store, one restaurant, and one deli, are empty. And the signs on these stores are all printed in exactly the same lettering. Not "Max's Deli" or "Vito's Pizza" but, get this . . . GROCERY (block-letter printing), DRUGSTORE (more block print), RESTAURANT (still more), TAILOR (and more yet still).

Yipes.

And did I tell you yet about the streets? How there was no traffic? Well, that's not completely true, because inching along every few feet were motorized wheelchairs driven by wasted men and women with limp hands that could barely press the "forward" or "stop" buttons on their machines, and who looked past us with dying eyes, and sucked on breathing tubes as their unsmiling and self-propelled neighbors dodged between or past them with the grim-lipped determination of people committed to pretending that it's perfectly normal to trip over fifteen wheelchairs and twelve paraplegics on the way home to one's apartment every day . . . and don't you forget it!

And these somber-looking residents, did I tell you about them? About how the municipal housing regulations for Roosevelt Island had specified clearly that this, being an equal-opportunity housing project, had to have an equal proportion of handicapped and unhandicapped, senior citizens (the only people on the island that looked as confused as we were), Negroes, Caucasians, single people, married couples, Latin Americans, and parents with children.

Nice place, David. A clean, totally integrated little Utopia, where the residents are so afraid either to like or dislike their neighbors that they ignore them, and instead emanate a vague and nonspecific hostility against The Whole World.

Which seems like a good place to tell you about Julian Solo's secretary. Her name is Melanie, and I don't like her. She not only looks as though she should live on Roosevelt Island, but she *does* live on Roosevelt Island.

We met this broad, Melanie, when the three of us trooped up to Julian's office to pick up him and Cynthia for lunch. She may have been nice enough to me in a cutesy-poo way (she was flirting like crazy with poor little innocent lamb Mathew), but once, when she didn't know I was watching her (David, you haven't fallen asleep reading this, have you?), I saw a nasty look that she gave Cynthia, and I swear that there was pure hatred in it.

Cynthia and Julian say that I'm imagining things, and Mathew is infatuated with the little wimp, but when I brought it up to Laffy, he nodded in that Guardian of the Public Justice way of his, and said, "Yes, she bears watching."

Anyway, the rest of the afternoon was an absolute ball. We all wanted to explore the abandoned morgue and castle, but we didn't have time, so Julian said that next time I come in, he'll bring along his revolver (for the rats), and put a necklace of garlic around my neck (for the vampires, ha!), and we can all go wandering through the wrecked-up buildings and LOOK FOR GHOSTS.

I am *wild* about Julian Solo. He is so bright and clever and unfacetious and enthusiastic and handsome (not as handsome as you, of course), and he loves Cynthia so much that I'm surprised she doesn't melt under the hot glances he passes her from his icy blue eyes (if all of those temperature combinations are possible).

Anyway, that darling little peanut, Dr. Humphries (I want to adopt him! He's about a million years old), joined us for lunch, and then we all went back to Julian's house in Brooklyn (it really *is* a bloody Gingerbread House) for cocktails and tea sandwiches, and I got to play around on this wonderful revolving thingamajig for cars at the bottom of the driveway.

After the nibblies, I gave Cynthia and Julian the wedding-present painting that I had done of Cynthia (she cried when I gave it to her; and Julian's eyes teared up, too), and I must say, it is a fine piece of work, and I don't know how I did it, but the damn thing is not only as beautiful as the original, it even has the same serene, wise green eyes that seem to be following you around the room with the same slight, but not very insistent, questions in them, that are usually in the eyes of my best and now Most Happy Friend.

Finally, my dear, sweet husband, that is about all. Tonight I'm sleeping over at Cynthia's apartment. Tomorrow we were going to go shopping, but she didn't feel well at dinner, and I think she's coming down with the flu, so I'm making her stay home, and *I'll* go shopping. The day after that, I'll have to do some color corrections on a silk screen down at the Thirty-ninth Street Studio. Then, after I admonish Mathew to write me every last detail about the wedding, I'll hop onto the airplane that will fly me back into your warm and snuggly strong arms.

Do you miss me wildly? Are you still madly in love with me? How is our little itty-bitty infant girl-child?

I bet I get home before this letter does. I love and love and love you.

Your amiable wife.

Memo from Dr. T. Gideon Humphries to Julian Solo, dated June 12, 19—.

My Dear Friend:

I cannot express to you my delight at having been selected as your best man. However, as the auspicious occasion encroaches, I fear that I am beginning to assume the qualities of what I hear is called "stage fright fever."

Alas, Julian, I am averse to admit it to an apple as polished as yourself, but for a man like I am, who doesn't know even if both of his socks are the same color, and if they match his shoes, and if his shoes match his tie or his suit . . . Julian, the consternation I feel is overwhelming.

What if I should lose the ring? Or lose my way on the highway and appear in Far Rockaway for a graduation instead of in Brooklyn for a wedding? You think maybe you could draw me a map? Or maybe you could still manage to change your mind, and for your best man, you could choose a younger man whose wife knows about such ecclesiastical subjects as should the socks match the tie or should the socks match the trousers?

You think that I am joking, but the stress I feel is axiomatic.

Maybe on the way home tonight from work, you could stop up and see me for a while for the purpose of going through my closet and rehearsing with me what I am supposed to do.

Julian, it's not easy being a color-blind bachelor on the eve of his colleague's matrimonial occasion.

Have mercy. Assist me!

Letter from Mathew Wylie to Nancy Lee Meyers, dated June 17, 19—.

Dear Nancy Lee, David, and Judy (if you're old enough to read this):

I know you've all been waiting anxiously for word about the wedding, and if I could describe it with just one word, that word would have to be *magical*.

I don't know how Julian did it, but the whole affair was something out of a fairyland. And it was all his doing, too, as he planned the entire day so that Mother wouldn't have to lift a finger.

The ceremony was held outside in Julian's big backyard, and instead of decorating with tents or ribbons or Chinese lanterns, Julian had a bower built out of the palest yellow and almost beigey-pink roses, and it was in this bower that Julian and my mother exchanged wedding vows.

Mother (as you see, I am obeying your orders to describe *every last detail*) wore a lacy, ivory-colored dress that came down to just below her knees. The sleeves were tight and ended mid-forearm, and the neckline was round or oval, and very pretty, although it was too complicated to describe. Oh, and the dress had a wide belt, and Mother didn't wear a veil, and she carried a single branch of cymbidium orchids.

Before the wedding, Julian had given Mother a four-strand pearl choker with an emerald clasp, and matching emerald earrings. She wore this, with her hair piled on top of her head, and she truly looked like a fairy princess or an elfin queen. Instead of me walking her down the aisle toward the altar, one almost felt as though Mother should have floated toward her betrothed on a lily pad, as any true heroine of a fairy tale must.

Julian, wearing a tuxedo and bow tie, looked somehow the way I had expected him to look — virile and manly, completely self-confident and in charge, but somehow surprisingly quiet. One might almost say hushed.

When the two of them met in front of the rose trees, one almost expected the very heavens to burst into a solemn and passionate song, and when the judge began:

> Friends, we are gathered together here in the presence of this company to join this man and this woman in the bonds of matrimony, which is an honorable estate and is not to be entered into inadvisedly or lightly, but reverently, discreetly, advisedly, and soberly . . .

when the judge intoned those truly weighty and awesome words, in a voice majestic in its power and depth, one felt that instead of a human being marrying them, it was God Himself.

Of course, everybody was crying before Mother even said "I will." I was crying. Laffy was crying. And when I looked up and saw Julian standing beside his wife-to-be, I was moved to see that despite his serene expression, there were tears in his eyes.

After the judge pronounced Julian and Cynthia Solo man and wife, someone (I don't know who) let out a wild hoot of satisfaction, and from that moment on the mood of the party changed from one of reverence to one of merriment.

I had a wonderful time, although I'm afraid I drank too much, and I am told by Mother, who remembers these things in the way that *mothers do*, that someone took a photograph of myself and Dr. T. Gideon Humphries, who was also imbibing a bit of the grape, and that in this photograph we are said to have had cymbidium orchids behind our respective ears and been perched in the arm of an enormous chestnut tree, reciting Rudyard Kipling poems to each other.

By the way, did you know that Dr. Humphries speaks Estonian? Or, at least, he says he does.

The entire day was an enchantment. The reception was held both inside and out, with the buffet table in a large dining-type room that opened onto a terrace, where a cheerful quartet played romantic melodies to which Mother and Julian danced.

Mother also danced with me and Laffy and Dr. Humphries (he came up to her chin), and Julian danced with several alarming and unmemorable matrons who seemed to have had some reason for being there; but it was the sight of Mom and Julian dancing together that really got one feeling all choked up. He was so straight, strong, and handsome, and she was so graceful, radiantly beautiful, and in love.

Watching them made me wish that I were *old* like you and my mother, so that I could live happily ever after, too. I mean, after watching those two, my peer-group role models just don't make it in their skintight blue jeans with their "I don't give a damn whom I sleep with next" attitudes on life, love, and . . . I was going to say "romance," but I'm beginning to get the horrible feeling that there *is* no romance for people under forty—an ironic twist of fate.

In any event, the party went on for hours, although Mother and Julian left immediately after she cut the cake (and *she* must have been drinking too much champagne, too, because she dropped the knife when she was trying to cut the first piece, and eventually Julian had to cut it), and the two of them drove off to someplace lush and private and no doubt exotic for a three-week honeymoon.

I hope that the piece of wedding cake that I enclosed in this package wasn't too squashed by the time it got to you. Judy will probably like the frosting. Also enclosed is a clipping from the local newspaper announcing the marriage of Brooklyn resident, Julian Solo, to Manhattanite, Cynthia Wylie; and as soon as they are printed, I will send you a set of the wedding photos.

Other than that, Nancy Lee, there really isn't much to tell.

Laffy and I miss you, but you already know that.

Mother said she'd be writing from wherever she went, and if you hear anything before I do, let me know.

Meanwhile, regards to David, and love to the prodigy.

Postcard from Cynthia Solo to Mathew Wylie, dated June 18, 19—.

Darling Son:

I am basking in the sun on this lovely beach, which looks exactly as it does on the reverse of this card. After three days, my marriage is still wonderful, and Julian spoils me in a most congenial manner. Oh, oh. No more space. More tomorrow.

Take care, love. Mom.

Postcard to Mathew Wylie, dated June 19, 19—.

Dearest Mathew:

This morning visited the ruins at Joaquin, and this afternoon, skin diving in the bay. Nights here are balmy and mild. Days clear, warm, and delightful. Julian tans. I burn. Otherwise, we remain compatible. Tomorrow, a *real* letter. I love you. Mom.

Postcard to Mathew Wylie, dated June 20, 19—.

Darling Matt:
　　Things are too idyllic. I can't concentrate to write an entire letter. My mind is filled with the scent of lilies. This morning, we did nothing Oh so nicely. This afternoon, we water ski. Maybe tomorrow, I'll write a real letter. But, Oh, it's so hard to be responsible. What a lovely man I married. Julian says Hi! Love, Mom.

Letter to Mathew Wylie from Cynthia Solo, dated June 22, 19—.

Darling Son:
　　At last I have the time and level of concentration to write you a real letter. But alas, it is at a price.
　　I am propped up here on my terrace, and from my lounge chair I can see both arms of the bay, as they almost completely circle the little harbor. There is a delightful mixture of yachts, fishing boats, and some oddly shaped seagoing vessels that remind me of Aladdin's lamps with sails, and these last are particularly romantic things on which one can imagine all manner of piratical deeds being done.
　　Now, as to the "alas" that I sneaked so dramatically into the first paragraph of this epistle, it refers to your apparently less-than-graceful mother's water-skiing accident of two days (or so) ago, in which I cleverly managed to trip while climbing from the pier to the boat, before I even got up on a pair of skis!
　　How's that for an undramatic accident?
　　In any event, the sprain is not bad. Just a great deal of swelling (which has already gone down considerably), a lot of tenderness (I would not like to be dragging a ball and chain on a chain gang just now), and a curious lassitude that seems

to have either preceded or followed my accident, but that I am thoroughly enjoying.

Julian is sitting here beside me on the patio, and continually pops up to get me pencils, stationery, exotic drinks that flow out of orchid-covered coconuts, and pillows. In a way, the little accident has been a blessing in disguise, as now that we can't *do* anything, at least for another few days, we are finding so many things to talk about. I even told him about your father, and the words were hardly out before he told me a story about his college roommate, a man whom he, too, loved. And the stories, indeed, ran parallel.

Perhaps there is a psychological type that men like your father and Julian's roommate represent. I am just so terribly happy now, that I find I have been thinking of your father for the first time in years, and hoping that if he is alive somewhere, someone believes that he really is a spy or a fighter pilot or a captain in the French Foreign Legion.

The day has been so lovely, my beloved son, and now, my thoughts turn to you, and to the exquisite luck I have had in enjoying your company all of these years. I thank you for the manly way in which you walked me down the aisle. I thank you for having tried, and succeeded, to care for the man that I married, and I thank you for being so happy on my behalf.

I was always blessed with you, but now I am twice blessed with Julian here at my side.

And he is at my side right now as I write this. His feet are propped up on the balcony, a straw hat covers his face, and from the way the book is lying open on his lap, I would venture to suggest he is having a little siesta.

I'm afraid the power of suggestion is drawing my eyes shut, too, and perhaps I will join him in his nap.

Otherwise, all is well here, although the pace has slackened considerably.

The day after tomorrow, we begin a two-week cruise of the Outer Islands, and all the way down the coastline, stopping at the main cities along the way. We are hoping my foot is well enough to trek to a few ruins, but I frankly don't think either of us really cares, as long as we are together.

Mathew, may you someday love and be loved the way that I do and am.

Meanwhile, take care of yourself, and remember that I *truly* treasure you.

Letter from Cynthia Solo to Mathew Wylie, dated July 4, 19—.

Matt:

I know that we are flying out tomorrow night, and that I will get home before this letter reaches you, but it feels strange being out of the country for the first time on the Fourth of July, and since nobody is celebrating down here, I just wanted to do something patriotic to commemorate the occasion.

So wish America a Happy Birthday for me, and may she have many happy returns.

Love, Mom.

P.S. Wait until you see the wonderful presents we bought you. You'll have to rent a warehouse! You *do* need a quarter horse, a mule, and an adobe hacienda, don't you?

Narrative by myself—Mathew Wylie.

Of course Mother and Julian did not bring me home either animals or a house, but they were laden with wonderful trinkets both for me and for themselves. They brought me an intricate and colorful Aztec mosiac calendar, the type that one often sees in museums, although this one had neither grimacing gods nor monsters on it. Since I did not have a spare wall on which to hang it, all of my other walls having been taken up with either window, doors, or hallway entrances, I had to move Nancy Lee's painting up a bit too high, and hang my mosaic down a bit too low, so that they could both share the same wall.

Mother and Julian also brought me mohair sweaters made by Indians; attractively carved primitive sculptures of elephants, monkeys, and eggs; turquoise cuff links; and a colorful woven rug.

They got off the plane looking tanned and healthy, and if I could throw my mind back to that date and make an ominous forecast based on their appearance, the only thing on which one might have been able to foredoom disaster was my mother's thinness, for although always a slender woman, on her honeymoon, she appeared to have lost even more weight.

To say that at the time this weight loss made me either suspicious or apprehensive, however, would be to misconstrue the facts. My mother, Cynthia Solo, looked more beautiful than I had ever before seen her. Again, part of this beauty may have come as a contrast to the tall, handsome man who walked beside her, and much of it may have resulted from the glowing love for him that she felt and that was illuminating her eyes. Nevertheless, her beauty that day was of the kind where strangers stop in their paths (they did) and stare at her.

Her skin, instead of having tanned or burned, seemed to have taken on a glow. All of her natural colors were intensified, rather than changed. Her hair had been bleached by the sun into the almost translucent gold — or was it white? — that had been its color in the photographs that I had found from her modeling days. Her green eyes seemed to have become both greener and more speckled with yellow, as though they had gone almost overnight from emerald to a particularly compelling shade of hazel. Although she wore no makeup, her naturally dark eyelashes and eyebrows framed her eyes bewitchingly, and as one looked at her, one felt one understood for the first time what songwriters meant when they wrote songs to gypsy eyes, witches' eyes, eyes in which one could drown. And so on.

Mother was wearing a pale-blue denim shirt tucked into white linen pants. Julian was wearing a white open-collar shirt over khaki slacks. They walked off the plane holding hands, and as they moved toward me, I remember thinking two thoughts almost simultaneously. One, that I loved these two individuals; and two, that they looked like the perfect couple, and that unlike most "perfect couples" these two were as pure and lovely inside as they were outside. Contrary to the popular bromide, there has never been any doubt in my mind that Julian Solo could be as much a hero to his valet as Cynthia Solo could have been a heroine to her maid, if either of them had had either of them. Nor, and this may interest you, has there ever been any question in my mind about Julian's love for and devotion to my mother. I have never seen such love of any man for any woman.

Perhaps the problem was that Julian loved his wife just a little bit more than his wife loved him. And perhaps his wife already loved him to the rational limits of a human emotional response.

Regardless of the nature and depth and the ultimate course of their passion for each other, it was obvious in watching them as they debarked from the plane, that they had had a wonderful honeymoon, and that they were still having a wonderful time.

Julian went back to work on Roosevelt Island the Monday after he got home, as did my mother to the piano showroom. She did not intend to resume giving private piano lessons, though. All of her students lived in Manhattan, and she now lived in Brooklyn. Besides, she had never particularly enjoyed teaching the piano to children, but had done so because she needed the additional income. She did plan to resume teaching, but this time through a university, and only to adults.

Cynthia Solo did not intend to do this, however, until she and Julian had redecorated the house. For the first time in her life, she had both money and options, and she intended to enjoy herself to the fullest, exercising the latter, with the former to pave the way.

I can remember so clearly those first few days back from her honeymoon, how completely delighted she had seemed with her new life, and how, when I came over for dinner, she dragged me from room to room, telling me where the melon carpets were going to be, and how the sheer, embroidered curtains were going to delicately offset the heavy velvet drapes.

Even toward the end of the week, when her energy seemed to have waned, when her enthusiasm dissipated, and when she took so long just to compose a single note to be left for the mailman, I did not realize that there was anything wrong with my mother, because the smile on her face for me and for Julian was still so warm and real, so genuinely happy and loving.

It was not, in fact, until Nancy Lee had come and gone that any of us suspected that something might be seriously amiss.

Letter from Nancy Lee Meyers to Cynthia and Julian Solo, dated July 11, 19—.

Dear Lovebirds:

Here comes the Mama Hen to check out her little chicks and make sure that you aren't mistreating each other. YOU KNOW WHAT THAT MEANS, JULIAN! When I arrive, Cynthia had better be positively dripping with diamonds and emeralds. She had better have an upstairs maid, a downstairs maid, an in-my-lady's chambermaid, and a butler, a chauffeur, a gardener, a butcher, a baker, and a candlestick maker.

In fact, when I visit your domicile, I want to discover that the woman who married Julian Solo has transformed herself from a useful, productive, purposeful, and intelligent individual into the spoiled and frivolous plaything of a wealthy man.

Enough is enough already, kids. I mean, when after forty years you finally manage to get it, FLAUNT IT!

Are you making her flaunt it enough, Julian Solo? She's a stubborn woman, you know. At least, for heaven's sake, make sure that you've made her hire a full-time maid or two and a cook. I mean, that gothic cookie jar you live in could whack the breath out of a full platoon of charwomen.

O.K. Enough lecturing. You want to know why I'm bothering you, right?

Well, it's just more good news, of course. I mean, when you're hot, you're hot.

My publisher (I bet you didn't know I had one), *but*, my agent is married to Bob Greenberg, who isn't an editor himself, but whose sister, Marge, works in the children's book section at Harbour House, and she has a writer named Shari Seufert, who just wrote an insipid children's book called *Jennifer Takes a Leap*, and they (meaning everyone in the whole wide world) want me to illustrate the book.

Of course, I'd pay them for the opportunity to do anything that will eventually bring me a royalty check, but my agent (who doesn't tell her husband everything because he *does* tell his sister everything) has told me to fly to New York, at Harbour House's expense, and negotiate tough, as though they need me (ho ho) more than I need them. Did you get all that?

Ain't life grand!

Anyhow, save ALL DAY SUNDAY for me. And I don't even have to sleep over at Matt's this time. Harbour House is paying my hotel bill. And, no, I will *not* sleep over at your new house. At least not yet. After you've been married four months, you're fair game.

But now, for the first few months, at least, the whole damn thing is still SACRED.

Meanwhile, polish the silver and put a light in the window. I can't wait to see you.

Oodles of love.

Entry into personal diary of Julian Solo, begun on July 12, 19— .

I have never kept a personal journal, and I've always been somewhat suspicious of those who do, particularly of those brooding individuals who hunch over narrow ruled pages in dimly lighted rooms to do in-depth analyses of the lint that did or did not appear in sufficient or insufficient quantities in their belly buttons.

To expand my disclaimer, I have always considered the purity of the motives of these literati suspect when informed that they make entries into these journals at those intimate times of night when their spouses are sitting across from them, ignored, as the diarist sits intently over his journal in full view of the mate who is forever barred from perusing the thoughts penned therein.

Indeed, I think diaries are rightly the psychological playthings of late adolescence, wherein one secretly discusses with oneself the mortification of one's first blemish or most recent rejection.

I believe that a diary—an intimate dialog in which one reveals his innermost angers, outrages, excitabilities, and ecstasies—has no place in an unhappy marriage, and even less in a happy one.

I believe that there is an element of sadism in the diarist who, after a fight with his wife, turns his back on her and begins to scribble furiously about that to which she is forbidden access . . . but which she knows is about herself, and which she knows is filled with venom, hatred, or wrath.

Just as foolish is the man who has shared delight with his beloved, who then walks across the room, turns his back, and shares with the senseless, deaf pages the exhilaration of his delight.

In both instances does one deny from the man or woman most entitled to it, the awareness of his or her mate's thoughts, feelings, and intentions.

It is in no way my intention to deny anything to you, Cynthia, who are my wife, my life, my soul.

Rather than a diary, this is but an open letter to you, which may bore you to death, since the recurring theme is always the same—the love that I bear you; and I write here rather than speak these words to you only because my heart is still overflowing with love and my mind is brimming over with things both nonsensical and adoring that I want to say to you, but can't, because you are asleep.

God, how I love you.

I can remember back now to the first time that I saw you. As I think of it now, I can't help but smile over the line Noel Coward wrote about the potency of cheap music. There we were, surrounded by concert grand pianos. In the next room, someone was playing Grieg. On our other side, we could hear strains of Rachmaninoff's Second.

But what words and melody come to my mind when I think of that moment? Remember the Rodgers and Hart song that went like this:

> I took one look at you
> That's all I meant to do
> And then my heart stood still.

Isn't it silly. And isn't it true. Cheap music? Cheap sentiments?

Cynthia, my darling, my wife (beautiful word, *wife* . . . it should be carved in marble someplace over an important doorway to somewhere) . . . Cynthia, have you ever wondered why all of the world's great music is either sorrowful, brooding, ferocious, or, if less darkly passionate than the norm, written for eunuchs to sing to a nonexistent celestial being?

Do you realize that were it *not* for so-called cheap music, we few fortunate souls who are happy—and not just happy, but exquisitely in love—would have no preexisting medium with which to express our sweet joy?

> Though not a single word was spoken
> I could tell you knew

> That unfelt clasp of hands
> Told me so well you knew.

And my heart *did* stand still. Sometimes I think that before you even turned around, the moment I walked into the room and my skin touched the same air that your skin had touched . . . I knew.

I was in love with your back, first. So slim and graceful. So soft. Cynthia, how can anyone so slender be so soft? I am a scientist, and I say that it is biologically impossible!

And yet it is true. You are soft, and you are true.

And after I had finished falling in love with your back, lingering a moment over your legs, I fell deeply and madly in love with your hair, which I feel, in its own way, is beginning to love me, too.

There is this one strand at the base of your neck (have I forgotten to tell you how I adore your neck?), and when I put my forefinger up below your ear, this one strand of hair inevitably leaps toward my finger and curls around it, just like a baby's hand.

See, I told you that your hair loves me.

Cynthia, I cannot go on now about your face. I cannot tell you how, when I first saw your face . . . when our eyes first met . . . how I died for a second because what I was feeling, what I instantly knew in that second about us both, was too much. Too intense. Too exquisite. Too big. I must have died for that second, in order to summon up the strength to live through that next moment when the vision and meaning and force of you . . . of your essence, exploded in my heart like a . . .

Like what?

My Cynthia. Cynthia Solo, née Wylie. Cynthia Solo. It sounds good. Beautiful, but strong. Like my wife. MY WIFE. God, how I love the words.

God, how I love MY WIFE.

Cynthia, do you know what an absolute disaster you are to my work? Do you know that the amount of work I did this week on my cryo-scientific experimentation was considerably less than zero?

Do you know that I spent the entire week gazing out the window of my office, staring at a sprig of wisteria and humming?

And I wasn't even humming anything specific. I was just humming, in general—metaphysically. Like a happy vacuum cleaner or a refrigrator generator or a field full of inefficient crickets.

Penelope and Horatius are outraged at my behavior, or lack thereof. They are accustomed to my rigid policy of regimentation. I come in at 8:00 A.M. "Good morning, Herr Doctor," they squeak in unison. "And what will be our duties and responsibilities for the day?" Followed by blood sampling, pulse taking, maze running, chart filling, and the whole gamut of laboratorial minutiae that fills up an experimenter's day.

Now, however, when I come in, usually after 9:00 A.M., and when pretty Penelope and brave Horatius squeak "Good morning, Herr Doctor," I inevitably amble over to the cage, lift the lid, give the little beasties a treat of honey and Cheerios—they're mad about Cheerios, don't ask me why—and then proceed to scratch the scruff of their necks and rub their little tummies until interrupted by the first telephone call of the day.

Alas, I fear that as a result of this bizarre behavior, any day now, as I walk past their cages, rather than being greeted by my customary "Good morning, Herr Doctor," Penelope and Horatius are going to remain slumped sloppily in their cage, scratch themselves under their armpits, and slobber out disrespectfully, "Hey there, Doc. What's happening, Man?"

And all because of you, my darling. Thank the stars; all because of you.

You know, it's curious, Cynthia, about motivation, and despite what I have just written, I am not really spending my days mired in sloth. But about motivation, it is interesting that since meeting, falling in love with, courting, and marrying you, the entire thrust of my work has shifted dramatically away from my Cryogenic Catalystic Serum and to the biochemical interaction of cerebral molecules during the act of creation. I am wondering if there mightn't be a way to chemically enhance the creative process. Aside from the obvious applications of making people brighter and more productive and improving the learning potential of Down's syndome children, I wonder if this might not be the exact avenue for which we've been searching, and which might lead us to the breakthrough we need to interrupt the progression of Alzheimer's disease, also known as premature senility.

But that's not what I want to write about or say to you now. I can babble on about my theories anytime. Here, now, in the gentle lassitude of the night, with you lying almost within touching distance of me on our bed, your beautiful hair, which is in love with me, framing your face like a blessing, I think about mortality — yours and mine — much differently from how I ever did in the past.

I think not of prolonging life, but of savoring it; I think not of minideaths that would add years to life, but of life itself, long and not always smooth, with its ripples of sorrow and leaps of joy, moving along gently in a continuum from being born to dying; I think of life, now, not as that which exists in defiance of death, but as a celebration and a sharing. Perhaps even before you came along I had known that life is supposed to be a celebration. But you know what it's like to go to a party alone. How even though all of the trappings of joy are there, and you are ripe to partake of them, they don't seem to have been put there for *you* . . . when you are alone.

A celebration *and* a sharing. And now, since I have found you, I may share, and therefore, I can finally celebrate completely.

> Take my heart; I shall have it all the more;
> Plucking the flowers, we keep the plant in bloom.

Those aren't my words. They were said by Cyrano de Bergerac to Roxane.

These, now, are my words.

Wife. My wife. Cynthia. My beloved. Love me. Live with me. Allow me to give to you, and give to me. Hold my hand when we go walking together down the street. Let me worship and adore you. Share with me my zest in being alive. In my potency. My creativity and my intellect. Smile with me and beside me as we grow old together, from year to year to year. Stand with me, our heads thrown back and laughter in our hearts as we face the highs and lows and quirks and fate of a life that will overflow with gladness like a cornucopia of lilacs tumbling over the edges in an exuberance of joy.

And now, at last, to bed. I am finally tired enough to go to sleep. I am finally aware of how rapidly discovering the "Secret of Life" has become a deadly bore to me, since life itself has been revealed in the person of the woman I love. And if you should ever become curious enough about what I have written here to read these pages, I again borrow a line from Edmond Rostand:

> . . . unto you my whole heart gives one cry.
> And writing, writes down more than you receive;
> Sending you kisses through my finger-tips —
> Lady, O read my letter with your lips!

Narrative by myself—Mathew Wylie.

A little less than a week after Julian began to write his open letter or diary to his wife, Cynthia Solo received a handwritten note from Dr. T. Gideon Humphries. (Although my mother showed it to me at the time, I have been unable to locate it among her things.) It began with a cheerful paragraph or two thanking her for her hospitality at a recent dinner and complimenting her on the change she had wrought in Julian Solo.

The latter part of the epistle discussed the nature of the work that Julian was performing at the Roosevelt Island Psychiatric Hospital, and the nature of the scientific inquiry in which he was engaged. Although I cannot quote it verbatim, I do remember one sentence from the end of the letter, which struck me as being intriguingly melodramatic and uncharacteristically grammatical.

It went something like this:

"The allegedly fine line between genius and madness is actually far wider than fine and much thicker than a mere line; the gulf that separates an angel from an opportunist, however, is often no wider, at its origin, than the uninspected passion to do the right thing, without the intellectual analysis required beforehand to determine what, exactly, right is."

The point of Dr. Humphries's letter was that since Cynthia had come along, he no longer felt compelled to constantly oversee Julian's tendency toward philosophic laxness, and that her presence seemed to have made Julian less eager to batter down the doors of nature's secrets and more eager to ferret out the key, turn the knob, and walk in like a gentleman.

Written in Dr. Humphries's curiously convoluted style, the effect of the letter was charming, despite or because of his ever-reiterated theme of philosophy, philosophy, philosophy as man's moral means of survival, as well as his salvation. In thinking about the letter now, I wonder if Dr. Humphries always tried to get Julian Solo to read Aristotle, as he had me.

In any event, my mother had been delighted with the correspondence, and told me that after we finished lunch she was going to go up to her room for a half hour and pen him a quick reply. Mother suggested that I read the newspapers, and that by the time I was finished, she would be down.

Two hours later, after having finished both newspapers *and* both crossword puzzles, and after an impromptu nap, I climbed the stairs to her room.

Cynthia Solo was sitting at her desk with a pensive, determined, and slightly slack-jawed expression on her face. When she heard me at the door, she looked up and smiled.

"Come on in, son."

I walked across the thick, plush carpet and looked over her shoulder to her desk to peruse what she had written. In wide, sprawling, uncoordinated script, I read these few words:

Dear Dr. Humphries:
Thank you so much for your flattering and charming

"Mom," I said, "is that all you've written?"

"Yes, Mathew. Why? Is there something wrong?"

"You've been up here over two hours."

"Oh, I'm sorry. I didn't mean to leave you alone so long."

"What have you been doing all this time? Daydreaming?"

"I don't think I was daydreaming. I've been writing to Dr. Humphries."

"Are you feeling all right, Mother?"

"Well, I am a little tired."

I took the pen out of my mother's hand and refused to leave the room until she had taken off her shoes and lay down on the bed. I think she was asleep before I had even closed the door behind me.

I determined, at that point, to call up Julian that very evening after he had gotten home from work and tell him that I was concerned that Mother had become overtired from the excitement of too many changes in her life in too brief a time. I felt that up until her marriage, her life had moved along fairly consistently in one direction and on one plane for approximately twenty years, and that the marriage, the honeymoon, and the move to Brooklyn, all within a matter of months, had worn my mother down.

Oddly enough, the deterioration in her handwriting barely touched my consciousness and thus caused me no apprehensions whatsoever. I considered that merely a symptom of exhaustion, and I thought that a good night or two's sleep would instantly bring that gangly, ill-formed lettering back to its gently refined norm.

Before I had an opportunity to call Julian that evening, however, I met with another cause for alarm in the form of a

104

letter addressed to both myself and my stepfather. It was from Nancy Lee, dated the day before.

Letter from Nancy Lee Meyers to Mathew Wylie and Julian Solo, dated July 17, 19—.

Dear Matt and Julian:

I am writing this on the plane, because it wasn't until I literally left earth and was staring at the monotonous clouds that I guess my brain had the peace and quiet it needed to sort out all of my impressions of the week, and click them into a meaningful panic.

And what I feel now is exactly that: panic. Maybe it's a good thing I'm nine or ten thousand feet from a telephone, or else I'd be calling you up and probably not making any sense. And it is most important that I *do* make sense, and present my evidence to you calmly, clearly, and logically.

I will mail this off to you by guaranteed overnight delivery the minute I land, so that you get it first thing in the morning. The reason I sent just this one letter to the both of you is twofold: One, it concerns the both of you equally (perhaps you a bit more, Julian, as you are both her husband and a man of science); and two, because if trying times are ahead, you will desperately need each other's support, and so you may as well start out together now.

Now, remember, IT MAY NOT BE ANYTHING TERRIFYING, and I am PROBABLY OVERREACTING. But . . .

The very first change I noticed in Cynthia was her speech. Usually, words spoken by her are perfectly formed and enunciated. I remember once, after I heard a record of beautiful French poetry, I thought that although French was a wonderful language to slobber about love in, English, when spoken the way Cynthia did, was the language best suited to communication; the language of clarity and definition.

105

I've always thought of Cynthia's speech per se as pieces of cut glass. Not that she spoke coldly or abruptly, but that each syllable she formed seemed, before it was spoken, to have first been precision cut, designed, and polished.

When Cynthia met me at the airport last week, her lips seemed almost to struggle before she could pronounce a single word, and the words that she did pronounce came out slurred and imprecise.

Granted, it was hardly noticeable. In fact, nobody else did notice . . . certainly not the cabdriver when she competently gave him the instructions to get to my hotel. But *I* heard and saw the slur.

That was the first indication.

The second was the deterioration in her handwriting. Have you seen anything that she's written lately? She writes like a mentally retarded ten-year-old in a bumpy car going over a landscape cluttered with craters. The letters go all over the page, and when she writes, she concentrates so deeply and intently that I almost expect her to start mouthing the letters with her lips, the way a child does when he is first learning how to handle a pencil.

And worse than any of the above, Matt and Julian, is that CYNTHIA DOES NOT NOTICE THESE THINGS IN HERSELF. It took her an entire hour to write a note to her maid that said: Mrs. McIver, please defrost the refrigerator.

Not only did she not know that it had taken her so long, she also did not realize that her handwriting had become sprawling and infantile.

I've also noticed that Cynthia is tired. All of the time, she is tired. When we went together to purchase lingerie, she said that she wanted just to sit quietly for a moment while I shopped; at my hotel, she fell asleep on my bed while I was putting on my makeup; and when I dropped her off at the showroom on Fifty-seventh Street, Mr. Hazard, that darling old man who also works there, took me aside when Cynthia had gone upstairs to put away her things and asked me if my friend was all right. "I fear," he said, "some neurological dis-

106

order, as her piano playing and state of mental acuity have deteriorated so rapidly in the last two weeks."

And that, kids, is it in a nutshell. If I have noticed it before either of you, the reason is obvious. Distance gives one perspective. Slight changes can become drastic, and go unobserved, if they happen slowly enough and over a long enough period of time. The time *is* long enough, now, though, and the change *has* become drastic. There is something very wrong with our friend/mother/wife, and I am afraid about it.

Terror was struck in my heart just before we parted, at lunchtime, when I asked Cynthia to pass me the salt. She picked it up, awkwardly, and as she passed it to me, she did not do so with fingers extended toward me, as she normally would have, but with fingers pointed backward, and with her hand leading by the wrist.

You know what jerky, uncoordinated hand movements this brings to mind.

I urge you to take Cynthia to see a neurologist AT ONCE.

I was never one for praying, but right now, in my heart, I am already down on my knees.

Call me *as soon as you find out anything*. Anything, do you hear? ANYTHING!

Narrative by myself—Mathew Wylie.

I did not even stop to telephone Julian after I had read that letter. I folded it into my back pocket and ran to the subway.

An hour and a half later, Julian and I were sitting at the kitchen table and he was reading Nancy Lee's ominous warning. Mother, prophetically, was already in bed, sleeping, although it was only 7:00 P.M.

When I think back now on Julian's reaction to the letter, I seem to see him as if through the glass barrier of an aquarium. Everything about him during those tense, heart-shattering minutes had a quality of alien and terrible beauty about

107

it. I don't know why I think of an aquarium, a gigantic thing filled with shimmering, exotic life forms, gracefully twisting plants, and fairy castlelike projections of rocks, but I do. And I see Julian as if he were standing on the far side of this glass enclosure, the golden scales and flowing tails of fish darting past him in streaks of luminescence, as his head is bent, ever so slightly, over the letter.

I see the letter itself, not as something written from a girlfriend in California that I, an unemployed, undirected stepson had given to my stepfather. I see the letter as a vital missive, wax sealed with the insignia of a king, sent secretly to Julian, and concerning a matter of grave and royal concern.

Julian I see as the bejeweled, rich-beyond-riches prince, king, or maharaja. Cynthia is his wife, his queen, and his consort. The letter itself is a correspondence of vital concern to them both, read with the seriousness of intent of a conquering hero by an individual who had the strength of character, the awesome wealth, and the intellect to deflect an attacking army with the elevation of an eyebrow or the calculated flick of a wrist.

Perhaps Julian, simply by virtue of being Julian, lent to all of his actions a particular quality of majesty. Perhaps in his nature and being there was a certain ineffable something. That same something that makes some men follow other men into battle, or makes unruly gatherings hush to an awed murmur when a man of this caliber walks into a room.

I don't know what it was. I do know, however, that without rank emotionalism, dramatic outburst, or even minimal gesturing, Julian conveyed to me, by his posture, by the way he held the letter in his hand, by the ripple of muscles in the area of his clenched jaw, the dread seriousness with which he treated this terrible information.

I became, in that moment, Julian's lackey . . . messenger . . . aide . . . whatever you want to call it. I recognized not only that he was in command of both himself and the situation, but also that he was best suited to be. In that instant, I seem to have volitionally given up all of my rights as Cynthia's son in deference to what I considered Julian's far superior judgment in determining the course of her treatment. It seemed to me then much more sane and practical to subordinate myself to an individual who so obviously knew exactly what he was doing.

And that is what Julian was like in those days. Do you think now that it was irresponsible of me so willingly to suspend my own judgment to that of Julian Solo?

Ha! Had you known him at the time, had your loved one's life been in jeopardy . . . I defy you to have resisted the compelling force of Julian Solo's competence.

Without a word, Julian placed the letter on the kitchen table and went to the telephone. Within seconds, I heard this half of the conversation:

"But I must speak to him immediately . . . my name is Julian Solo. I've been a colleague of Dr. Ziegler's for twenty years . . . Thank you, I'll wait . . . Solomon? This is Julian . . . Thank you. I'm fine . . . No. It's my wife . . . I'm not sure, but it appears to be neurological in nature . . . slurred speech, jerky hand movements, constant exhaustion, loss of manual dexterity . . . Not that I can remember, except for a touch of the flu just before we were married . . . about two months ago . . . Yes, I know. I'm worried too . . . No, Solomon, I can't wait until tomorrow . . . No, she isn't in any pain, but I couldn't make it through the night not knowing what we are up against. Once I know, I can devise an appropriate course of action, and proceed accordingly, but . . . That's right, Solomon. I have never been a patient man . . . Very good. At your office in an hour and a half . . . Thank you, Solomon. I do appreciate this."

Dr. Ziegler, I found out later, not only had a reputation as the top neurologist in the country, but he had also received the Nobel Prize for Medicine when he was only thirty years old for his contribution in discovering the striatal deficiency of dopamine in all types of Parkinson's disease.

My mother's attitude, when we woke her and told her of our concern, was almost one of relief. Unbeknownst to us, she had been extremely bothered by her recent state of almost constant exhaustion, and, particularly, her clumsiness at the piano.

In contrast to the terror that we felt, Cynthia Solo faced the thought of this late-night doctor visit with considerable good cheer and enthusiasm, suggesting a series of alternative causes of her symptoms that ranged from a possible thyroid deficiency to hypoglycemia.

Oh, if only . . . if only one of those had been Dr. Ziegler's diagnosis.

Despite the late hour, we were greeted at the door of Dr. Ziegler's office by a thirtyish nurse-receptionist with an unmemorable face and a snippy attitude; and I must admit that if, even way back then, I had any reservations about the famous Dr. Solomon Ziegler, they arose when I observed that the nurse did not speak with curt disrespect only to her helpless patients, but also talked to Dr. Ziegler in the same tone of voice.

The office in which Dr. Ziegler had his practice was located on Fifth Avenue and Eighty-first Street, across from the Metropolitan Museum of Art. The waiting room was decorated with dark, glossy antique furniture and faded Oriental rugs. Dr. Ziegler himself was a pleasant-enough looking man, easily in his late seventies. He had a full head of dull gray hair, a wide strong jaw, watery but friendly brown eyes, and competent, strong hands. He was short, only about five feet three inches tall, and he wore old-fashioned, wide-cuffed, tweedy-looking trousers. On the way into the examining room, Cynthia whispered to us, "His wife must have died years ago. She'd never have let him out looking like that."

Dr. Ziegler put Cynthia through a series of tests requiring her to walk a straight line, touch her nose with her right, and then her left forefinger, breathe, and squeeze his hand. He tested her strength, her coordination, her blood pressure, her reflexes, and her eyes.

110

After approximately twenty minutes alone with her, he came out into the waiting room to speak to me and Julian. His face was somber. Again, I felt that thrill of fear as he turned to Julian.

"I can't be sure after a superficial examination, but it could be bad."

"How bad?"

"We have to put her in the hospital immediately for testing."

"How bad?"

"The tests will tell us that."

"Solomon, I'm a doctor, too. Tell me what you suspect."

"Of course, one can't be sure."

"*Please*, Solomon."

"All right. I suspect one of the neuromuscular diseases."

"That's what I was afraid of."

"But the symptoms could also be the result of a brain tumor. Has she had any accidents or falls recently?"

"Yes, but not on her head."

Dr. Ziegler shrugged, hesitated for a moment, and then looked Julian in the eyes. "Pray for a brain tumor," he said, and walked out of the room.

Narrative by myself—Mathew Wylie (continued).

I will spare the reader the details of my mother's stay in the hospital. That it was an agony of anticipation, and that we both welcomed and dreaded the results of every test that was inflicted on her, should go without saying.

My mother's response to her hospital stay was an unhappy mixture of bravery and apprehension. She feared each new element that seemed to be locking her into that terrible prognosis. But she bravely endured it all on the chance that the horror might be averted and the disease prove to be temporary in nature.

"I won't tell you not to worry, dear," she said to me one bleak afternoon before a CAT scan, "but if you could just show it a bit less, I might be able to muster up a pleasant enough facade to help you survive this entire unpleasant experience."

Whether it was a facade or not, my mother's demeanor was consistently undespondent, courageous, and gallant. One felt, in observing her as she faced her ordeal, that there was about her an air of heraldry. The dignity with which she met each tribulation belonged to another time and another day . . . an era in which it was expected of one that he or she would slay the dragon that threatened outside the gate and, as a matter of course, be knighted for the effort.

Every morning of every day, Cynthia Solo braced herself to face and destroy another fire-breathing dragon, and each evening of each day, after she had returned to her bed, she bestowed yet another knighthood on herself for having achieved this.

When, after eight days of testing, Cynthia Solo was finally released from the hospital—with the preliminary diagnosis confirmed—her determination was simply "to go on with it" as well and for as long as would be possible.

The depth of this determination became obvious to me on her first day home, when she sat down at the piano, and despite her fumbling fingers, resolutely continued to practice hour after hour, until she had done all her scales.

After she had finished, she looked over to Julian and me, smiled, shrugged, and, quoting Shaw, said, "He who can, does. He who cannot, teaches." Then she proceeded to the telephone and began to make arrangements with the local community college to teach piano to adult members of the student body.

That is what my mother, Cynthia Solo, was like.

Her days after she resumed teaching were as activity filled as before, although they were now divided by a mandatory nap. "Orders of Dr. Solomon Ziegler."

112

Cynthia also continued to work four days a week in the piano showroom, where she turned potential buyers over to Messrs. Hazard or Fullerton-Peabody for the piano demonstration, but reclaimed them in time for the sales pitch and commitment.

When she was at home, Cynthia managed neatly and untraumatically to circumvent each problem that arose as a result of her increasing physical disability. Instead of writing letters, my mother typed, telephoned, or made a recording on a cassette and mailed that to whomever she had wanted to say it to. All of her rotary telephones were replaced with touch-tone, her bathrooms were fitted with support railings, her soap was attached to ropes, and in such a way did Mother enable herself to maximize her mobility without decreasing her independence.

Despite her apparent ease in accepting her disastrous diagnosis, though, my mother did show her level of concern by beginning to read assorted books on neuromuscular diseases. This is interesting, because aside from the reading, one might have thought that she had completely put her medical problems out of her mind. She did not discuss them with me; and Julian told me that she did not discuss them with him, either.

These books that Mother read and reread, though . . . I do not know what she expected to find in them. A cause or a treatment? Both were and remain unknown. An alternative prognosis? There is none. Although the disease sometimes goes into temporary remission, the prognosis is always the same: muscular deterioration followed by death.

Perhaps in reviewing this material, Mother gained a kind of strength in affirming to herself that she could face whatever lay ahead. And perhaps Cynthia Solo merely sat with the books on her lap and pretended to read the highly technical manuals from which she knew that she would find absolutely no consolation.

Narrative by myself—Mathew Wylie (continued).

I think you can tell in reading these reminiscences how *I* dealt with the sudden discovery of my mother's illness. I overreacted, which means I reacted; because everyone else seemed to be underreacting. I cried a little bit when I was home in my apartment; and I cried over a beer or an Irish coffee every few Saturday nights in the back booth down at Donovan's Pub. But adhering to both my mother's and Julian's unverbalized dictum, I betrayed no sorrow and projected no gloom in my mother's presence, and I told no one of Dr. Ziegler's prognosis. Not even Mike Laffy or Nancy Lee.

From the moment that Dr. Ziegler spoke alone to my stepfather and myself in his office, and explained to us the unrelenting nature of this terrible disease, it was as though an impenetrable barrier came down between our day-to-day reality and the ugly inescapability of the future.

"Mother may be dying, but that has nothing to do with anything," seemed to be the tenor of the times.

Julian's attitude toward Mother's illness would have seemed incomprehensible to any but those who knew him well, and of those who knew him well, I felt that I knew him better than anyone alive, for I had seen him, and watched over him, when he was dead.

It is because of this particular intimacy that I recognized the depth of Julian Solo's affliction by my mother's disease, for, when Dr. Ziegler pronounced those fatal words, I saw on Julian's face that same unbearable tension . . . that same tightness and repressed strength . . . that same almost enraged vitality that preceded by only seconds Julian Solo's resurrection.

Seeing this . . . seeing that this attitude, which had saved his own life, was now being brought to bear on that of my mother, I felt a tremendous flood of serenity wash over my being. I knew nothing about Julian's plan at that point in time, other than that he had one, *because he had to.* And I knew nothing about the nature of that plan other than that

114

it would succeed, *because it had to*. Perhaps, since I did not believe in God, and since I then so very much needed something to believe in, I made Julian Solo into my personal deity; and I ascribed to him unerring wisdom, omnipotence, and benevolence.

More's the pity.

Memo from Dr. T. Gideon Humphries to Julian Solo, dated August 20, 19—.

Julian, Julian, Julian.

This work schedule of yours cannot persist without causing undue strain to the body, the mind, and the human spirit. What is going on now with my star researcher? You have not ever heard the expression called "too much of a good thing"? You think a man can spend his whole life bent down over a microscope lens, and then when he gets up he is still in focus for the rest of reality?

My friend, what are you doing to yourself again, with these late hours? And a newly married man, yet. And to such a beautiful, intellectual wife (who, I should remind you, thinks that I am a very nice guy!), that you cannot be seeing enough of, since you are spending all of your time in the lab?

And for what, I ask you?

So, you're excited about a new idea. Good. Fine. Stupendous. I understand. Congratulations and whoop-ee-do. But enough is enough, already. So you come in an hour or two early in the morning. For science, I admit, it's worth it. And you stay maybe an hour or two—maybe even three—late at night. Even that I can go along with. Who knows? Maybe someday you'll get a Nobel Prize.

But what can be worth the hours you are putting in now at your lab? I have heard reports of two o'clock . . . three o'clock . . . even five o'clock in the morning.

Can this be good for your health? No.

Can this be good for your marriage—and to such a lovely woman? No again.

Julian, my friend and colleague, here is where we always differ, for I ask, can this be good for your work? And you answer, yes! And I answer, no. No. A thousand times, no!

An eye to a microscope or an ear to a stethoscope does not increase the expanse of human knowledge. No man who looked through a lens and saw a star ever gave one iota of length or breadth or depth to our greater awareness of the *meaning* of things—of how things are, of why things are, of how they work.

All an eye to a microscope can acquire is *data*. It can focus, observe, and record.

Look up. Star.

Look down. Amoeba.

So?

So, what do you know?

Not until you see one amoeba, and then another. And record these data, and observe the structure, color, movement, habits, dividing, subdividing, renting, subletting, and co-oping of these creatures, and make from these data a meaningful conclusion—do you *know* anything.

You think that I am a crazy old man, don't you, one who harps over again that before science can *achieve*, philosophy and morality must guide. But there is no absurdity in my position. It is those who only achieve—who acquire data to pile on data, like the bones of sacrificed corpses—who do most of the harm in the world, when the acquisition of those facts, those statistics, that input, is not done for a moral purpose.

Need I remind you, my friend, that that nation which had the highest literacy rate in the world was the same nation which set genocide as one of its priorities, and justified that genocide in the name of science . . . as did the scientists in the Reign of Terror who performed human experiments in order "to increase the storehouse of human knowledge."

How much heat or cold can a human being endure before he dehydrates and dies? Or freezes and dies?

How long can a human being live after his pancreas has been removed?

How much voltage can a human being endure before he dies of shock?

How many times can a pregnant woman be raped by "laboratory assistants" before she (1) aborts the fetus, (2) bleeds to death, or (3) kills herself?

Data. Volumes and volumes of data. In the name of science.

And so, what is the result of all of this so-called scientific research? What do we know, Julian, as a result of all of these poor, violated, dead, and tormented souls?

Nothing. From these monsters in lab clothing we have learned not one single, human thing. We have learned not one iota of knowledge about human behavior, because humanity itself was violated in the very formation of the question.

Do you understand what I'm saying? Do you see?

If a scientist puts a gun to my head and tells me to suck my toe while I am whistling "Yankee Doodle Dandy," do you think the scientist has learned anything about *me* when I do it?

For heaven's sake, there's a gun to my head. It doesn't matter what *I* do, because I haven't any choices. To be human is to choose, and I have been stripped of my humanity. So how could one possibly think that observing *me* under such circumstances could give one any information at all about being a human being?

But I'll tell you something, my dedicated young scientist; I tell you that you *can* learn something about human nature when you watch me with the toe in my mouth whistling "Yankee Doodle Dandy."

You can learn a great deal about that scientist. You can learn how he has suspended all morality, all philosophy, and

117

all ethics, and has, in the name of "science," disregarded all of the rights of others as being subordinate to his own.

And so I warn you to beware, my friend. I do not know what you are doing here, now, so early in the morning and so late at night. I do not know what can suddenly be so important to you that even your beautiful new bride is being neglected to it as a consequence.

But I know that in you a fire of genius burns, and I also know you possess two qualities other than your amazing intellect: impatience and benevolence.

Julian, you are a good and generous man whom life has never really tested. I have always feared that someday your lackadaisical attitude toward philosophy might get you into hot water, because you will act first and think about the consequences later.

If you are doing that now, my friend and colleague, may I implore you to stop and *think*. Many a good man has been brought to ruin for want of a moment's hesitation.

I think, Julian, that we should talk. I think, perhaps, that it is time for another one of our most agreeable, if too early in the morning, discussions at the Plaza Hotel. A little bit of philosophy with our breakfast, if you please. And I will even permit you to foot the bill!

Maybe a dish of eggs Benedict, a cup of coffee, a wink at the elderly lady with the delightful ankles who is sitting beside the potted palm, and after forty-five minutes you will have reassured the anxieties of an affectionate old man.

Tomorrow, what do you say? At 7:00 A.M.?

Memorandum from Melanie Graice to Dr. T. Gideon Humphries, dated August 20, 19—.

To: Dr. T. Gideon Humphries
From: Melanie Graice
      Secretary to Dr. Julian Solo
Re: Breakfast

Dr. Solo has asked me to inform you that due to circumstances beyond his control, he will not be able to meet you tomorrow morning for breakfast.

He has also asked me to convey to you that he is quite capable of looking after both his wife and his professional ethics without your interference, but that since you are the chief of psychiatry and he is only a department head, he will take the concern that you expressed in your letter as a direct order, and will cease working overtime in the laboratory facilities of the Roosevelt Island Psychiatric Hospital.

Handwritten letter from Dr. T. Gideon Humphries to Cynthia Solo, marked "Personal" on the envelope, and mailed to her attention at the piano showroom on Fifty-seventh Street, dated August 20, 19—.

My dear and lovely lady:

You will excuse in me please the impertinence of writing to you at your place of employment. However, I fear that I must do so at the insistence of my conscience and out of love for your husband and affection for yourself.

Can you explain to me perhaps the nature of his most recent and unaccountable behavior? He is becoming tense, unorthodox, and unpredictable. He came suddenly into the habit of working unusual hours in the morning and far too late into the night. When I mentioned to him this too fervid schedule, he then stopped working all hours but the most conservative for a period of seven or eight days, but he has since forgotten my remonstration and is now back in full force.

He is rude. When I invited him to obtain with me a breakfast wherein we would be enabled to discuss these changes, he had his secretary write me a curt refusal.

With my years invested in the field of psychiatry, for any other man I would suspect drugs or alcoholism, but my love for your husband grew out of our mutual love for reality. I know that Julian's tendency when encroached upon with a problem is not to seek out a simple or a chemical means of escape, but rather to face the problem, solve and conquer the impending difficulties.

Dear lady, I fear though that in his courage there may be a component of rashness, as with the brave man who would save his community from the threat of an attacking army by brilliantly setting a fire around the outskirts of his fortress, but not taking the time to calculate beforehand what might happen to his own people if there is a derogatory shift in the wind.

Something of great consternation must be affecting him, but I do not know what it is or how to communicate my apprehension.

Surely you, too, have noticed this change.

What can be done, my dear lady? And is there any way you perceive that I might be enabled to assist him?

Letter from Cynthia Solo to Dr. T. Gideon Humphries, dated August 22, 19—.

Dear Dr. Humphries:

I shall have to keep this short, as you can see by my hand-writing how difficult it is for me to write.

Herein is the explanation you sought for my husband's state of mind.

I have been diagnosed by Dr. Solomon Ziegler as having the same illness that Julian informs me a colleague of yours, Dr. Lewisohn, had. As you know, this disease is both progressive and terminal, and although Julian is unfailingly kind, gentle, and attentive in my presence, I am afraid that the stress of watching me deteriorate has taken its toll on him during his hours away from home.

Please do continue to try to get my husband to confide in you. He will not let me help him, and the burden he is carrying is far too much for any man to have to bear alone.

Typed letter from Dr. T. Gideon Humphries to Julian and Cynthia Solo, dated August 25, 19—. This letter was hand-delivered to Julian's office. It was found, opened, in its original envelope, locked in Melanie Graice's desk. It is logical to assume that Melanie never delivered this letter to the Solos, and that they were never made aware of the contents.

My dear children:

How I admire your courage and fortitude!

Yet, as I said to Cynthia on the telephone, to be resigned to one's fate is often not the solution, for yet another answer may be waiting for you beyond that which you perceive to be a brick wall.

Without meaning to cast aspersions on the professional competence of Dr. Ziegler, might I suggest that despite his significant reputation, one has heard words spoken now and then that give one pause to wonder.

Therefore, I have contacted Dr. Jon A. Von Peterson, a young man with much experience in his field. It would make me very happy if you would both consult him for a second opinion with regard to the diagnosis and prognosis of the disease in question.

Dr. Von Peterson's telephone number and address are attached.

Letter from Dr. Eric Lilljigren in Norway to Dr. Julian Solo, dated August 26, 19—. This letter also was found opened, but still in its original envelope, in Melanie Graice's desk drawer. We can be certain that it, too, never reached Julian Solo's eyes.

Dear Julian:

Please excuse my delay in responding to the announcement of your wedding. Although I am aware that Heidi has conveyed our regrets at our inability to attend, I have long wanted personally to convey to you my very best wishes and congratulations. If, at any time, you and your bride shall be traveling in Europe, I insist that you descend on us for a visit. And if it is true, as Phillip Block says (he mentioned that he met your lovely wife at a seminar last spring), that Cynthia is a pianist of the first order, we shall insist that she honor us with a performance. Should she hesitate to do so, I propose to negotiate an agreement with you, as follows: If your talented wife will enchant us with a small concerto or a long sonata on our piano, then in exchange for this performance, we will promise to prevent our daughter, Veronika, from doing irreversible damage to your nervous system by singing for you an extremely long and tedious passage from *La Bohème*. That is my deal. Unless Cynthia plays, Veronika sings.

To change the subject, I just reviewed an article by a colleague of ours in Florida entitled "REM and Sanity." A photostatic reproduction is enclosed. The gist of the article, as you will readily apprehend, is that both an important and a necessary component of mental health is the fifth level of sleep in which REM dreaming occurs. As the article so clearly delineates, the progress of our sleep descends through five levels. The first level is that of light sleep, during which our muscles relax, our heart rate slows, our breathing evens out, and our brain activity engenders a floating sensation during which we seem to peaceably meander in and over the events of the day. At this stage, we are easily awakened, and can just as easily drift back to sleep.

At the second stage, our heart rate lowers and our blood pressure goes down. The frequency of our brain waves increases, however.

In the third stage of sleep, which occurs only minutes after the second, our blood pressure and body temperature go down even further. At this stage, slow delta waves also begin to emerge from our brain.

Ten minutes later, we reach stage four, during which we achieve true oblivion. This is the stage of deepest sleep, and one that we maintain for about twenty minutes.

After stage four, the plot thickens, as it were, and we enter the fifth and most tempestuous stage of sleep. This is the REM state, named after Rapid Eye Movement, which accompanies this phase. Here, heartbeats quicken, breathing becomes irregular, and hands and feet begin to twitch. The flow of blood to our brain increases and our brain temperature soars. Fast, erratic waves replace the gentle delta waves of only minutes before, and the brain is at its highest pitch of arousal and excitement. This condition persists for about five minutes, during which time the body remains paralyzed.

At the end of this hectic REM dreaming, the brain returns to its quiet mode and begins the entire procedure all over again. A complete dream cycle takes from seventy to one hundred and ten minutes, and in an eight-hour period we experience four or five complete sleep cycles, with each REM phase at the end of the cycle growing longer and longer as the night progresses.

I mention these things to you now, Julian, because certainly they are of great concern to our particular areas of expertise. REM appears to be inextricably entwined with our psychobiology. That period of REM dreaming, by releasing high concentrations of stimulating hormones and chemicals into our bodies, and drastically increasing the flow of oxygen to our brains, appears to have a vital and positive effect on maintaining our sanity. The high temperature of the brain in this state implies a high rate of brain metabolism, which is necessary to the keen functioning of the mind.

Interestingly, the absence of REM dreaming is often the first indication of mental disturbances. Volunteers who were prevented from attaining the REM stage for over five nights in a row developed alarming symptoms of mental degeneration. They lost control of their impulses, became antisocial, irritable, uncoordinated, listless, and inefficient; they experienced hallucinations, blurred vision, lack of memory, anxiety, and entire personality alterations.

In effect, deprived of REM sleep, normal, moral, socially integrated individuals began to exhibit the personality characteristics and behavioral traits of borderline sociopaths.

When the volunteers tested were again permitted to experience plenty of REM sleep, all of the above-mentioned negative symptoms disappeared, after only one night.

The reason I bring this so urgently to your attention is that these findings appear to put a natural and insurmountable barrier to the length of time at which one can safely sustain a state of cryogenic death. That is, regardless of how useful an artificially induced hypothermic response might be in terms of one's long-range *physical* well-being, these benefits are far outweighed by the mental damage that would be incurred by individuals who, deprived of their REM dreaming, are then put in a position where they may manifest the same symptoms of the insane.

Therefore, if one indeed could reanimate individuals who had been "frozen" for weeks, months, years, or perhaps decades, although it is more than possible that the body might well survive the ordeal, we begin to suspect that the mind most likely would not.

Alas, Julian, I am beginning to ramble. Surely all of this will be obvious to you after reading the enclosed article.

Now my friend, I must console Heidi about the breakdown of our social ambitions. After all, I *had* promised her that you would marry her sister, and I fear your willful insubordination must be explained, if not effaced.

Please give my salutations to your lovely wife, and tell her that my mercenary motives in no way interfere with my admiration for her sterling characteristics.

Fondest regards.

Diary entry of Melanie Graice, dated September 1, 19—.

Dear Diary:

I once read an article about death, and it made a very clear point about how there was an important legal difference between an act of commission and an act of omission.

The article was about medical malpractice, and explained how if somebody was horribly ill and dying, that if this person had been put on a life-sustaining system, and then the doctor turned it off, that was murder, because the doctor did an act of commission, by turning off the machine. In other words, because the doctor *did* something, he was guilty.

Here's the interesting point, though. If the doctor had *never* put her on the life-support system in the first place, and she just died on her own, then he is *not* doing anything. That is an act of omission, and a person can't be guilty of something that she didn't do, and that's *not* a crime.

So, even though I'm not giving to Dr. Solo those two letters from various individuals about various subject matters that might or might not concern the health and well-being of his wife, it's not as though I'm actually doing anything to hurt her by not doing so.

I mean, it's not as if I know for a fact that she's sick or anything, because I can swear on my honor that nobody ever told me that Mrs. Solo was sick, and I certainly have no reason to believe that she's dying.

So no matter what happens, and I certainly don't *expect* anything to happen, it's not as if I'd be responsible.

I mean, letters get lost in the mail all the time.

Entry into Experimental Log of Julian Solo, dated July 27, 19—.

0600 hours: This log is resumed from last entry posted April 25 of this year. Status of experiments at that time were deanimation of lab mouse Horatius for a period of five hours, and successful reanimation.

Follow-up tests indicated that Horatius suffered no deleterious side effects from cryogenic death state, and all mental, physical, and physiological functions remain satisfactory to date.

Original plans to study effects of Cryogenic Catalystic Serum on mouse Penelope have been altered, as full term of pregnancy is complete. Penelope has been retired from service, and experiments will proceed on alternative mice, as well as on larger mammals in response to urgency of investigator involved.

This writer will eventually be using himself as primary subject, and therefore a new means must be discovered to deliver CCS to hypothalamus gland. Progress of experiments will henceforth be maintained in strict confidentiality. Secretary will be employed to assist in laboratory and to transcribe and record numerical data provided; however, she will remain uninformed about the nature and purpose of the work.

Locks have been changed on office doors, and I arrive at office early every morning, and work until late every night, not only to push experiments forward, but also to admit secretary and cleaning personnel, so that administration does not discover change of locks.

Video- and audiotape equipment have been delivered and installed in lab room located adjacent to my office, and all doors to lab other than that behind my desk have been permanently sealed.

Log, notes, video cassettes, and memoranda on experiments from this date forward shall be kept in top drawer of locked, fireproof file cabinet beside bookshelf on east wall.

Additional laboratory/office is currently being constructed in Brooklyn home convenient to anticipated patient. Attached guest house is being converted for this purpose.

Projected method of delivering CCS to hypothalamus is injection of molecule containing minute transmitter directly into gland itself. This is one-time operation after which and upon injection of CCS, the receiver will automatically pass through bloodstream and deliver serum to hypothalamus.

Tomorrow morning, tests of above method of delivery to hypothalamus will be made on lab mice Trudy and Joseph. If said experiment succeeds, same will be repeated on two succeeding days.

Subsequent to devising proper method of injection and delivery of CCS, I will proceed on day three to test short- and long-range benefits and/or drawbacks of serums in progressively higher mammals.

Log entry, dated July 31, 19—.

EXPERIMENT D.   Purpose of experiment: to measure rate of progress of diseases and effect on tissue, cellular structure, and metabolism where disease is arrested by Artificially Induced Hypothermic Response.

Secretary Melanie Graice will assist with injections. She was told that we are testing new virus strain AB negative vaccine.

Test will begin this date, and proceed seven days. On day eight, medication will begin after reacceleration to normal state of metabolism, and continue uninterrupted for one additional week, or until cure or death is achieved by test animal.

0900 hours: Injections prepared. Animals separated by aisle. Four control animals on south side of corridor; four test animals on north side.

0945 hours: Injection sites shaved, sterilized.

1000 hours: Rebel and Hoppy injected simultaneously with cancer cells.

1002 hours: Sissy and Gussie injected with tubercle bacillus.

1005 hours: Candy and Tootsie injected with pneumococcus.

1008 hours: Otto and Franz injected with influenza virus.

Test Animals	Control Animals
Name: Rebel Description: Mongrel. Six-year-old male Disease Induced: Cancer	Name: Hoppy Description: Mongrel. Six-year-old male Disease Induced: Cancer
Name: Sissy Description: Spaniel. Four-year-old female Disease Induced: TB	Name: Gussie Description: Spaniel. Four-year-old female Disease Induced: TB
Name: Candy Description: Chimpanzee. Eight-year-old female Disease Induced: Pneumonia	Name: Tootsie Description: Chimpanzee. Seven-year-old female Disease Induced: Pneumonia
Name: Otto Description: Chimpanzee. Eleven-year-old male Disease Induced: Influenza	Name: Franz Description: Chimpanzee. Nine-year-old male Disease Induced: Influenza

Control animals Hoppy and Tootsie will be unmedicated throughout the entire length of these experiments, to exhibit the natural course of these diseases.

Control animals Gussie and Franz will begin medication at 0600 hours, tomorrow, August 1.

Test animals Rebel, Sissy, Candy, and Otto will begin receiving Cryogenic Catalystic Serum also at 0600 hours tomorrow; however, Rebel and Candy will be treated only by Artificially Induced Hypothermic Response, whereas Sissy and Otto will receive a combination of CCS *and* medication.

Log entry, dated August 4, 19—.

Experiments proceed on schedule. All animals exhibit definite symptoms of induced diseases. Too early to make distinction in results of therapies.

Additional experiments to begin today and tomorrow, as follows. Test and control animals will be mice, except where otherwise noted.

EXPERIMENT V. Purpose of experiment: to test whether use of CCS in conjunction with transfusion improves survival opportunity for victims of poisonous bites.	
Test Animals	**Control Animals**
1. Inject subjects with lethal venoms.	1. Inject subjects with lethal venoms.
2. Inject poisoned subjects with CCS prior to venom reaching heart.	2. Treat with conventional antitoxins.
3. Drain veins and arteries.	
4. Infuse with new blood supply.	
5. Reanimate.	

EXPERIMENT P. Purpose of experiment: to test whether pregnancy can be prolonged without endangering life, health, or mental state of mother and/or fetus.	
Test Animals	**Control Animals**
1. Impregnate mice. 2. After formation of fetus, inject CCS for fifteen minutes at eight-hour intervals for three days. 3. On day four, inject serum for twelve-hour stretches, alternating with reanimation. 4. Check growth of fetus, temperature of pregnant mice, heartbeat, respiration, etc. 5. After two weeks, allow pregnancy to proceed uninterrupted full term.	1. Impregnate mice. 2. Allow pregnancy to proceed unimpeded.

EXPERIMENT S.   Purpose of experiment: to test whether life span can be extended by substituting natural sleep with Artificially Induced Hypothermic Response, and to test whether said state of deanimation affects health, emotional state, intellect, and disposition of subjects. Experimental animals used will be *Mustela Angriosa* of the rodent family. I have chosen these animals as they are rapidly growing mammals, large enough to operate on, but with a life expectancy of only thirty-six days.

Test Animals	Control Animals
1. At 2000 hours on day one, inject subjects with CCS to induce one hour of cryogenic death.	1. Allow normal sleep patterns.
2. At 2000 hours on day two, increase dosage to induce three hours of cryogenic death.	
3. At 2000 hours on day three, increase dosage to induce five hours of cryogenic death.	
4. Each day hereafter, increase time by four hours until a total cryogenic death state of twenty hours is achieved. Maintain at this rate until death of *M. Angriosa* from control group.	
5. Reanimate and allow metabolism, sleep, and all other activities to proceed uninterrupted.	
6. Record characteristics of mental activity, emotional state, disposition, life spans, etc. Differentiate from control group.	
7. Record life spans.	

Log entry, dated August 10, 19—.

EXPERIMENT D. Measurement of progress in CCS treated and untreated animals.

Test proceeds as expected. Rate of deterioration so far corresponds to time spent in state of Artificially Induced Hypothermic Response.

Diseases have spread throughout systems of untreated animals, Hoppy and Tootsie. They exhibit lethargy, irritability, and depression, depending on the extent the disease has spread throughout their bodies.

CCS treated animals are divided into two categories: those receiving medication, Sissy and Otto; and those not receiving medication, Rebel and Candy.

Disease in nonmedicated CCS animals has progressed farther than in medicated animals.

Both exhibit same mental/emotional characteristics. Slight decrease in speed of reflexes. Slight decrease in decision-making capacity. Moderate increase in crankiness. Dispositions of *all* animals have deteriorated; however, CCS treated animals are irritable out of proportion to the invasions of their bodies by disease, i.e., CCS seems to act as psychological irritant while at the same time impeding progress of disease.

Do psychological follow-up on this.

Log entry, dated August 30, 19—.

Summary of experimental results to date.

EXPERIMENT D, which tests the progress of four diseases (cancer, tuberculosis, pneumonia, and influenza) in four dogs and four chimpanzees:

Results to date clearly indicate that most favorable treatment is combination of CCS *and* medication. Use of CCS alone on Rebel and Candy halted progress of diseases by 65% and 72% respectively; whereas the addition of medication to the treatments of Sissy and Otto lowered the rate of the diseases' progress by an additional 22% in both cases.

Conclusion: An Artificially Induced Hypothermic Response reduced disease symptoms in test animals by a minimum of 65%, and with the addition of medication, reduced it to at least 87%.

EXPERIMENT V, which tests the advantage of CCS injection plus transfusion over conventional methods of treating victims of poison bites:

Conclusion: There is no advantage to the use of CCS injections over the conventional methods. In both instances, the purpose is to prevent the venom from reaching the heart. If that is achieved, either method is satisfactory, and neither is as good as one might wish.

EXPERIMENT P, which tests the effect of Artificially Induced Hypothermic Response on pregnancy:

Results to date, both in natural and CCS injection pregnancies: mothers and fetuses are progressing normally.

CCS fetuses are retarded in growth by exactly the amount of time that they spend deanimated. When reanimation occurs, pulse, heartbeat, and vital signs are all excellent.

A normal birth fetus on the twenty-third day in the womb is 11.74 percent completed with its prebirth development.

A CCS fetus conceived on same date is a perfectly healthy, developing embryo, the size of a fetus that is only twelve days old, as per the proscribed restrictions on its growth.

Conclusions: Pregnant women who do not wish to abort could rely on Artificially Induced Hypothermic Response to delay pregnancies so that birth does not come until after termination of normal gestation period. If CCS could be converted to pill form, women could take in same way that they at present take birth control pills, at bedtime, to insure that when mother and fetus are apparently "sleeping" but actually in a state of cryogenic death, no growth occurs.

Advantages: Pregnant actresses who want to finish shooting a film but can't afford to let their pregnancies "show" yet; women stranded in foreign countries who want their children to be born on native soil; women whose husbands are traveling, and want to await their return before giving birth.

EXPERIMENT S, which tests whether life span can be increased by injection of CCS and replacement of sleep with nightly periods of total deanimation:

Results to date concur with results obtained in Experiment P. Growth was retarded in direct proportion to time spent deanimated.

Initial observations of test and control animals indicate good health and energetic vital signs for both groups.

I am as yet unable to make an appraisal of the effect of the CCS on the emotions, intellect, and disposition of the test group of *M. Angriosa*, as throughout their lives these animals are bad-tempered and fairly stupid.

Conclusion: Continued reliance on the Artificially Induced Hypothermic Response to inhibit aging appears to have no negative physical component.

The effect of cryogenic death on the mind, however, is as yet undetermined.

Advantage: Keeping one's loved one alive until a cure can be found for her disease.

Narrative by myself—Mathew Wylie.

I do not know what possessed my mother to do what I am about to describe, whether it was an attempt to enjoy what she saw as an isolated moment out of the rest of her life, or if her motive instead was to concretize her defiance of death, which seems unlikely, as despite Mother's love of drama, defiance never seemed to be one of her dominant characteristics.

But for whatever reason, Cynthia Solo decided that she wanted to have a big, elaborate, out-of-doors Labor Day party in the backyard of The Gingerbread House on Shore Road.

And not only did she intend to invite her own friends, but Julian was instructed to invite his staff and associates.

The party was planned to take place on Saturday, beginning at 3:00 P.M., and continuing late into the night, until everyone went home.

At 9:30 P.M., Mother had scheduled a pyrotechnic display that was going to last ten minutes. The party was to be catered; a small band was commissioned to play patriotic marches, waltzes, and melodious tunes from bygone operettas; and the overall ambience of the affair was to be gay, carefree, ebullient, and festive.

My heart broke when Mother told me about this.

Her beautiful, serene hazel eyes—they never went back to their original green after she got sick— seemed to perceive in me the pain I was feeling at this attempt on her part to ignore her illness. But although she *saw* my pain, she refused to acknowledge the reality or validity of what she was seeing.

There is a new psychological concept floating around, the idea of which is that one owes one's friends the inner workings of one's sorrow, anger, pain, and rage, and that in times of distress it borders on immoral to deal with these emotions by oneself.

Needless to say, Cynthia Solo did not share the attitude that pain diminishes when it is dispersed. Or perhaps she never even thought about the dynamics of what she was suffering, and how her friends, family, son, and husband might react to *her* reaction, because it would never have occurred to her to consult anybody about the proper way in which to deal with her own emotional responses.

Cynthia Solo's pain, just as Cynthia Solo's joy, was her business and her business alone.

And that is the reason why, when my mother, my flesh and blood, saw me suffering over her disease, she not only could, but *had to* ignore her perception of my pain.

Anything . . . anything at all that got in the way of Cynthia Solo's courage, when she needed courage, was not to be tolerated. If it made her stronger not to cry, she did not cry. If it made her stronger to cry alone, she cried alone. If it made me feel better to cry over her in her presence, then as far as she was concerned, god damn me, for how dare *I* lay that extra burden on her, when I so obviously had no right to do so?

My mother was a woman of incredible dignity. She would no more have joined a consciousness-raising session than participate in a form of group therapy for all of those in the area who were suffering from her same disease.

Cynthia Solo believed that there was dignity in everything, even sorrow. And that if that dignity could be preserved, sorrow itself could be overcome, and life, for as long as it lasted, would proceed on its merry way.

Over the weeks, I learned how to hide my own grief about her disease, from her at least, if not from myself.

And so, in the name of life and to the exclusion of sorrow, Cynthia Solo had a party.

There were many people at the party whom I did not recognize, and even more whom I did. Both Mr. Hazard and Mr. Fullerton-Peabody from the piano showroom were there. Mr. Hazard was eighty-five years old if he was a day, and he wore a bizarre pair of green plaid Bermuda shorts, with yellow socks and blue suede tennis shoes, and he seemed to be having a hell of a good time continuously refilling his glass by the punch bowl. Mr. Fullerton-Peabody, very dapper in a white gabardine suit with a straight-brimmed straw hat and a boutonniere in his lapel, chatted for a short time with Alberto, the maintenance engineer from the piano showroom's warehouse, and then as if to the tune of an ancient but insistent different drummer, Mr. Fullerton-Peabody took leave of Alberto to proceed from group of people to group of people, to "mingle" in the most gentlemanly and mandatory of ways.

Freddy Pappas and Marvin Kahn, two of Julian's students who had formerly worked in his lab, threw Frisbees on the west side of the yard, away from the buffet tables, while Dr. T. Gideon Humphries, remembering what I had told him about my childhood experiences with Detective Michael Patrick Laffy, had that unfortunate gentleman practically pinned against a wall, while he (Dr. Humphries) extracted from him (Mike Laffy) the principles behind and the methodology of picking a lock.

The party was an informal affair, and other than my mother's very old and very eccentric colleagues, everybody was dressed casually in shirts and slacks or blue jeans.

Everyone, that is, except Melanie Graice.

After Mike Laffy had extracted himself from the grasp of Dr. Humphries ("I gave him my pick set and locked him in the pantry," Mike explained), he ambled over to me.

He motioned toward Melanie. "That's Julian's secretary, isn't it?"

I nodded.

Melanie Graice had come to the party dressed in a frilly white sort of see-through top, not that there was anything to see through at, because she had a slip or something on underneath. Her dark blond hair was curled sort of wavy and soft, and she had a barrette in it that was made of a cluster of small pink silk roses. She wore white high-heel shoes, and the skirt of her dress was full and kind of floaty. Melanie looked very pretty and young that day, like something out of the past, when women were women and men were soldiers, and if I'd have blinked just then, I think, with the Strauss waltz playing in the background, I might have expected a parasol to materialize in her hand.

When an errant beam of late-afternoon sunlight fell across Melanie's face, illuminating her hair to the glossy shade of dark honey and highlighting her skin to a texture that I wanted to touch and breathe in and with which I was already irreversibly intoxicated, I took a step in her direction, but was stopped by the firm restriction of Mike Laffy's hand.

Melanie turned her head and stepped out of the sancti-
fying light. The urgency I had felt to be near her . . . to
breathe in of her deliciousness . . . receded, and I relaxed.
Laffy let go of my arm.

"Her name is Melanie Graice," I said. "You met her that
day we all went to Roosevelt Island."

"Yeah," Mike nodded. "And I didn't like her then, either."

I turned to him. "Why not?"

Mike lowered his eyes to mine, and seemed to bore into
me as he answered. "She hates your mother, and she wants
Julian for herself."

I threw back my head and laughed. "You've been watching too many soap operas."

Mike shook his head, make a "tsking" sound of either pity
or scorn, and then walked away.

I stayed right where I had been, and continued to watch
Melanie, who by now had walked across the lawn and was sitting on an old-fashioned rope swing suspended from a giant
mimosa tree. Melanie swung gently back and forth, back and
forth, and the breeze that she created barely rippled the ruf-
fles of her dress. As she reposed in the circle of this movement, her eyes fixed on a point not twenty feet from her,
behind the buffet table. I shifted my eyes to follow her gaze,
and encountered the handsome figure of my stepfather.

Hmmm, I thought.

I looked back again at Melanie, and I continued to watch
her as I felt the beginnings of a resentment against Mike Laffy
for putting unwelcome suspicions into my head.

I watched her sitting, immobile except for the slight
movement of the swing. Her eyes attached to Julian Solo as
though her line of sight were the beam of a searchlight, and
the object on the end of the beam must forever stay in the
circumference of its glare.

I watched Melanie's eyes as she stared at Julian, and I
admit that I did feel a shiver of apprehension at the almost
reptilian way in which she could stare, unblinking, with both

face and eyes expressionless, for minute after minute after minute.

I confirmed to myself that maybe Melanie was carrying a torch for my stepfather, but then I modified my position by thinking, "So what if she is?"

Something else happened almost immediately, however, which gave Melanie's absorption in Julian a new and suddenly ugly interpretation.

Julian and Mother were standing behind the buffet table. Julian was filling up the punch glasses and then carefully handing them to my mother, who, in turn, was giving them to random thirsty individuals.

Mother's disease had not progressed, up until this point, beyond the occasional clumsiness and exhaustion previously described, and other than the times that she had dropped the cake knife on her wedding day and tripped on her honeymoon, there had been no accidents or falls.

After Julian handed her the punch glass, though, and as she was reaching across the table to give it to a short, fat woman whom I didn't recognize, the glass seemed just to drop, almost gently and gracefully, one might say, out of my mother's hand to shatter on the ground.

Now, I don't mean to imply that any big deal was made of this accident at the time. For an instant, Mother had a startled, almost uncomprehending look on her face; and the short, fat lady immediately did a good bit of dithering and apologizing, apparently quite certain that it was she, and not her hostess, who had dropped the glass. But, other than these proper and predictable responses, only one person at the party reacted in a manner that was both unexpected and ungenerous. That person was Melanie Graice.

The instant the glass broke, my gaze involuntarily shifted across the yard. Melanie had not moved. She was still swaying back and forth and back and forth on the swing.

The wind still barely ruffled the gauzy material of her dress. Everything appeared to be the same. But it wasn't. Melanie was no longer staring at Julian Solo. She was now staring at my mother. And Melanie's face was no longer expressionless. Melanie was smiling.

"That's what I meant," Mike Laffy mumbled at my side. I hadn't heard him come up.

I didn't want to believe what I saw, though. "Maybe she's just jealous of Mother."

"She hates her. She wishes your mother were dead."

"Isn't that a little drastic?" I countered. "Would you consider the possibility that you might be overreacting?" Mike looked at me again with scorn. I went on, with considerably less vehemence, however. "What I meant was that being a police officer, you might be somewhat prone to see criminal intent everywhere."

"You mean like how immigration officers in California think that they see a wetback behind every tree?"

"Exactly."

"Mathew," Laffy said gently, the scorn in his voice now tempered with pity, "in California, there *is* a wetback behind every tree."

I changed the subject. "How's Dr. Humphries? Did he manage to pick his way out of the pantry?"

But Mike wasn't finished. "Matt," he began, and his voice had now become tender. I braced myself, because I knew Mike, and I knew there was only one subject that could make him soft and gentle and sentimental like that, so I started to walk away, because I didn't want to face it. But he yanked me back, and turned me around. His gray eyes darkened with intensity.

"What's wrong with her?"

"Who? What's wrong with who? I mean, with whom?"

"Tell me, Matt. I can't stand it anymore."

I tried to squirm away, but Mike's hand tightened on my arm.

"Mathew." His eyes grew soft again, and pleading. Now it was I who couldn't stand it anymore.

140

"All right," I broke down, and then began to speak rapidly, slurring my words and racing my thoughts across my mind as though they were being chased by phantoms.

". . . but swear to me, Mike, that you'll never tell her that I told you, and that no matter how hard it is and how much your heart is breaking, you will not reveal to her by thought or word or deed that you know or suspect that anything is wrong."

Laffy closed his eyes for a moment and stood motionless; he nodded his head. And then, trying to keep my face expressionless and the tears out of my eyes, I told this strong, gentle man who had always been my mother's friend all of the events and suspicions about Cynthia Solo's behavior and condition that had led us to this moment where I could not look at my mother without seeing her as doomed.

Just as I finished talking and was waiting for Laffy's response, I heard a voice at my shoulder that struck my heart numb with terror.

"Mathew," my mother said cheerfully, "who locked up Dr. Humphries in the pantry? And since we're on the subject, do you have any idea why he refuses to come out?"

Without skipping a beat, Mike Laffy turned to face Mother, looked down at her, grinned widely, and said, "Cynthia, don't get mad at me, but the little fellow wanted to learn how to pick a lock, so . . ."

"So you locked him in the pantry?" Mother asked, her enunciation of the letter *l* in *locked* and of the *t* in *pantry* being noticeably slurred, and her smile, as she became amused by the situation, angling crookedly down toward the left side of her face.

Mike smiled back at her. His eyes were clear, calm, strong, and mischievous. There was neither pain nor the knowledge of any pain anywhere in the world apparent on his face. At that moment, I knew how much he really loved my mother. He loved her with, for, by, and through his soul.

Mike threw back his head and laughed. He grabbed Mother by the arm and said, "Come on, Señorita. Let's let that cute little bugger out of there."

That laugh, and that act, was the most elegant and courageous thing I have ever seen performed by any man, before or since, in my entire life.

Entry into Experimental Log of Julian Solo, dated September 22, 19—.

As of this date, all experimental animals have been transferred by me to Yorktown Diagnostic for analysis by their Communicable Disease Control facility. I can invest no more effort in the study of the lower primates. In the limited time that the urgency of my situation has permitted me, I have had to surmise, based on clumsy and inconclusive experimentation, that the following can be said of the medicinal use of my Cryogenic Catalystic Serum:

1. It is effective in delaying the degenerative onset of symptoms in progressive diseases.

2. It can cure nothing. It can merely arrest.

3. When the effects of CCS have worn off, the disease progresses at a normal rate, neither accelerated nor slowed down by the serum's former presence.

4. Periods of time spent deanimated can be determined in either of two ways:

    a. CCS can be ingested in time capsule form, and reanimation can occur at predetermined hour.

    b. CCS can be injected hypodermically, and deanimation can be programmed to await the later injection of an antidote, at which point the patient will reanimate.

5. In future experiments I intend to use process "a," i.e., the time capsule method of sustaining cryogenic death and subsequent reanimation, on myself. This will enable me to retain complete control of both my experiments and my destiny, without the necessity to confide in or rely on any external laboratory assistance.

6. In treatment of . . . in treatment of my patient, I shall rely solely on process "b" to deanimate, with no predetermined reanimation scheduled. This will enable me to maximize the time during which the patient's disease can be arrested.

Although all experimentation performed to date has confirmed my tentative conclusion that there are no deleterious side effects from the use of CCS, I am fully cognizant that by the accepted (and quite proper) rigid standards of scientific experimentation to which we adhere today, my conclusions must be considered tentative and premature.

I therefore intend to provide one last check against error as I proceed on the drastic course to which I am committed.

For this, I shall employ a video-sound recorder. The unit that I intend to use can be preset to turn itself on and off anywhere from one to six times each day, and can also be set to record up to six months in advance. I shall review these videotapes to apprise myself of the psychological effects of CCS on its primary human subject. In other words, I will be able to study myself not only in a state of deanimation, but also when reanimated. I can observe my reflexes, my emotional responses, my intellectual behavior, my psychological condition, etc., as I increase both the dosage and the use of CCS in my body.

Thus, the one great unknown—the psychological effect of CCS on the brain—can also be studied, by me, and if said effect reveals itself to be negative, or if I perceive in myself any mental or psychological deterioration, I can reassess the effect of cryogenic death as an adjunct to life and discontinue CCS treatment at once.

Log entry, dated September 23, 19—.

Today I shall orally introduce the Cryogenic Catalystic Serum into my bloodstream in capsule form. The time I spend deanimated, if the dosage required is proportionally consistent with my increased body mass over that given to the lower primates, will be five minutes.

My log entries will consist of two parts. The first will be an *objective* description of the dosage taken and the time spent deanimated, as well as a description of the effects of deanimation on my body as observed by me when viewing the videotape after I have revived. The electrocardio, respiratory, and biochemical data that I also acquire during this segment will be appended to these notes, but not included in the journal per se.

The second part of my log entry will consist of my *subjective* responses to the CCS experiment. How do I feel? Do I reanimate groggy, as if from a deep sleep? Or completely attentive, as if on the far side of a prolonged blink? Do I experience any pain? Any confusion? Am I disoriented? Or am I able to maintain my posture as both subject and object of the experiment with, if not poise, at least equanimity?

I realize now, that I am delaying the inevitable.

0700 hours: I have entered my private laboratory. The door is locked. Other than maintenance personnel and a skeleton night staff, the hospital is still empty. I shall be undisturbed.

0705 hours: I have turned on and preset the audio-video recorder. I am positioning myself on the examining table. In a moment, I shall put aside this journal and lie down. Then I will swallow the CCS capsule. Within ten seconds, I will die.

144

0720 hours: It worked! The digital timer registered exactly four minutes and 46 seconds of deanimation. The video screen recorded my absolutely inert form. The cardiopulmonary monitors registered no pulse, no respiration, no neuroelectronic activity, and no detectable circulation. Body temperature (I exult at this) remained 98.6 the entire segment. I died, and yet I live. I ceased, and yet I exist. I was no more, but here I am.

And how do I feel?

How did Tchaikovsky feel when he heard his Piano Concerto Number One played by a full orchestra for the first time? How do I feel indeed.

I feel just fine.

Log entry, dated September 24, 19—.

0501 hours: I shall perform both this and all future experiments before the morning shift of hospital personnel arrives, and henceforth, I will also resume the outward appearance of a conventional staff member, leaving the lab on or about 5:00 P.M. daily. I have come to realize that as one deliberately departs from the norm for purposes that neither can nor ought to be made public, his outward appearance of conformity must increase in inverse proportion to his departure from the norm.

When the nightmare of this illness is over, as I am sure it someday will be, I shall have to remind myself with a laugh of this psychological quirk of nature, for by then I will no doubt have convinced myself that those who appear

145

conservative are actually outlandish, that those who are outwardly the quietest are inwardly the most berserk, that black is white, that bad is good, that odd is even, and that sane is insane.

Which last observation I should have written with less levity, as even those of us with the firmest grasp on reality can lose our grip if the pressure becomes unrelenting, or if the options open to us seem to merit less consideration than scorn.

Today, the time spent deanimated will be sixty minutes.

0508 hours: I am reclining on the examining table in my laboratory. I am reminded of a line from Shakespeare: If you have tears, prepare to shed them now. Odd, since I do not feel like crying. Or perhaps, I do. No human being alive has ever experienced what I am about to experience. I can be excused for embarking on this adventure with a sense of great trepidation.

However, I observe that, again, I delay. I avoid the cryogenic death experience. Let us take that as one psychological side effect of CCS.

NOTE: Patient resists death.

NOTE SUB-ONE: Patient would have to be a bloody lunatic to *welcome* death, though, wouldn't he?

Enough of this nonsense!

0515 hours: I am taking the capsule now.

146

0617 hours: I am alive.

I was dead for one hour. *All* of my bodily functions ceased and then revived, interrupted by
three thousand six hundred seconds during
which all metabolism, all vitality, all *process*
ceased.

Now I am crying. Why am I reacting this way?
Because I died? Or because my wife may live?

I am crying and I am trembling from the emotional impact of what I have just endured, as
well as from fear of what I know looms ahead.
I can see the ramifications of this successful
resuscitation, and it is all too much for me to
bear. I cannot possibly continue with these
notes.

1400 hours: Almost eight hours have gone by since I made
the above entry. I have spent that time avoid-
ing the necessity to continue with these reminiscences. Why? How do I feel?

I am not sure. I do know that during the time
I spent deanimated, nothing of a malevolent
nature transpired. No bad dreams. No drop in
body temperature. The audio-video record of
the experience evidences no loud noises. No
attempted interruptions. The cardiopulmonary charts and records of neuroelectrical activity progressed exactly as I had projected.

However, the emotion I experience in being
called on to look back at that hour—those sixty
minutes spent deanimated—is one of dread.

147

I can only assume that I am suffering from an exhausted body and an overworked imagination.

Tomorrow I shall remain deanimated for six hours.

Diary entry of Melanie Graice, dated September 25, 19—.

Dear Diary:

Sometimes, when you love a person very much, you have to do things that you wouldn't do if you didn't think that that person were in trouble and needed you to think for yourself and do something that he probably wouldn't want you to do, if he knew you were doing it. Or else I never would have made a duplicate of his keys.

Dr. Solo . . . Julian . . . he told me not to come in today. He told me that he was going to be conducting some experiments all day in his lab, and that he wouldn't need my help, and that he didn't want to be disturbed.

He never makes any jokes anymore. He hasn't called me Nurse Ames in I don't know how long. And he never laughs. Ever since he met *her*, he doesn't have any fun.

Everything's all mixed up, and I'm all mixed up, and I don't know why I went into the office even though he told me not to. But I did, and I didn't hear anything, so I tiptoed over to the door of his laboratory, and I listened for fifteen minutes, and I was quiet, as quiet as a mouse, but not even a chair moved, or the sound of someone reading a book, and I swear that before I knew that I had done it, and I never would have intended to, but the key was in the lock of the door, and the doorknob was turning in my hand.

I almost screamed when I saw what I saw on the other side of the door. I felt the scream rising in my throat, but I caught it just before it reached my lips, because somehow I knew. I just knew that he wasn't really dead. Dead people don't have electrodes attached to their chests; dead people aren't hooked up to machines with blinking lights and buzzing motors.

But even though I knew that he had to be alive, Dear Diary, I was afraid. I was terrified. My heart was beating in my chest so loudly that I was afraid he would hear it across the room and wake up; so instead of getting hysterical, I kept my calm, and I quietly closed the door.

It was awful, though. To see Dr. Solo . . . Julian . . . to see the man I love laid out on that table like a corpse on a slab of concrete.

Why would somebody like that do something like that to himself? Terrible. It's just terrible.

I am sure that it all has something to do with *her*, and that whatever it is, it's all her fault.

Entry into Experimental Log of Julian Solo, dated September 27, 19—.

Cynthia's disease progresses at an alarming rate.

Today I experienced six hours of complete cryogenic death. A self-examination has revealed that all vital functions are normal. Although prior to ingesting the CCS this morning, I again experienced a momentary panic and feeling of dread, I find I am able to think back on and write about the experience without my initial aversion.

Shortly, I will go on an extended leave of absence from the Roosevelt Island Psychiatric Hospital. The guest house in my home has been converted into an office, and I have equipped it sufficiently with medical supplies to treat both my wife and myself as we embark on a therapy of Cryogenic Catalystic Serum.

Additional haste will be required because I became aware today that somebody has observed my experiments. The timing device on my video recorder indicates that at 8:15 A.M. the door to my laboratory was unlocked and opened. As the camera's eye was trained on the examining table, rather than on the room's entryway, I observed only the shadow of the door as it fell across my body. The door remained open for exactly seventeen seconds. I believe that I know who the intruder was. I will not say anything, though. The very same words that can affirm innocence might also be twisted into a breeding ground for suspicion and disbelief. Guilty people make excuses. The righteously indignant do not.

It is clear to me now, however, that I must suspend all further tests and experimentation at this facility. I must also disconnect my video camera, assemble all of my records and notes, and begin to put them someplace where they will never be found.

Diary entry of Melanie Graice, dated September 28, 19—.

Dear Diary:

He knows what I did. I can tell by the way he looked at me this morning. But why isn't he saying anything? Why isn't he questioning me? If he'd only just yell at me or say, "Melanie, how dare you spy on my experiments?" Or something like that. If he'd only just *do* something, then I'd know that it couldn't really be all that bad.

But this . . . this silence. This way that he stares at me when I walk into a room. This disgust on his face. This disregard in his eyes. This contempt.

"Dr. Solo," I begged. "If you'll just listen, I can explain everything."

But he wouldn't listen. All he said was, "Not now, Melanie," and he said it quietly, the way you would talk to a sick person in a hospital, and that was all. "Not now, Melanie," just like that.

Oh, Dear Diary, how *could* he treat me like this?

How *could* he, when he *knows* that I adore him. He *must* know. He *has to* know. He *does* know.

But "Not now, Melanie" is all that he said.

Doesn't he realize that you can't brush off someone who loves you as if she's a fleck of dirt on your shirtsleeve?

"Not now, Melanie."

Oh, my God, I don't think I can stand it. It's all too much. I love him too much. I swear that I think I'm going mad!

Entry into Experimental Log of Julian Solo, dated September 28, 19—.

I have found the perfect place to hide my records. I fear that either a hitherto unsuspected macabre humor, or a sense of the ridiculous on my part . . . or even, perhaps, a bit of mischief, has compelled me to wander toward the derelict and uninhabited portion of this island and seek sanctuary for my notes and memoranda among the ruins.

And such ruins! Here we have yet another instance of fact far outreaching fiction in the realm of the spectral, the eerie, the haunting, the absurd. Here in the bustling metropolis of New York City, center of art, commerce, fashion, industry, energy, and drive . . . Here, no more than one thousand feet from the clamor and din of the United Nations, and at the very foot of the Fifty-ninth Street Bridge . . . Here, I have come upon a setting of such gloom, and evocative of so much evil, that one could easily believe either that he was wandering about in a dream, or that in the middle of the night a malicious demon had waved a nasty wand and transported him, unawares, into the very heart of Dracula's homeland.

An appropriate setting, no doubt, for my formulas, my journals, my diagrams, and my notes. I can no longer leave these items in my office, since the security there has already proven itself to be easily compromised; nor can I take them home, where Cynthia might either come upon them unawares, or perhaps ask me questions about their content which I would prefer to remain unilluminated by the light of day.

No, my ruins are where they belong. I have discovered a building that I believe to have been constructed over a century ago to incarcerate the insane.

As one approaches it, a gaping hole opens into the earth and divides on either side into two broken stairwells. One of these descents is impassable. Brambles and thorny branches clot the way.

The other passage is free of foliage. Neither branches nor twigs nor clinging tendrils of ivy enliven this gloomy byway into the depths. My flashlight revealed a crudely painted skull and crossbones on the lowermost corridor wall, and beneath that a faded, barely legible sign beside the door that spelled out the word MORGUE.

Beyond the portal, the room that I entered is a shamble of collapsed beams, ensnared pipes and wiring, fallen plaster, and splinters of glass. Just inside the door, both protected by the collapse and almost completely hidden from sight are six metal-sheathed shafts that extend horizontally backward for approximately six feet. I had inadvertently come upon the cellar in which the bodies of the dead lunatics from the insane asylum had been held in cold storage as they awaited autopsy, embalming, and burial. These body drawers consist of two columns containing three drawers each. In the second column, the middle drawer was obscured by jagged boards, clumps of rubble, broken bricks, and dust, all of which were encased in a thick, matted gray spiderweb that testified to the length of time that the drawer had remained undisturbed.

I studied the precarious balance of the debris, selected one brick on which no other object seemed to be balanced, gently pried away the spiderweb, attempting not to tear it in the process, and lifted out what I hoped was the pivotal brick.

I had chosen correctly. I now had a small opening to the body drawer on the other side. A dry, inaccessible, absolutely safe hiding place for my secrets.

I assured myself that even the most brazen trespasser who walked down the same steps that I had just decended would never, never overcome his revulsion to death by reaching into a drawer that had once contained a corpse.

I assured myself that my notes and memoranda could be safely hidden here, and I inserted the airtight cylinder into which I had placed them through the aperture that I had made. Then I replaced both the brick and the spiderwebbing.

As I shone my light against the carefully reconstructed debris, I saw the skeletons of generations of bugs clinging to the spiderweb, and I found it easy to believe that no one in his right mind would dare to disturb such an ominous and digusting heap.

This was an ugly place. A forbidding place. And yet, it was a hiding place so perfect that despite myself I began to laugh; but the sound of my laughter in that catacomb was jarring. It was too loud. Too resonant. Too alive.

I had to get out of there. I heard a rustle coming from behind me. What could it be? A stone that I'd dislodged? A rat whose territory I had invaded? The spirit of some poor imbecile whose soul was doomed forever to haunt this awful place?

I climbed the stairs. The sun was shining with the cold, white rays of autumn that shed light without imparting warmth. I moved away from the cellar entrance and looked up at the massive, broken building before me. Its walls are composed of thick, gray slabs of limestone. Its windows rise in Gothic arches. Its roof is crenellated, like the battlement of a castle. Broken staircases hang in midair and lead to nowhere. Trees that long ago took root in small, ground-level rooms thrive and grow so tall that their trunks punch through the flooring above, and grow yet taller and bigger and more rangy, until crazed by the confinement of the place, they stretch their branches out the windows and wave frantically, as though attempting to attract the attention of a passerby.

This was a wonderful place. It suited my present mood and disposition, just as a clammy, damp mist suits a grave digger at a grave.

I chose in that unguarded moment to revel in the gloom to which my present circumstances had conveyed me. I chose, for that brief interlude, to be neither rational, courageous, nor brave. I chose, for a hair longer than an instant, not to fight the depression that threatened to overtake me, but to wallow in it, as one does with Shakespeare when we steep ourselves in the convoluted griefs of a Portia, an Othello, a Cordelia, or her father, the king.

I was sad, and here was a wretched place of grief and tears to enshroud me. For a moment, my guard was down. And for that moment, I could not but let this terrible place be my tormented soul's home.

Entry into Experimental Log of Julian Solo, dated September 29, 19—.

I have not subjected myself to CCS for two days. My head is clear and my spirits are up. I have reread my log entry of September 28 with both horror and surprise. I feel certain that those ravings cannot have been mine. And yet I know for a fact that they can have originated with no one else.

Perusal of my journal convinces me that I must get off this pernicious island. I view with dread my actions of yesterday. Surely one would have to have been mad to secret his scientific papers in an abandoned morgue. Surely I had taken temporary leave of my senses, and as surely, I can attribute it to the pressure under which I have been functioning, as well as my repressed dismay over the rapid physical deterioration of my wife.

I am surrounded by too much grief: That which pervades the hospital in the persons of the sick and dying; that which envelops the island, with its history of incarcerating the lunatic, the raving maniac, the incurably deranged; and that which emanates from my own exhausted soul.

I will not retrieve the cylinder from its dismal abode, despite the illogic of having put it there. Nothing untoward can befall it. Should I need my notes, they can be readily obtained. Should I never again desire to review those unfortunate pages, none but myself knows of their whereabouts or existence, and in their abandoned crypt, surely they can rest in peace.

Diary entry of Melanie Graice, dated September 29, 19—.

Dear Diary:
He is gone, and I am lost without him. What can have happened to my wonderful Dr. Solo? One day he is a whirlwind of activity, ordering: Melanie, do this; Melanie, do that. Then, all of a sudden, I see him lying on a table with electrodes attached to his skin like some kind of an experimental . . . thing. And then, after that, I follow him when he sneaks off to the deserted buildings south of the hospital.

There is a tear in the cyclone fence that cuts off these buildings from the rest of the island. NO TRESPASSING signs are posted all around, so I had never gone there before.

I was able to follow Dr. Solo without being observed. I had to walk carefully to avoid stumbling over rocks and ruts in the ground and puddles and fallen branches, but I saw where Dr. Solo went, and I could even follow his flashlight after he went inside.

I know what he did, and why he went there. I don't know what he hid, but I suspect that it has something to do with his experiments, and I expect that they have something to do with his wife. Or else, why would someone hide something in an abandoned morgue?

Julian doesn't know that I was watching him. And now I am bewildered, confused, and unhappy.

What should I do? Is there anything that I *can* do? I *must* do something.

Letter from Cynthia Solo to Nancy Lee Meyers, dated October 1, 19—. This, and all subsequent letters written by Cynthia Solo, were found, unmailed, in the drawer of my mother's bedroom vanity.

Nancy Lee, this uncomfortable prose, which I hope and pray you are *not* reading, is done at the insistence of my most incorrigible son. Why has the Good Lord plagued me with a loving son who persists in bullying me and ordering me around as if I were a wayward child? If you asked Matt, he'd say, "You're just lucky, I guess."

In any event, and despite my feeble protests, this is by way of being—to quote Mathew—"a written account of the progress of my symptoms." Since I have out and out refused to keep a journal of these accumulating characteristics, Mathew suggested that I put them in letter form to you. I have agreed to this for reasons that are beyond me. Perhaps my illness has begun to affect my maternal brain.

Mathew's brain has recently been affected by television. I fear that a medium which, in the past, one could count on for pleasantly predictable mediocrity at best, has upgraded itself to the point where even the terminally ailing aren't to be left in peace. For what has inspired Matt to his current fervid burst of activity? A documentary on television describing the frequency at which people are medically misdiagnosed in this country.

That Julian, Dr. Ziegler, and I have all concurred about the nature of my illness has not deterred Mathew in the least.

Hence, I have been instructed by this enfant terrible to record my symptoms on these pages so that Mathew at some unspecified time in the future can send me, and them, to an expert of his choosing, for a second opinion.

I find I have become a bit tired. I shall finish this tomorrow.

Letter to Nancy Lee, dated October 3, 19—.

Hello, Nancy. I am back from the showroom, and very tired. When one isn't ill, "being tired" is a description. However, when one is ill, "being tired" is a symptom. There, won't Mathew be proud of me. I am doing as he instructed. I have written down a symptom!

It should also be apparent that my handwriting does not reflect that I am the flower of womanhood, which goes to show how duplicitous the written word can be.

Other symptoms?

Oh, *must* I do this? I really do not see the sense!

Letter to Nancy Lee, dated October 4, 19—.

Horror of horrors. Mathew has read what I have written, and I have been vigorously reprimanded and reproached.

It is, indeed, all my fault, for after Martin abandoned us when Mathew was a child, I insisted on exposing the lad to male role models so that he could learn masculine assertiveness. And see what it has gotten me! If I had only thought faster, I might have been the mother of an amiable and affectionate doormat, instead of the fire-breathing tyrant who has threatened, tomorrow, to read these pages.

Therefore, Mathew, here are my symptoms, and a plague on your house if you remember any of them either after I am gone, or in the event that I get well:

1. Increasingly slurred speech.

2. Intermittent loss of balance.

3. Jerky hand movements.

4. Heavy footed-ness (to coin a phrase). I cannot seem to walk lightly. I seem either to lurch or stomp.

5. Pleasant disposition in the face of filial pushiness.

Nancy Lee, while you still have the time, take your infant child, put her in a basket, and hide her in the bullrushes for somebody else to raise. I am warning you, after they reach a certain age, they insist that one do the most astonishing things.

Letter to Nancy Lee, dated October 6, 19—.

You know, Nancy Lee, perhaps Mathew is right. Last night the television network showed a replay of the documentary that had impressed him so much. I found the show extremely interesting and informative.

One case that was represented concerned a young woman experiencing symptoms not unlike my own, except I am experiencing no tremors. This young woman was tested and retested by over *thirteen* different doctors and medical institutions, and all to no avail. Universally, the findings were the same: There was absolutely nothing physically wrong with her, and therefore it must be all in her head.

Knowing that she was not the psychosomatic type, however, she persisted until she found a doctor who finally made the appropriate test for her very rare hereditary disease. The patient was then put on a strict diet and given the correct medication and physical therapy. Her current prognosis is that she will live to a ripe old age, provided that she eats properly and continues to take her pills.

It seems that there is much to be said for at least a second opinion, and perhaps even a third or a fourth.

I shall certainly discuss my misgivings tonight with Julian. Ever since he moved from the lab at the hospital to the lab in our house, I have seen less of him, rather than more.

Can that be another one of my symptoms? The stress that I am imposing on my dear husband?

I'm afraid that my disease is wearing poor Julian down.

Entry into Experimental Log of Julian Solo, dated October 8, 19—.

There is much to be said for never falling in love. When one loves life and its inhabitants—but none too much—he is spiritually fearless and free. He may take daring expeditions to the North Pole or foolish safaris in search of the Fountain of Youth. He may, like Icarus, bind wings to his shoulders and fly too high, or he may plunge into abysses beneath the sea in the hope of encountering Atlantis.

When one loves the world and all that is in it—but none too much—he may take chances. Although he wants to live, and he does not want to die, he is not afraid of dying. He has no long-range commitments and no psychological debts. There is nobody to grieve over him, and nobody over whom he must grieve. Life for such a man is fruitful and amusing, but it is still, by and large, just a jolly affair.

And then, such a man meets and falls in love with the woman whom, over all else, he worships, cherishes, idolizes, and adores, and life is no longer just fruitful and amusing and jolly.

Life, and the object of his love, and his commitment to her, have become sacred. And then, suddenly, he becomes aware of his own mortality. For in order to love, he must live.

And in order to love, *she* must live.

He who, before, was complete unto himself, is now dependent for his happiness and well-being on the happiness and well-being of another.

Lives have become interlocked.

Purposes have become entwined.

Actions, once so simple and direct, often now seem to backtrack on themselves to make sure that they have not overlooked a fortuitous fact or an opportunity to aid in and increase the happiness of the object of his love.

I am writing drivel because I am trying to avoid doing what I know that I must do.

But, it is oh so hard to make myself do it.

I closed my office on September 29. Melanie has left my employ, and I believe that she has been transferred to Administration. Although she pleaded to come with me, I was adamant in my refusal. I do not need her, and I believe that she has been spying on me. Also, although Cynthia has not said anything, I suspect that my wife does not like Melanie. In all honesty, I am coming to dislike her myself.

I had intended, before removing my things from the hospital, to drop into Dr. Humphries's office to say good-bye. However, as the time came to do so, I found that I could not make myself knock on his door.

Good-byes are final.

I do not want to say good-bye to Gideon. I do not want to believe either that I will never be working with him again, or that I won't be back.

I have been here, in my laboratory in my home, since September 30. Cynthia thinks that I have been busily at work on my experiments.

However, I have been sitting here doing nothing but staring at the walls, at my hands, and at my soul for the past nine days. I have been paralyzed by the options open to me, and the fear of acting, coupled with the greater fear of refusing to act.

My only consolation has been that the decision I make will be made for both of us. One does not send one's love into a tunnel of darkness alone, even though he can project for her a panoply of iridescence on the other side.

Nine days and nine nights I have sat here, white-knuckled and filled with terror and anxiety.

This morning I silently observed Cynthia at the breakfast table. She did not see me watching her. She lifted a cup of tea to her mouth. Her hand jerked, and some tea splattered against the table. Then her lips closed over the rim of the cup, and a rivulet of liquid dribbled out of the corner of her beautiful mouth, down her chin and her neck, and made an ugly brown stain on the breast of her white silk blouse.

When one is in love, one is bound to earth. One is bound to mortality. One cannot be happy if the one that one loves is in jeopardy, or dead.

Cynthia is dying. That is an irrefutable fact.

I can prevent her from dying. That, too, is a fact. I think.

If I do not act, she has no chance.

Tonight I take the risk and inject both myself and my beloved wife with my serum. I do this that her life may be prolonged until a cure has been discovered for her disease.

I am an atheist.

There is no God to whom I can appeal for guidance.

The rightness or wrongness of this decision must rest on my soul alone.

Continuation of Cynthia Solo's narrative to Nancy Lee about the progress of her disease, dated October 9, 19—.

What a terrible night I had last night. As though I had fallen into a void. No dreams. No tossing and turning. Nothing. Just having disappeared into a vortex and awakened from one, without a twilight approach either to or fro.

Letter to Nancy Lee, dated October 10, 19—.

I am afraid. I dread going to sleep. Last night, I remember Julian's arms around me, a sensation of a pinprick at the back of my neck, and then . . . nothing.

Letter to Nancy Lee, dated October 11, 19—.

Is Julian changing, or am I? What is going on? Tonight he literally forced me into bed, rambling something about God, mortality, and saving me. Tomorrow, Nancy Lee, I'm mailing these letters to you. Perhaps I *am* going mad. Write me or call me. Be objective. What is happening? Am I going insane? Is Julian? Help me!

Entry into Experimental Log of Julian Solo, dated October 12, 19—.

Has my wife become suicidal? I just barely prevented her from mailing letters to Nancy Lee . . . letters that surely would have brought a stop to our treatment. I say "our" because over the past three days, I, by capsule form, and Cynthia, by injection of my Cryogenic Catalystic Serum, have been suspended for approximately eight hours per night in a state of Artificially Induced Hypothermic Response. Together we have experienced that nightless night which I so dreaded, in order that she may live. Together we are embarked on this treatment. Yes, treatment, not a cure. A time-buying device. A necklace of garlic . . . a white lily . . . a cross that I hold up defiantly against the Draculean specter of death.

Tonight, again, Cynthia resisted going to sleep. My unfortunate, beloved wife. You must allow me to take the lead. You must temporarily suspend your judgment and rely on mine. No more letters to Nancy Lee. And more sleep. Yes, much more. Today your tread was heavier, your limp was more pronounced. I increase the dosage. Longer periods of "sleep." Less time for the disease to progress.

Narrative by myself—Mathew Wylie.

In looking through Julian's log, my mother's frantic letters to Nancy Lee, and my own calendar, I can place the date that

162

I arrived at their home, unannounced, as October 13. I had no particular purpose in this spontaneous visit other than the desire to see how my mother was doing, and to continue to exert pressure on her to seek out the opinion of other medical diagnosticians.

This intention was strengthened when I called Julian Solo's former boss, Dr. Humphries, with whom I had developed such a pleasant rapport at my mother's wedding. I questioned him about my mother's disease and discussed with him my eagerness to obtain a second or third opinion. His response was complete shock that she had not already sought one out. Apparently, and I had to wait while Dr. Humphries shuffled through carbon copies of his correspondence to look this up, he had written to both Mother and Julian as far back as August 25, recommending exactly what I suggested, and that they confer with a Dr. Jon A. Von Peterson with regard to Mother's symptoms.

When nobody answered Dr. Humphries's letter, he assumed that they had, indeed, sought out the consultation, and that Dr. Von Peterson had confirmed Dr. Ziegler's dismal diagnosis.

After I hung up from Dr. Humphries, however, I called Dr. Von Peterson's office and asked his secretary if a Mrs. Cynthia Solo had ever made an appointment to see the doctor. The secretary stated that she was certain that my mother had not.

So in the early afternoon of October 13, as I approached The House on Shore Road, my eagerness to see my mother was somewhat muted by bafflement over why she had not followed Dr. Humphries's advice.

I was still in this distracted state as I rang the front doorbell, and when seconds later, Julian Solo pulled the door wide open, stood firmly blocking my entry, and suddenly seemed to be glaring down at me, I was momentarily at a loss for anything to say.

"Well," Julian glowered. He was wearing a long-sleeved, pale-blue tailored shirt, with the cuffs rolled up up to his

163

elbows, and khaki slacks and bedroom slippers. His hair was ruffled. Not messy, but somehow . . . I don't know how to describe it. As though it were experiencing static electricity. It almost didn't quite cling to his head. His icy blue eyes were cold and depthless. His lips ran across his expressionless face like a grimy underlined sentence. The most noticeable thing about him, though, was his arms.

As Julian stood blocking the door, I could see his hands clenching and unclenching into fists, and I could see the pronounced veins of his forearms rippling and protruding under his skin. For the first time since I had known him, I thought that I was seeing the full force of the indomitable power of the man. And for the first time, I wondered if that power would always be directed at and for my mother's good.

It is difficult to know what to say when your mother is gradually but insistently dying, your stepfather is barring your entrance and glaring at you with undisguised resentment, and you have picked that moment to pop in with all sorts of cheerful little suggestions about how you think you can assist them in reorganizing their lives.

Julian continued to glower.

"Ah . . . uhmmm," I sputtered. "Uh . . . hi, Julian."

"What do you want?"

"Well, uhm . . . I was in the neighborhood, so I sort of thought I'd kind of drop in to say hello."

"Hello."

"Aren't you going to invite me in?"

"No."

"Why not?"

"I'm busy. You should have called first."

"Well, I mean, it's not that I don't *want* to see you, Julian, but actually, well, uhm, as a matter of fact, I didn't really come to see you, so you can just go back to what you were doing." I took a step toward the door. Julian continued to block the entryway. I cleared my throat and attempted to sound decisive. "Julian, I'd like to see my mother."

"You can't. She's asleep."

164

I looked at my watch and expressed great surprise. "Why is she asleep at one-thirty in the afternoon?"

"She wasn't feeling well today. She was tired."

Again I tried to more or less insinuate myself through the doorway. Again Julian didn't budge.

"Couldn't you wake her up? Just so I could kind of wave to her . . . or maybe wink, or shake her hand?" As I look back on the interchange, I have to admit that I must have sounded like a complete moron.

"She needs her rest."

"Julian." I was becoming irritated and suddenly angry. I mean, who was this man to speak to me in such an arrogant and peremptory fashion. "I want to see my mother, and I am going to see my mother."

At that point Julian must have realized that he had gone too far and that I was getting ready to do something drastic, and indeed I was, although to this day, I have no idea what it would have been. However, Julian's eyes suddenly softened, his fists relaxed, and his lips parted in, if not a smile, at least not a snarl, either.

"I am sorry, Mathew." He reached out his left arm and looked at his watch. "I'll tell you what. You come back for dinner at eight o'clock, and both your mother and I will be good as new."

As he spoke, I was completely unaware that Julian had taken me by the arm and was leading me down the front walk to the gate. And before I realized what was happening, I discovered that I was walking toward the subway station after having agreed with Julian Solo to come back later.

Narrative by myself—Mathew Wylie (continued).

I don't know what an afternoon of anticipation can have led me to expect, but whatever it was, I was unprepared for the nervous irritability and tension which, throughout the evening, my mother displayed to both myself and to Julian. From

165

what little I had read in medical textbooks, languidness and depression are occasionally symptoms of her disease, but crankiness, excitability, and rank emotionalism absolutely are not. Nor had these personality traits ever been part of my mother's makeup for as long as I had known her.

It was not, however, until I observed Mother snapping at Julian that he knew it was stuffy inside, so why hadn't he opened the window, that I began to suspect the obvious: Mother was taking drugs, and Julian was administering them to her.

As the evening progressed, I became more and more convinced of my suspicions, for one simple and obvious reason. People's personalities don't change overnight. Or, to translate this into a high school syllogism:

> Nice people don't suddenly act creepy
> unless they have a reason.
> My mother was a nice person acting creepy.
> Therefore, she must have had a reason.

What about the reason, though? Can it really have been a reaction that Mother was experiencing because Julian was fooling around with drugs? Or was Mother's disease suddenly taking an ominous and unexpected turn? Or, since Julian's personality was also becoming inexplicably and unpleasantly changed, did it mean that my mother and my stepfather had, overnight, become secret drinkers?

Wanting to get to the bottom of whatever it was, I asked Mother to come for a walk with me, half expecting Julian to try and prevent her. On the contrary, though, Julian exhibited that loving care and almost heart-wrenching tenderness for his wife which, since the onset of her illness, had been so characteristic of him. He made her change out of her pretty evening slippers and put on a pair of woolly socks and sneakers. He wrapped a cashmere scarf around her neck, helped her tuck into a thick, warm sweater, kissed her lightly on the lips, and then admonished me to hold onto her arm and make sure that she didn't fall.

In fact, Julian's loving behavior all but vanquished my suspicions, and if half a block from the house Mother hadn't begun to tug at her neck and mutter under her breath that she didn't know why Julian was trying to suffocate her with this idiotic scarf, I would have completely forgotten about her irritability.

We continued to walk arm in arm beneath the trees on a virtually abandoned Shore Road. The night was glorious— one of those warm, magical evenings in Indian summer that make one's heart hold its breath at the whimsical ballet of a falling leaf or at the familiar crackle and rustle of dead leaves underfoot. Autumn is a strange season. It is a season of endings. The end of summer. The end of growth. The end of harvest. Yet despite all of these endings, it is the gentlest and kindest of seasons. It is the season of repose, during which all living entities may experience their well-deserved hour of rest, prior to winter's sleep and spring's rejuvenation.

Thoughts such as these were running through my head as Mother and I walked, and it wasn't until many minutes had gone by that I realized we had gone all the way up to the Verrazano Narrows Bridge, down the path to the promenade, and were now leaning against the wrought-iron railing overlooking the harbor.

There is a solemn and serene beauty about the scene I beheld which, perhaps, is unequaled anywhere in the world, for the Verrazano Narrows Bridge is a towering engineering expanse of unusual delicacy and incomparable grace. Some whim of some magistrates in City Hall had caused the bridge to be painted pale blue, and beholding this elegant giant with its slender back arched across the river and its colossal legs plunked firmly up to the ankles in water not more than twenty yards off the shore, is like seeing a pastel-hued creature from *Fantasia*, poised momentarily against the horizon, that might any minute rear up on its mighty hind legs and gallop off into the sunset.

That night in the moonlight, however, the bridge hung motionless. Its bright necklace of lights was impressionistically mirrored in the water, as though one had before him reality both as it was, and as it might have been interpreted by a Van Gogh or a Monet. On the rocks below us, the water lapped silently against the shore.

I realized that, for a long time now, Mother had ceased her mutterings. I looked over at her face.

The lines of tension and irritability that so recently had dominated her features were now gone. The woman standing next to me was no diseased, drug-ridden victim; she was the mother I had always known, admired, and loved.

She released my arm, grabbed onto the iron railing, and took a deep breath. Then she exhaled, closed her eyes, sighed, and said, "Oh, Matt. What a relief." She turned to me and smiled. "I have been an intolerable monster, haven't I?" And then she threw her arms around me in a big hug. "Oh, boy. Is it good to be awake!"

She led me to a park bench.

"Awake?" I asked.

But Mother didn't answer. Instead, she took another deep breath and looked all around herself with every evidence of satisfaction.

"Mother, are you all right?"

She smiled at me. "I am now." And then she shook her head, "But I know I've been behaving badly."

I took my mother's hands. "That's what I wanted to talk to you about. You *have* been acting funny. Not at all like yourself."

"Well, I haven't been feeling like myself, so I'm not surprised. Lately I—"

But I interrupted. "Mother, I'm concerned about Julian."

"So am I. He worries too much, and I don't think he's getting any sleep."

"That's not what I mean. What I mean is that I'm concerned about Julian's treatment of you."

Mother dropped my hands and turned to look at me in shock.

"Julian's treatment of me? You know how Julian treats me. You saw tonight. That wasn't an act for your benefit. Julian is always painstakingly devoted and kind. Even when I snap at him and hardly deserve such solicitous concern. Frankly, if I had to put up with the way I'd been acting lately, I'd have been tempted to strangle me with this scarf, instead of tucking it around my neck."

I took back my mother's hands. "That's exactly what I mean. Your personality is changing. Not now, but all through dinner, and up until the air seems to have cleared your head, you weren't acting like yourself, and that's what I'm concerned about. I mean, Julian is a scientist, and I wondered if maybe you were worried that he might be tampering with your medications, or surreptitiously giving you some mood-altering chemicals."

But Mother shook her head. "I don't think so. Sometimes after a very bad night, I might think that Julian is being too domineering, and I might resent everything that he tries to do to help me, or accuse him in my mind of somehow sabotaging my cure, but when I'm feeling better, like now, I realize it's not Julian that I'm afraid of."

"Then you are afraid of something?"

"Yes. I'm afraid to go to sleep."

"Afraid to go to sleep?"

"Uh huh."

"But why? Bad dreams?"

"No. No dreams."

"Then why are you . . ."

Mother took away her hands and clenched her fists. I could see her nails digging into her palms. "I don't know, but lately the mere idea of sleeping terrifies me. I feel that every time I lie down it isn't to go to sleep—it's to die."

"That's horrible!"

169

The sound of my indignation must have shocked her out of her reflective mood, for she suddenly relaxed her hands, looked over at me, and smiled.

"I know. I just said that." I could see the tension drain out of her, and as her smile grew warmer and more affectionate, I realized that my mother was now looking at me in that way that mothers have of looking at their children after they have just flubbed a line in the school play, but it doesn't matter, because they still think that you're the neatest kid in the whole wide world.

"Why are you smiling, Mom?"

"I'm smiling because you are so cute."

"I am?"

"Yes. And you are determined to protect me against all manner of fire-breathing dragons, goblins, and demons, aren't you?"

"Of course. Isn't that all right?"

She reached over, pinched my cheek, winked, and then stood up. "I think it's just dandy."

I stood up, too. "Then can I sleep over tonight?"

"Of course. But whatever for?"

I shrugged, and again Mother smiled, and this time she patted me on the hand. "By all means, my son. Patrol the corridors for goblins, and with my blessings. Maybe with you here, Julian and I will finally be able to get a *good* night's sleep."

Narrative by myself—Mathew Wylie (continued).

When we arrived home and told Julian that I was going to sleep over, at first he seemed unpleasantly surprised and on the verge of protesting, but before Cynthia had even stopped speaking, Julian's whole attitude toward me altered drastically, and he appeared to be genuinely delighted that I was going to stay.

170

Nor do I think that it was an act, for Cynthia's personality had undergone such a complete transformation since dinner that both Julian and I could not fail to attribute her current ebullience to my presence.

Indeed, the latter part of the evening took on an aspect of vitality and gaiety that put one to mind of earlier and more lighthearted days, and by the time we were ready to go to bed, my suspicions had also been put to rest, and my intention, for the remainder of the night, was just to more or less go through the motions of a man who still had his doubts.

From my bedroom windows I could see the west wing of the house and the lights in the master bedroom, as well as the shadows of Cynthia and Julian moving behind the curtains as they prepared for bed.

At exactly 1:30 A.M., their light was turned off, and from that time on, other than the sigh of an occasional wind in the trees or the far-off moaning of an occasional foghorn in the harbor, the house, the area, and the very world that we inhabited seemed to have gone to sleep.

What I had planned to do was to take my penlight, carefully open my bedroom door, and explore the house in search of . . .

In search of what?

I had absolutely no idea. And as soon as I stood in the hallway, light in my hand and foolish expression on my face, I realized that I would be exhibiting a good deal more common sense if I either went back into my room, or if I turned on the hall light and tromped openly down the stairs to the kitchen and raided the refrigerator for some cookies and milk.

But, of course, I did neither.

I had committed myself to this midnight reconnaissance, and neither good sound healthy reason nor common sense was about to deflect me from my appointed task.

Luckily, the entire house was heavily carpeted.

Unluckily, I had no plan, either of attack or of the architecture of the building, and so the only course open to me was to wander down hallways, quietly opening doors and peeking inside, until I felt that I had explored and eliminated the entire place.

At this point, I suppose that if I were a conscientious narrator, I would draw a diagram of The House on Shore Road, so that later on, as the events unfold, the reader could refer back to our movements like chessmen on a game field, and better follow that which occurred. I will not do this for two reasons. One, I cannot draw and/or read maps or schematics, and two, anytime I have ever read a book in which one appears, I either lose hours and my temper in trying to figure it out, or I just skip the page entirely and find that my enjoyment of the plot has in no way been hindered by my ignorance of the relationship of rooms and corridors to each other within a given perimeter.

Therefore, the reader may stumble blindly along with me and get a true feeling for, at first the anxiety that one feels as he knows he is violating somebody else's private territory, and then the feelings of confidence, assurance, and just plain curiosity that replace the fear after the first forty or so minutes, when he has managed thus far to proceed successfully without either screaming at the sight of his own reflection as it leaps out at him from a mirror, banging into the fireplace set of irons, pokers, and brushes that somebody had left too far in the middle of the room, or just plain tripping over his own feet.

It is true that doing something furtive for a good cause can give one a warm and giddy feeling of exhilaration. Surely the fear combines with the excitement, and somewhere in your bloodstream they both go crashing into your adrenaline, at which point they all mix, and you feel this cocksure, irresponsible smile begin to form on your face as you reach for the next doorknob.

Julian Solo's home . . . the vast (by New York standards) gingerbread, wraparound house in which he lived and which he inherited from his eccentric uncle, Howard Craven Solo, proved, by my inspection, to be far more tastefully decorated than I could have anticipated (even the laundry room hadn't escaped the application of hanging plants, cheerful wallpaper, and a Spanish-tiled floor and plush area rug). Until I entered the guest wing at the rear of the house, I encountered nothing that could in any way be interpreted as at all spooky, creepy, suspicious, malicious, or malign.

As I knew, Julian had transformed the guest house into his office. This was located adjacent to the servants' wing and directly over the garage, three quarters of which (the garage, that is) was actually below street level at the bottom of a steeply inclined driveway. The entrance to all of these areas is in a small hallway on the far side of the kitchen. The hallway is enclosed by doors, and it is very easy to become confused about where you have just been, where you are on your way to, and where you'd really rather be going. Presumably, servants, who often exhibit a higher degree of intellect than those whom they serve, can easily punch their way through the right opening in record time. I had no such self-confidence, and so propped open the kitchen door to assure myself that, without having to drop bread crumbs behind me, I would at least be able to find my way back.

To the left of the kitchen door was the doorway to the staircase that led up to the servants' wing. I did not even bother to mount these stairs, for just that evening Mother had asked me to run up there and get a sweater that she had forgotten, and at the time I could see that the formerly residential rooms had been gutted and that Julian had turned the quarters into a complete and efficient gymnasium, with hot tub, sauna, and the like.

Across from where I stood and diagonally to the right was the door to the garage, which also held little of interest for me. Directly across from the kitchen door was the small alcove and staircase that led to Julian's office. On the wall between the garage door and this staircase, there was a complex panel of switches and dials that I had always found incomprehensible. From this wall plate one could turn on the backyard lights, the front door lights, the kitchen and hall lights, the interior burglar alarm, the exterior perimeter alarm (never used), and the car turntable at the foot of the driveway in front of the garage.

I gave that panel a wide berth. To me it was as mysteriously unintelligible as a blueprint or an architectural drawing, and I knew that if I even brushed up against it, sirens would screech, walls would quake, and the whole house would scrunch up its face at me and kick and scratch and spit.

I tiptoed across the narrow foyer and up the seven short steps to Julian's office and laboratory. Then I turned the doorknob.

Or, I should say, I tried to turn the doorknob. It wouldn't open. Under normal circumstances, a locked door would present no obstacle to a surrogate son of Detective Michael Patrick Laffy of the New York City Police Department. In my time, I had opened gym lockers, girls' diaries, safety-deposit boxes, lockets, lunch boxes, bus terminal storage bins, police and Medeco and double-bolt locks. I never went anywhere without my handy dandy lock-pick set; and I had always been confident that given the time and the opportunity, there was nothing short of a bank safe (for which I would need explosives) that could keep me out.

I took out my pick set and shined the flashlight on Julian's laboratory door. The first thing I noticed was that although the solid oak door to the guest wing had not been replaced, the exterior hinges had been reversed and were now on the inside. This was my first indication that Julian had upgraded his security, for any competent burglar will tell you that the strongest locks in the world are meaningless if all you have to do is remove the hinge bolts, and . . . poof, like magic, you're in.

But nobody was going to get into Julian Solo's lab and office that easily.

I then flashed my light against the locks and discovered that Julian had outsmarted me there, too. For a burglar with simply his wits, a lot of time, and a pick set is never going to get past a three-dimensional Fichet lock combined with an electronic card insert lock. These extremely sophisticated

174

means of security thrust themselves into my awareness like two smug lips.

I shook my head. Why, I asked myself? What can Julian Solo be guarding that requires such an impenetrable barrier? I knew that in the daytime, Julian housed a full staff of servants. Even so, weren't all of these precautions excessive, just to protect a few formulas, some file cabinets, and the like?

Or was that door shielding more than just the usual accouterments of a doctor tinkering in his lab on a bit of inoffensive this and that?

Did this lab conceal the clue to my vague uneasiness about what, if anything, Julian might be doing to my mother?

I heard something. I don't know what. A click or a footstep or the closing of a door. Something.

My heart stopped.

I was afraid to breathe.

I turned off my light and stood there in the dark.

My heart began to beat again. To pound. I knew that whoever it was that had made the noise would discover me. I knew that whoever it was would be able to hear my heart beating a mile and a half away.

I waited.

I counted the seconds.

When I looked down at my watch, the luminescent dial sat at 3:12 A.M.

I counted more seconds and tried not to breathe.

I waited.

I prayed.

When I looked down again at my watch, I read 4:01 A.M.

I hadn't heard anything since that one, remote click almost an hour before.

It had probably just been a pipe creaking, I assured myself. Or the house settling. Or a mouse. Or I'm imagining things.

I flicked my penlight back on and I carefully threaded my way back up the stairs to my bedroom.

After I locked the door behind me, I staggered across the room to my bed and collapsed in a dead faint.

And I don't remember a thing more until, at around eight o'clock in the morning, I heard a knock at my door and my mother's cheerful voice. "Breakfast, Mathew. Up and at 'em," and I awoke instantly, absolutely convinced of what I had to do.

Narrative by myself—Mathew Wylie (continued).

Breakfast was delightful. The maid had laid out a veritable feast of date nut breads, hot croissants, fresh pumpernickel, and bagels, among platters heaped with scrambled eggs, assorted cheeses, lox, onions, shrimp, caviar, creamed chipped beef, and bacon. We sat down to this sumptuous array in a glass-walled atrium at the back of the house. The room was a jungle of plants and brightly colored fabric pillows on yellow wicker furniture. We ate at a glass-topped wrought-iron table, and the sunshine streamed in at us from all sides.

Both Julian and my mother were positively sparkling with charm, wit, vitality, and warmth. There was an air about us of relief and celebration, as if either a great disaster had just barely been averted, or a terrible premonition had suddenly proven to be untrue.

We talked of the new dance company that had just been formed in Spanish Harlem; of the Rodin exhibit that had been lent to the Metropolitan Museum by a highly respected collector out west; and of Mother's dream one day, if she were ever rich or well enough, to found, form, and direct a New York City repertoire company devoted solely to the revival of American musical comedies, specializing in the Gershwins, Rodgers and Hammerstein, Lerner and Lowe, and Comden and Green.

It was a festive meal, and in the merriment I detected no false or forced behavior; and if anything even remotely unusual could have been noticed about the three of us as we sat there, it would have to be simply that we clung to the sunlit room, and the table, and one another's company like inadvertent misanthropes who had spent half a lifetime alone and were now positively drunk with the pleasure that could be derived from the company of one's fellow man.

Throughout our breakfast together, I found that I was equally able to participate in the lighthearted conversation, and at the same time to formulate a plan to investigate why both Julian and Mother seemed suddenly to be so prone to these wide and almost manic mood swings. What was hidden behind Julian's locked laboratory door? And what, if any, relevance did that have to my mother's current state of health and/or the prognosis for her disease?

The sunlight streamed. Julian was telling an amusing anecdote about Dr. Humphries; Mother was laughing; and as I pretended to listen, I began to outline mentally the letter that I would shortly write to Nancy Lee, and the unanswered questions I would raise that very afternoon to Mike Laffy, when I enlisted his aid on the telephone.

Entry into Experimental Log of Julian Solo, dated October 15, 19—.

My wife's son slept over last night. Although I at first resented the intrusion, I now realize that his youth and vigor and naturally buoyant spirits are exactly what we both occasionally need. I shall encourage the boy to visit us regularly, and on those days, I shall abstain from the CCS treatment for the day prior to his arrival and continue to resist using it until after he has gone.

Although I do not know the nature of the stress that my CCS therapy is imposing on us, I suspect that our endurance is being tested; and I know that even I desperately long for a respite.

177

But one cannot always have that for which he wishes. I wish to live happily ever after. I wish my wife were healthy. I wish. I wish. I wish. What is it that Cynthia sometimes says?

"If wishes were horses, beggars might ride."

So where does that leave one?

Tonight we make up for lost time. I increase the dosage. We will remain deanimated for fourteen straight hours.

Letter from Nancy Lee Meyers to Mathew Wylie and Michael Laffy, dated October 18, 19—.

Dear Guys:

My response to the situation Mathew has described in re: Cynthia and Julian, is: "What the hell is going on?"

Matt, to be perfectly honest, nothing of what you said in your letter is really out and out *suspicious*, and it can all probabily easily be *explained*. We are living in a free society, and certainly a man has a right to lock his own door, and a married couple living UNDER STRESS because the wife is dying (for God's sake) has the right to act irritably, unpredictably, antisocially, and obnoxiously; and if you look at the whole thing *objectively*, we are ALL PROBABLY LOSING OUR COLLECTIVE MINDS.

But . . .

But, Julian did work on Roosevelt Island, and I have always believed that insanity is contagious; and THAT PLACE has always been a containment bin for stockpiling nut cases; and Julian does live in a house that even he calls a Gingerbread House, and even though gingerbread houses conjure up warm and toasty images of loving families and baked apples and turkeys and Christmas Eve, the gingerbread house that is the granddaddy of all gingerbread houses was the one that Hansel and Gretel stumbled into, and *that* house was owned by a witch who pushed Hansel and Gretel into an OVEN; and Julian lives in a gingerbread house; and I'm sure

178

we're all behaving perfectly ridiculously, but I've got a gallery opening on October 25, and I have to fly in anyway, so I'll come in on October 21, flight 67 at La Guardia.

Laffy, meet me at the airport. Matt, I'll bring along a sleeping bag and can camp out on your floor, but for God's sake, please *spray for roaches* every five seconds until I arrive!

Narrative by myself—Mathew Wylie.

On October 22, 19—, Nancy Lee Meyers, Detective Michael Patrick Laffy, and I all met in my studio apartment.

We discussed exactly what we wanted to accomplish, and then argued about the courses that were open to us to gain the information we would need to set our minds at ease.

As to what we wanted to accomplish, that was easy: establish that Mother was safe, that Julian was innocent of any sinister involvement; and if he wasn't, immediately effect my mother's escape. Our goal was to get inside Julian's laboratory and determine for ourselves that nothing nefarious was going on. Failing that, our plan was to confront Julian openly and en masse, in front of Cynthia, about all of the peculiarities of their behavior, and get from him an explanation and justification for it, if he had any to give.

Although we could all agree on what we wanted to accomplish, we disagreed strongly on how to set about doing it.

Mike Laffy wanted to lure Mother and Julian out of their house on some pretext, and then when it was empty, have the leisure to search both the house and the locked laboratory (he thought he could bypass the alarm and get in through an outside window) before we did anything drastic. All Mike's instincts, background, and training rebelled against precipitate action. He believed that fools rush in, and angels case a joint before they dare to tread.

Nancy Lee and I understood Laffy's appreciation of caution, but we were both far more frightened than he, and far more convinced that the situation required less planning and greater haste. Nancy Lee and I favored immediate action. We wanted to call up my mother and Julian, tell them that Nancy Lee was in town, and suggest a little reunion party at The House on Shore Road for that very night.

Our idea was that we would all pretend to leave, but one of us would stay behind, and then later on, after everyone had gone to bed, I (I suppose this meant that I had been elected to stay behind) would come out of my hiding place and let Nancy Lee and Mike Laffy back in, at which point we could again search the place, and Mike would break into the lab.

But Laffy absolutely refused to proceed. He insisted that we call Julian and Mother, and continue at a more careful and calculated pace.

Narrative by myself—Mathew Wylie (continued).

As of 6:00 P.M. on October 22, after Mike Laffy had been calling at intervals of approximately fifteen minutes for the past seven hours, Julian Solo finally answered the telephone at The House on Shore Road.

Mike said that although Julian's voice lacked any real warmth or recognition, he was polite enough to his wife's friend in a distant and extremely formal way.

No, Julian explained, Mike could not talk to Mrs. Solo, because she was unavailable; and yes, Julian continued, he was certain that Cynthia would be very glad to know that Nancy Lee was in town; but no, tonight was absolutely out of the question, for it was far too late for all of us to come over, since Cynthia had had a trying day and was already in bed; and yes, since Nancy Lee was staying only one more night, Julian thought that he would be able to rearrange their plans; and yes, Julian would see to it that accommodations would be made for Mike Laffy, Nancy Lee, and "my stepson Mathew" to join him and Cynthia for dinner at . . . shall we say 7:30 on the following night.

Mike Laffy hung up the phone.

"I don't like it," he said.

"Don't like what?"

"Don't like he won't put Cynthia on the telephone. Don't like she's already sleeping. Don't like we can't come over until tomorrow night."

"So?" I asked.

"So," Laffy said, "we do it your way."

Letter from Cynthia Solo scrawled to Nancy Lee and dated October 22, 19—. This letter was found on the floor beside my mother's bed by Nancy Lee the day after Mother wrote it. The handwriting was barely legible.

I *shall* mail this. I am desperate. I need help. Julian is changing. He is too tense. Too intense. He talks too much about saving me. Talks too much *about* me, but not *to* me. As if I play no part in being myself. He will not listen. I am afraid of him now. Not because I fear he would hurt me, but because if I were hurting, he might not hear my pain. He is moving about in a delirium of purpose that he will not realize is defeating his own aim. I am afraid, and he will not comfort me. I live in fear, not of death, but of sleep. To sleep is to enter into the realm of sheer terror. It is a bottomless black hole of nothingness. A void. It is worse than death, for in death there is rest. There is peace. But this . . . this sleep I am sleeping is a torment, a punishment, an empty hell of negation from which I awaken angry, hostile, irritable, and exhausted. I know that I am being misdiagnosed by Dr. Ziegler. I *must* change doctors, but Julian won't listen. He thinks Dr. Ziegler is God. He thinks that *he* is God. Someone *must* listen. Mathew will listen, Nancy Lee. Tell Matt. Oh, no. Here comes . . .

181

Note written by Mathew Wylie on sheet of blank paper, dated October 24, 19—.

I write this at six o'clock in the morning.
I am in jail.
Julian Solo is dead.
I killed him.
Mother is dead.
Julian killed her.

Sworn statement of Detective Michael Patrick Laffy, describing the events of the previous evening, dated October 24, 19—.

The events that led to the alleged crime that was committed at 2:05 A.M. on October 24, 19—, and that resulted in the death of psychobiologist Julian Solo Jr. of Brooklyn, New York, began at approximately 11:30 P.M., at which point myself and my companion, Nancy Lee Meyers, departed from the residence in which the incidents described later on occurred. Myself and the aforementioned Mrs. Meyers and a third party named Mathew Wylie, age twenty-one years, who is accused of perpetrating the alleged crime, had been dinner guests of the deceased and his wife, Cynthia Solo, who is also deceased.

Myself and Mrs. Meyers were friends of Mrs. Solo, having known her for over fifteen years; Mathew Wylie, being Mrs. Solo's biological son, was also known to us for approximately that length of time. Dr. Solo was the second husband of Cynthia Solo, and he had been known to us for less than one year.

We, the aforementioned dinner guests, had obtained an invitation from Dr. Solo to visit his home, as certain facts had come to our attention that caused us to be suspicious that Mrs. Solo's life and health might be in jeopardy.

It was our intention to depart from the premises and create the impression that we were leaving, but in actuality to return after the lights had gone out and search the residence for evidence that Mrs. Solo was or was not in danger.

Mathew Wylie, the female deceased's son, had been left behind for this purpose, earlier in the night having pretended to be tired, and saying that he would let himself out the door, but actually secreting himself in a large closet underneath the stairs.

Myself and Mrs. Meyers did leave at 11:30 P.M., as we had planned. We entered my automobile, and by means of vehicular transportation were conveyed to an all-night diner on Fourth Avenue, at which I obtained two cups of coffee. We then drove back to the Julian Solo residence, parked, and drank coffee until 1:30 A.M., when we observed that the lights had been extinguished in the upstairs bedroom.

By prearrangement, the extinguishment of said illumination was the signal I and Mrs. Meyers were waiting for to leave my vehicle and proceed on foot to the front door of the Solo residence.

We waited in the shadow of a large tree at this aforementioned door for approximately fifteen minutes, at which time Mathew Wylie opened the door and let us in.

Prior to departing for the Solo residence for dinner that evening, we had prearranged the manner in which our search of the premises would be conducted.

It would be my assignment to search the second- and third-floor bedrooms, including establishing whether Dr. and Mrs. Solo were actually in residence and in their room and in bed at the time of the search. Since this would be the most sensitive area, because it was assumed that Dr. and Mrs. Solo might hear any unusual movements, I assigned myself this task, being the most experienced at breaking and entering and at undetected surveillance.

It would also be my responsibility, after the second and third floors had been investigated, to return to the first floor and find a means to compromise the locks and alarms that protected Dr. Solo's office and laboratory, and to effect entry into said location.

Mrs. Nancy Lee Meyers had been assigned to search all of the ground-floor rooms to the left of the main entrance hall. This included parlor, living room, formal dining room, music room, library, sun room, two storage rooms, and servants' lounge.

Mathew Wylie was assigned to search the small dining room, kitchen, pantry, butler's closet, garage, and gym. He was also to try the door to Dr. Solo's office again, and if he could effect entry, to wait for us inside.

Our plan further incorporated a rendezvous at the foot of the main staircase to the second floor. This aspect of the plan was never accomplished.

We did follow our initial arrangement for the preliminary stage of the search, fanning out to our various assigned areas.

I had completed my inspection of two second-floor bedrooms, and was establishing that Dr. and Mrs. Solo were not occupying the master bedroom, which was empty, when I heard the sound of something heavy, similar to a large piece of furniture, crash. This was followed by the additional sounds of what appeared to be glass breaking and a scream. I looked at my watch. The time was 2:05 A.M. The sounds came from the area of the garage or kitchen.

I ran out of the master bedroom, down the stairs, and through the small dining room to the kitchen, where I turned on the light. As nothing was out of order in the kitchen, I proceeded to the small corridor between the kitchen and the rear wing of the house, at which I began to turn on various switches on what I assumed was a light panel against the far wall.

Lights immediately came on in the hall, outside in the backyard, in the front yard, and in the gymnasium. I believe that at that time I also inadvertently turned on the turntable in front of the garage, which had been installed to rotate an automobile so that it can face forward, instead of backing out.

I proceeded through this rear corridor up a small set of stairs into a large, brightly lighted office.

The first thing I saw in that office was the body of my longtime friend, Mrs. Cynthia Solo, lying on an examining table. She was dressed in a white nightgown, and her long blond hair was hanging over the edge of the table. Her hands were folded across her chest, and she appeared to be lifeless.

I immediately rushed to her side, whereupon I shook her several times and shouted for her to respond if she was all right. Upon receiving no response, I checked for breathing and pulse, which I could not detect. So I shouted out to Nancy Lee, knowing she could not be far away, to call an ambulance, and I began to administer cardiopulmonary resuscitation.

It was not until the ambulance drivers arrived that I noticed that her son, Mathew Wylie, was sitting on an overturned desk in a state of shock. I then inspected the laboratory and discovered that there appeared to have been a struggle in the room, for lamps, files, and chairs had been knocked over. The window had also been broken, and one of the large casement frames was hanging by one hinge.

I walked over to the window and looked down. I saw, splayed on the turntable at the foot of the driveway below me, the body of Dr. Julian Solo. From the distance, it appeared that he had fallen or been pushed out of the window, and that he had died as a result of the fall.

Apparently, I had, as I suspected, activated the driveway turntable, for as I looked out of the window, I could see the body rotating around in a 360 degree circle, its arms and legs at odd angles. Dead, but still moving.

Then I threw up.

Sworn statement of Nancy Lee Meyers describing the events of the previous evening, dated October 24, 19—.

The three of us had gone our separate ways to look through rooms, and I was poking my way through the library. It must

185

have been just after two o'clock in the morning when I heard a piece of furniture crash and some other loud noises over on the other side of the house. I dropped everything and started to run toward the commotion, but I took a wrong turn somewhere around the parlor and landed up in a closet. That's when I heard Laffy call out to get an ambulance, so I figured that whatever was going on, it was all out in the open and I didn't have to play hide-and-seek anymore. So I groped around until I finally found a light and a telephone, and I dialed 911, and then opened up the front door and waited for the medics.

They arrived about five minutes later, and I went with them through the kitchen to the little hallway in the back, where we could see Mike Laffy working on Cynthia where she was lying on that table.

Mike wouldn't stop giving Cynthia CPR until the ambulance drivers promised that they would keep working on her on the way to the hospital, and Mike got them to let me come along so I could keep an eye on them.

It all happened so fast that I wasn't sure what had happened, but before I left Laffy told me that Julian was dead.

Matt was slumped over in the corner, but sitting upright, so I knew that he was O.K., but other than that, nobody told me what was going on.

When we got to the hospital, the emergency-room nurse told me that Cynthia was Dead On Arrival.

Now it's six o'clock in the morning, and I'm sitting here in the police station and I still don't know what's going on.

Notes written by Mathew Wylie, dated October 25, 19—.

I am out on bail, and I am writing this for two reasons. First, I want to clarify in my own mind what actually happened; and second, I want to assist my attorney in my defense in the event that the grand jury indicts me.

186

When I try to think back on what happened, as I am doing now, my mind clicks into gear exactly the way the holes on the frame of a film click into the sprockets on a projector just before the motor goes on.

And when the motor does go on, and the lights, and the action, what I see in my mind now, and what I saw last night, was like a slice out of life — not a slice of life. It was events that would not, should not, and could not have happened.

I walked into a scene surrealistic in its detachment from what actually exists and what is possible and what could have occurred, like walking through a wax museum of murderers where a handsome cad is bent over the body of his beautiful victim; and all is static, and all is stationary, and none of it, thank God, is real. And then all of a sudden, the wax villain hears your footstep, and turns around and looks you in the eye, and you recognize that he isn't made of wax after all, and he isn't some caricature of a madman. He is Julian Solo, a man whom you admire, your mother's husband, your step-father, and your friend, and he has a hypodermic needle in his hand, and he has just taken it out of the back of your mother's neck.

You are in shock, and you do not believe what you are seeing. For even if this is all happening in your imagination, and if these really are wax characters who have come to life, then why is the wax woman lying on the table still not mov-ing? Why hasn't she come back to life, like the others? And why is the wax man holding the wax lady's head as though if he were not holding it, it would flop back, and she would be dead?

Why is the wax lady's skin so white? And why don't you see her chest rising and falling in that ever so subtle but noticeable way that means she is breathing?

And then, suddenly, you know that this isn't a wax museum, and you aren't watching a movie, and you hear yourself make some loud, inhuman animal sound, and you leap into the room and push the wax man . . . the murderer . . . away from your mother.

"You killed her!" you scream at Julian Solo. And you know that you are out of control.

You lean over the body and begin to search for a sign of life. But you don't find any, so you turn and grab your stepfather's shoulders. "What did you do to her?"

You begin to shake him violently. He tries to pull away, but does not fight back.

"Take it easy, son. She's not dead. I'm actually saving her life."

"Like hell you are. And don't call me son. I saw you take that needle out of her neck. I saw . . ."

"Look, Mathew. I only appear to have killed her. Actually . . ."

"Get away from her, you madman. You're insane. If you try to touch her again, I'll . . ."

And then, what I think I did was lower my head like a bull or a moose or something, and I rammed into my stepfather at such a terrific force that I crashed him over the furniture and up against the window, and I kept butting my head against him until I heard something crack, and I don't know what it was, my head or his ribs or the window, but the next thing I knew, Laffy was across the room giving Mother CPR, and I was under arrest for killing Julian Solo.

My attorney's name is Dominic D'Amato. He is a short, squat man with black eyes like hot marbles that you don't want to look at too closely because you're afraid that they'll singe your mind. He is a no-nonsense guy whom Mike Laffy recommended, and although I can't say that I like him, I have to admit that he inspires trust. For one thing, he really wants to know what happened. For another, he absolutely doesn't want me to lie. Laffy says that both of those attributes are unusual for a criminal defense attorney.

D'Amato is talking about either temporary insanity or justifiable homicide as our defense plea if the case comes to trial.

Laffy is sure that no matter what happens, I'll get off.

Nancy Lee and Laffy are taking care of the funeral arrangements for Mother, but since this is a criminal case, the funeral will have to wait until an autopsy has been performed.

I am home now, in my apartment. When they visit, Nancy Lee and Laffy look at me from time to time as though they're waiting for me to break down or cry.

I wish that I felt something, but all I feel is empty and boneless, as if all of my insides were taken out and stepped on and crunched and jumped up and down on until they were all loose and messy, like hamburger meat, and then all of this stuff was put back inside of me, without my bones, and someone propped me up in the corner and still expected me to be a person and cry.

How can someone whose insides are made of messy pulp cry?

Handwritten notes by Detective Mike Laffy for Attorney Dominic D'Amato, dated October 26, 19—.

O.K., Dom. Since I spoke to you, this is what happened. Around 1700 hours yesterday, I get a call from Mohammed Torres, the deputy chief medical examiner for the borough of Brooklyn, and he says to come right down to the M.E.'s office, because he can't tell me anything over the phone.

So fifteen minutes later, I'm hammering away at his private door, and he looks at me funny and shakes his head. So I ask him, "What do you want, Mo?" But he just shakes his head again, and then precedes me out of the room, and I follow him down the hall to this other room with an aluminum door, and he pushes on the door, and I say, "I ain't going in there," so he comes out again and he says, "What's wrong, Mike? Are you getting squeamish in your old age?" And I say, "No. I've always been squeamish. Now I'm just letting it show."

So he walks across the hall to a small room with two plastic chairs and a dirty sink, and we sit down, and Mo says, "How many dead bodies have you seen since you've been on the job?"

And I answer, "Too many."

So Mo goes on, "Well, do you know anything about the physiology of death?"

"Like what?" I ask.

"Like rigor mortis. Lividity. Body temperature. Decay."

"Yeah, I know all that crap. Back nine years ago when the civilian employees of the M.E.'s office went on strike, I was assigned to chauffeur and assist the chief medical examiner for the worst two weeks of my life."

Mo nods, and then pulls out a pack of cigarettes from his shirt pocket. He hands me one, and I take it. We light up. I hadn't had a cigarette in over thirteen years.

"You knew the deceased, Mike, didn't you?"

"Yeah. I knew 'em both."

"I heard that the woman was a friend of yours."

I don't say anything.

Mo goes on. "I'm sorry if this is painful to you, but I understand that you're a friend of the family, and I wanted you to hear it from me."

I cough and crush out the cigarette. "It ain't fun anymore," I say. Mo looks at me dumbfounded. "Smoking," I explain. And Mo continues.

"I received Mrs. Solo's body late last night. As you know, because it was involved in a suspicious death, I am required by law to perform an autopsy. In the course of preparing the body for my postmortem examination, I noticed several things of interest. The first was that despite over twenty-four hours in a reclining position on her back, the victim showed no evidence of lividity. Lividity is caused by the settling of blood due to gravity, and it occurs in *all* deaths. I next observed that although Mrs. Solo had been dead for many hours, there was no cyanosis, which, as you know, is the characteristic bluish discoloration in the mucous membranes of the deceased's mouth, lips, and nail beds, which results from a lack of oxygen in the blood. I next observed a lack of post-mortem rigidity of the skeletal muscles of the head, neck, and lower extremities, which indicated that no rigor mortis had set in; and then I observed the most peculiar fact of all." Mo Torres stops talking and stares at his fingernails.

"Go on, Mo," I say, and I pull another cigarette out of his pack and light it. The slim, intense deputy chief medical examiner looks up. He bites his lip.

"Go on, Mo," I say again, but this time, I hear a mean overtone in my voice.

Again, Mo Torres shakes his head. "It's the body temperature."

"What about it?"

"Well, you know that we refrigerate the bodies, don't you?"

"Yeah. Go on."

"So, we refrigerated hers. But even when it's out of the refrigerator, a dead body's temperature never goes above fifty-eight point six degrees Fahrenheit."

"So?"

"So before I was about to make the first incision, I touched Mrs. Solo body." He pauses. I lean forward in my chair and throw the cigarette on the floor.

"Tell me."

"And it was warm. Her body was warm. So I took the body's temperature, and . . . " Mo Torres looks up. There is a help-less, pleading look in his eyes. "It isn't possible, Mike, but her temperature was ninety-eight point six degrees Fahrenheit."

I clench my teeth and stand up. "You didn't cut her, did you?"

Mo also stands up. "No. Of course not."

"Do you think she's still alive?"

Mo shakes his head. "No, I do not. But I *know* that she isn't dead."

Handwritten notes written by Nancy Lee Meyers for Attorney Dominic D'Amato, dated October 27, 19—.

We are all sick to death with shock. Our emotions have been roller-coasting now for days, and half the time I don't know whether to cry demurely like a sissy or get hysterical and tear out someone else's hair.

Thank heavens for Laffy. I absolutely can't believe the man. I mean, here's this old faithful lug who's been plodding along in this predictable True Thomas way for about four hundred years, kind of looking like a cross between a mongrel that's grateful for the absence of a kick, and a dray mule that trudges through its days more or less just waiting until someone tells it that it is O.K. to die . . . and then all of a sudden, Crisis with a capital *C* enters into his life by way of Cynthia, and SHAZAAM, what happens, but the Old Gray Mule turns into a big, black, mean old stallion. I mean, the man has turned into a veritable dynamo in front of my very eyes.

First, he drags Dr. Humphries out of bed at about midnight, for God's sake, and makes him come down to the *morgue*, of all places, to give Cynthia a going-over, because the big honcho down there isn't sure that she's really dead. Then the two of them, Laffy and the little grape-nut flake doctor, commandeer an ambulance down there, and hightail it off to the Herbert Fischman Medical Center, where Cynthia is lying in a private room, not alive and not dead, like a sleeping beauty from a fairy tale, waiting for Prince Charming's life-giving kiss.

But Prince Charming is dead, and the evidence is beginning to point to him having put her in this condition in the first place, instead of some wicked old witch, and the whole thing is so damn sad and confusing and just so plain WRONG, that it'd break your heart if you let it.

But with Laffy running around like a maniac, still believing by some trick of his imagination that he can *save* Cynthia, who has the time to be bitter or angry or sad?

This morning Laffy has already ransacked Julian's house and laboratory. He's dumped a pile of notebooks, letters, and memoranda in my lap, and I'm supposed to sort it out by date and subject before he gets back. Meanwhile, he's gone rampaging across the river to Roosevelt Island to take apart Julian's office *there* and scrutinize his files and records and so on, and he's already come across two real humdingers in Julian's secretary's desk. One is a letter from Dr. Humphries implying that Dr. Ziegler may have gone a little bit gaga, and that Julian and Cynthia should go to another doctor for a second opinion. The other letter sent Mike Laffy into a paroxysm of anxiety, because it's to Julian from a scientist in Norway and it refers to experiments that Julian is making that may or may not have a bearing on Cynthia's condition, and Laffy wants to show it to Dr. Humphries as soon as that little guy gets back to Roosevelt Island.

Now, why Dr. Humphries is not at the hospital with Laffy is another story completely. Laffy put Dr. Humphries on Dr. Ziegler's track this morning, to get ahold of Cynthia's medical records, but when Ziegler started to do an old soft-shoe about doctor/patient confidentiality, Dr. Humphries practically *flipped* his highly educated wig! I have never *heard* anybody so *mad*. Dr. Humphries started to zap things out to Ziegler like "unconscionable bungling" and "gross misdiagnosis" and "criminal negligence," and ended up in a very quiet tone of voice with sentences including "medical malpractice" and "revoke license" and "lawsuit," and before you knew it Dr. Ziegler had snapped out something like, "If you want them, come and get them yourself." So Dr. Humphries is on his way to Manhattan to pick up Cynthia's file.

With the stuff they've dug up already, it still looks bad for everybody and hopeless for Cynthia, as far as I'm concerned. But "hope springs eternal," as Alexander Pope said, and who am I, of all people, to get into a fistfight with hope?

193

Letter from Dr. T. Gideon Humphries to Detective Mike Laffy with a blind carbon copy to Mathew Wylie's attorney, Dominic D'Amato, dated October 29, 19—.

And so, my good Detective Michael Laffy, could we have considered only a short while ago that not only would you have unraveled for me the secret of unlocking doors, but that together we would be seeking the solution to unlocking the mystery of my beloved friend Julian Solo's behavior, and to hope that our efforts might combine to help his beautiful and possibly still yet living wife?

It is a sorrowful purpose we are engaged upon. Certain facts have been revealed by my examination of Cynthia Solo and her treatment records, which give me great pain to communicate to you. For it appears that evil has come of incompetence, and but for the arrogant ignorance of one man, nothing would have been lost.

I will see to it that Dr. Solomon Ziegler never again will practice medicine. Never again will his reputation and esteem blind a good and desperate man like Julian Solo. Never again will this highly respected buffoon with no professional ethics be permitted to destroy, with his stupidity, a day, an hour, or even a minute of another human life.

My poor, poor unhappy friends. How unfair to them life has been. How pitiful that over their hearts was laid a burden of grief, when, at worst, it should have inflicted only a little bit of discomfort, maybe some annoyance. Some feeling "blue." But grief . . . tragedy . . . sorrow . . . Oh, no. For Cynthia Solo had no terminal illness. She suffered from no neuromuscular disease. I have gone over her case history with my colleague, Dr. Jon A. Von Peterson, and he said to me that there can be no uncertainty about it. Cynthia Solo had encountered an unusual case, for someone of her age, of Sydenham's chorea . . . or, to put it more simply, she just had rheumatic fever, and if left to its own progression, in a few months she would have been back to normal. One hundred and fifty percent well. The speech imperfections, the inability to coordinate properly, the necessity to indulge in great quantities of sleep, the illegible handwriting — all, *all* were of a nature most temporary.

Inside myself, I am feeling rage that one improper diagnosis can have resulted in the death of my valued friend. However, for both his sake and the sake of the beautiful Mrs. Solo whom he loved so greatly, I must put my emotions to one side and do what can be done to save Julian's wife.

It is true what the medical examiner has said, that she is not dead. How, then, can we make her come back to life? This is no case of coma or paralysis that we are dealing with, but a true breakthrough in medical science that Julian accomplished. Oh, I know from memory and conversation what my friend sought to achieve. And it takes no great mental conclusion to realize that his experiments with hypothermia were to the purpose of prolonging dear Mrs. Solo's life. But how can anyone have imagined that in so short a time Julian would have succeeded with his goals? How could even I, who believed so greatly in the genius of my good friend, have believed that so rapidly he would devise a technique in which the life process itself could be halted, and yet without any of the irreversible rearrangement of structural molecules that begins the deterioration of tissue characteristic of death?

One thing of which I am certain. Julian kept detailed records of his experiments and of his procedures; he will have somewhere instructions on how his beloved wife may be revived, and a serum to inject with which we can achieve this desired goal.

But where is it? And can we find it in time?

Tomorrow, my dear Detective Laffy, since your explorations have so far produced none of the material we need to accomplish Mrs. Solo's resuscitation, I suggest that I and my friends call upon the residence of Julian's former secretary, Miss Melanie Graice.

Perhaps in her possession is knowledge of the location of the information that we seek.

Narrative by myself—Mathew Wylie.

I hate Roosevelt Island.

I once took a course in philosophy, and the meaning of the word *hate* was explained to me. I learned that hatred represents a feeling in response to a metaphysical threat, i.e., something in *its* nature and substance and being is so awful that it threatens *your* nature and substance and being.

The point of the lecture was supposedly to explain to us that we consistently misapply the word *hate* to trivial and temporary things, instead of saving it up to use on something really worthy of an emphatic response. For example, when Joe Blow gyps you out of the money you lent him, you don't actually hate him; you just hold him in contempt. Why? Because Joe Blow, in his essence and being, is not a threat to you. He's just a jerk, and he got away with it once, but he certainly won't be able to take you to the cleaners a second time. Similarly, we *loathe* things that we find repulsive (like touching some slimy character's hand), and we *detest* things that we find unspeakably impertinent or annoying or irritating.

Hatred, however, or at least according to this philosopher whom I listened to at the time, we reserve for things that are so metaphysical in their terribleness that they infuse unadulterated malice into the very essence of being.

What, then, is entitled to our hatred?

Evil. We may hate evil.

Viciousness. We may hate viciousness.

Malevolence. We may hate malevolence.

And Roosevelt Island. We may hate Roosevelt Island. Because like evil and viciousness and malevolence, Roosevelt Island is in its nature and being . . . corrupt. It has, for so long a time, been a resting place for insanity, mania, and decay, that over the decades the rain has driven the corpuscles of corruption deeply into the very soul and soil of the place, and by now, instead of merely inhabiting Roosevelt

196

Island, evil has become an intrinsic part of the very island itself.

And so it shall stay, until some administration some day decides to tear down the entire mess. Evacuate the people. Raze the buildings. Desert it. Ignore it. Let it be. And then, maybe after thirty or forty years or decades or centuries of abandonment, the effects of wind and rain and clear fresh air and wildflower spores blowing across the river and settling in will have purged the wretched place of its malignancy. Then and then only, tabula rasa, like a smooth and clean sheet of paper, a new and happier history can be written about a once blighted and contaminated place.

Narrative by myself—Mathew Wylie (continued).

On October 31, 19—, at approximately 1:30 P.M., a delegation consisting of Dr. Humphries, Nancy Lee Meyers, and myself got off the Roosevelt Island tram and walked the half mile or so to the northern part of the island on which the newer housing was located, and where Melanie Graice lived.

The day was gray and gloomy, which the eve preceding All Saints' Day appropriately should be. As we walked down the carefully bricked and barely inhabited roadway into the city or housing project or town or community or whatever that conglomeration of grim-visaged buildings thought itself to be, we all felt the place, that afternoon, to be particularly repellent. A clammy wetness clung to our hands and faces and crept down the spaces between our collars and necks, and up the spaces between our wrists and sleeves. It was Halloween, and yet here, on an island that one would feel had been personally designed to revel in a celebration of the macabre, we saw not one outward manifestation of awareness of what day it might be.

We saw no jack-o'lanterns with candles lit to illuminate sardonic grins or gap-toothed faces. We saw no cheerful orange and black witches stirring caldrons in store windows

197

or hung by children on their doors as reminders of how much fun being scared can be.

And we saw no children wearing costumes. No three-foot-tall Tinkerbells or four-foot-high ghosts. No boys in oversized jackets wearing monster-hands and all-too-believably stitched and plugged Frankenstein faces.

We did see one little girl wearing a gray coat and carrying a quart of milk without a bag. She hurried out of a grocery store and ran across the street where there is never any traffic and disappeared into a beige brick building. And we saw two unfortunate, emaciated individuals of undetermined sex, sitting side by side in wheelchairs, not looking at each other and not talking to each other, as they sucked on their breathing tubes in unison; and we saw one elderly couple who held hands, had timid, threatened, rabbit faces, and didn't look from side to side as they walked too fast and disappeared into a different but similar beige brick building.

And we, too, hurried over the oh-so-beige and tidy streets until we found the right building, distinguished from all of the other buildings only by the right combination of numbers that told us that we had arrived at the residence of Melanie Graice.

The directory in the lobby informed us that she lived on the seventh floor, east wing, and when we rang her apartment and identified ourselves over the intercom, Melanie buzzed us in. It wasn't until she had opened her door and was facing us, however, that I remembered who Melanie Graice really was, and what she had meant to me, and how I had once been in love with the intoxicating ivory-smooth color of her skin, and the backlit sapphire of her eyes . . . but it all seemed so very long ago, surely no less than a thousand years, and anyway, her backlit sapphire eyes were bloodshot and red rimmed and underscored with dark, bluish-purple pockets, and none of that had any relevance now anyway. She pulled the door wide open so that we could come in.

One look at her, and there could be no mistaking the reality of Melanie Graice's feelings. Hers was not a face that had suffered just a casual sorrow, or one that sought to melo-dramatize its grief. And also, for the first time since I had known her, Melanie Graice was not dressed to enhance or to cultivate her image. She wore a faded pink nylon quilted bathrobe and matching mules. She shuffled into the living room, and we followed her. We all sat down. Clearly, our visit was a surprise. Clearly, we had interrupted her lamentations over the death of Julian Solo.

Melanie clasped her hands together and singled me out with her eyes. "The newspapers say that you killed him," she stated. But she didn't say it either harshly or as an accusation.

"I pushed him out the window."

"Why did you do that?"

"Because I thought that he had murdered my mother."

"Hadn't he?"

"No."

"That's strange," Melanie practically murmured. "And all along I thought that he had been trying to kill her, too."

I jumped to my feet. "You *what*?" I shouted.

But Melanie just shook her head. "What do you want? Why have you all come here?"

She disregarded me and turned to Dr. Humphries, who, being the head of the hospital where she worked, must have appeared to her to be the man in charge.

"Madam," he began formally, "we—"

"Call me Melanie."

"Melanie, then. We are here to visit you for a great purpose." There was absolutely no expression on Melanie's face. She looked at Dr. Humphries without curiosity. Without interest. Almost as if she was bored.

Dr. Humphries continued. "It has come to our attention that a good many papers and files are missing from the office of your former employer, Dr. Solo, and we have come to ask if they might be in your possession."

Melanie did not even blink. "They're not," she said flatly.

"Perhaps, then, you know where these records might be?"

"I don't."

"Maybe if you put your mind on the problem you could suggest to us a location where Dr. Solo might have thought of preserving these documents, or indeed any documents, notes, or papers that you feel may be of service."

Melanie stared through Dr. Humphries as though he weren't there.

"She doesn't know anything," I said to Dr. Humphries and Nancy Lee. "We're wasting our time."

But Nancy Lee suddenly stood up, walked over to the sofa where Melanie Graice was sitting, and sat down beside her. She reached forward, grasped Melanie's hands in her own, and made the girl look into her eyes.

"Now listen here, Melanie. You aren't my favorite person, and I'm sure if you gave it any thought, you wouldn't much like me either. But our mutual and personal aversions are more or less as important as the Peloponnesian Wars right now, because somebody whom I love is either already dead or dying, and you've got to snap out of that blur that your mind is in and help us. You're the only lead we have to the information that we need to save her."

Melanie tried to pull her hands out of Nancy Lee's grasp, but Nancy Lee held on tightly. A spark of interest invaded Melanie's eyes.

"So," Nancy Lee said, "you're waking up. I got your attention."

Melanie stopped trying to wrest her hands away.

"Save whose life?" she turned back to me and asked.

"My mother's."

"Oh," Melanie said softly, carefully, almost as though she were tiptoeing over the configurations of sharp-edged words. "You mean Mrs. Solo?"

"Yes."

"Dr. Julian Solo's wife?"

"Yes."

"And if you don't find these papers, you say that she'll die?"

"Yes."

Melanie shook her hands free and stood up.

"Poor Mrs. Solo," she said, and I thought that somewhere beneath the surface of her skin I saw the repression of what wanted to be a malicious smile.

Narrative by myself—Mathew Wylie (continued).

Needless to say, our trip back to Manhattan was a pathetic affair. None of us could think of anything to say. It was as if we had each individually replaced the hope we had carried in our hearts on the way to Roosevelt Island with irreversible death sentences that we carried in our pockets on the way back.

Melanie Graice had been my mother's last chance to return to being alive. And Melanie not only couldn't help us, but she had seemed pleased to have been able to offer us nothing more useful than belligerent and ignorant indifference.

Once we had gotten off the tram, we all got into a taxicab and went back to my apartment. Although subliminally I suppose we all remembered that we had promised to meet Mike Laffy there at 4:30 or thereabouts, we actually just drifted like zombies back to the place where I live, not really thinking of where we were going, or why.

Since, in our hearts, Dr. Humphries, Nancy Lee, and I were all attending a funeral service for Mother, it was more than a shock . . . it was on the order of a crass and insensitive intrusion to hear Mike Laffy's greeting as we got out of the cab and saw him sitting on the stoop. He sprang to his feet.

"What did you get?" he demanded.

But we were all tired and disheartened. It was too much of a burden to say anything. I stopped, looked Mike in the eye, and shook my head.

Mike grabbed onto my arms and squeezed them too hard. He shook his head as I had, imitating my gesture and facial expression. "What the hell does that mean?" he demanded.

"Mike," I pleaded. "I just want to be left alone."

201

"Alone, crap," he spat out, and then he released me and practically swooped down on Dr. Humphries. "What happened, Doc?"

Dr. Humphries shrugged. "I am sorry, my good policeman, but Julian's secretary could be of no use."

Laffy spun around to Nancy Lee. "So?"

But Nancy Lee, too, could greet his interrogatory with only a grimace and a shrug.

Well, I'll be goddamned," Mike Laffy finally exploded. "If you three aren't the biggest bunch of suckers that were ever sent out to do a man's job." He glared down on us with complete and unadulterated contempt.

"But, Mike," I protested, "we did everything you told us to do. We asked her if she had anything. Anything at all. Files. Notebooks. Journals. Notes. Any scrap of information. Any ideas. Any vague hints. *Anything*. And all she told us was that she didn't know a single, solitary thing."

"Of course she told you that, you idiot. What did you expect her to do? Tell you the truth?"

I was stunned. I looked at Dr. Humphries. I saw the sorrow suddenly begin to strip away from his face and be replaced by a more calculating and pensive expression.

Nancy Lee hit her forehead with the heel of her hand. "Idiot. I've been an idiot."

"You've all been idiots," Mike Laffy confirmed, and then he singled me out, as if for a special, personally merited castigation. "I mean the broad hates your mother, and she's always looking daggers at her, right? And she's wacko crazy in love with your stepfather, who happens to be married to your aforementioned mother, right? That's two. And it looks a whole lot like a couple of letters that a couple of people sent to Julian Solo never got to him, which, if he'd gotten them, maybe he'd still be alive today and Cynthia wouldn't be half or all dead, except that this secretary broad hid the letters in her desk and never delivered them to him, right? That's four."

"No, that's three," I interrupted.

"Shut up." Mike Laffy went on: "And anybody with half a brain can see that since the broad always wanted Cynthia dead in the first place, she ain't gonna do a damn thing to save her now, and that's three strikes and you're out. Come on." Laffy grabbed my arm. Nancy Lee leaped up after us, and Dr. Humphries trotted along, trying to keep up the pace.

"Where are we going?" Nancy Lee shouted.

Laffy stopped and whistled for a cab.

"Where do you *think* we're going, Bimbo?" he snapped. "Roosevelt Island?"

Laffy didn't even bother to answer. He got into the front of the cab. We got into the back. Dr. Humphries sat between me and Nancy Lee. "Our angry friend the policeman is correct in his assumption," he whispered to us intently. "We have, in truth, been foolishly naive."

Narrative by myself—Mathew Wylie (continued).

All I remember about our trip back to Melanie's was the anxiety of emotions running wild inside my chest like a mouse that had gone berserk on a treadmill. We walked the same walk that we had walked earlier in the day, but this time Mike Laffy strode ahead of us like some kind of a knight in shining armor or a cavalier carrying an embroidered handkerchief on his lance for the love of his lady and the greater glory of France. We all felt it. You could see it in our tread, in the way we hurried excitedly behind him, in the breaths that we caught as we followed him into the elevator, either because we had had a hard time keeping up with him or because the intensity of our emotions had caught us unawares.

The elevator doors opened and Laffy bounded down the hall. I felt that some triumphant music should be playing to accompany him, or at the very least, that the heavens should thunder forth in a tremendous and cacophonous din.

He slammed his fist against her door. No answer. He slammed his fist again.

"Who is it?" we heard Melanie's voice asking.

"Mike Laffy. Let me in."

"What for?"

"I want to talk to you."

"Why?"

"Let me in."

"No."

Mike turned to us. "Wait here," he commanded, which really hadn't been necessary, because a tempest might be interesting to observe from a distance, but nobody wants to get in its way.

Mike stepped back. He lifted up his right leg, and then faster than I could follow, crashed his foot just below the lock of the door and kicked it in.

Melanie stood cowering in the foyer. She was dressed now, wearing a nondescript sweater and slacks. Her hair hung limply around her face, and she was screaming like one of those banshee monkeys that you see on a *National Geographic* special about the wilds. Mike walked into the apartment and without hesitation socked Melanie one on the jaw. She stopped screaming. She fell back into the room, knocked over a table, and landed flat on her ass. Laffy moved in after her. Dr. Humphries, Nancy Lee, and I clustered in the doorway.

"Get up," Mike commanded.

"Wha—what do you want?" Melanie stammered uncomprehendingly. And then she saw the rest of us, and answering the question we had not yet asked, she suddenly regained her composure, threw back her head, and laughed sardonically.

"Not on your life," she said, and she groped at a table and pulled herself up. But this time when she had gotten back to her feet, she wasn't standing upright, like a person. Like a human being. Her shoulders were hunched forward, and her head jutted out; it was impossible to see her and not think of a snake, coiled, alert, and ready for an attack. I remembered back to my mother's Labor Day party, how Melanie had been able to stare at Mother seemingly continuously without blinking. I'd thought of a snake, then, too.

She took a step backward and laughed again.

Mike stepped toward her and looked at his watch.

"You have exactly no seconds left either to give me all of Julian Solo's papers or take me to them."

Melanie grinned at Mike and spat.

Mike left the spit on his face. He took another step forward, raised his fist, and clocked her again. Mike couldn't have been hitting her very hard, though, because there was no blood. But by now, both of her eyes were black and blue and her lips and cheek had begun to swell.

She fell back against the sofa. There was a telephone on the end table by her side. She reached for it. "I'm calling the police," she shouted.

"What for?" Mike asked quietly. "I am a cop."

The smug expression on Melanie's face quickly changed to fear. Mike yanked her forward, grabbed her around the waist, and ignoring her kicks and screeches, dragged her to the window. He pushed it open, hauled her over the edge, and literally threw her outside, keeping her from falling only by holding onto the waistband of her slacks.

"Let me back in," the voice out the window barely croaked.

"You know," Mike said conversationally, "I don't think the pants you're wearing were made to last. In fact, I think I just heard a couple of seams tearing." Mike turned back to look at us. "What about it, gang? Do you think her pants are going to go?"

We didn't say a word.

"Please," Melanie pleaded.

"Please what?" Mike Laffy asked.

"Please. . . . I'll give you what you want."

"Where is it?"

"I'll show you."

"You'll tell me now, lady, and then you'll show me."

We heard a quick tear of fabric. Melanie screamed.

"You're hanging by a thread," Mike said. "And you have about ten seconds left before you drop. Tell me where Julian Solo's papers are."

"They're in the morgue."

"What morgue?"

"Over at the asylum. In the basement. In the top drawer on the right-hand side. For God's sake, bring me in."

Mike Laffy reached down with his massive arms and hauled Melanie back.

"You're in," he said solemnly. "But not for God's sake. For mine."

Narrative by myself—Mathew Wylie (continued).

I have never experienced anything quite like the thrill and the terror that I felt when I followed Mike Laffy past the NO TRES-PASSING sign and under the rent in the cyclone fence surrounding the time-ravaged wilderness of abandoned buildings on the southern end of Roosevelt Island.

The sun had long since departed, but it was possible to pick a path through the rubble by moonlight. The moon was full and only partially and infrequently obscured by a stream of clouds that hid no more of its face than a veil hides the seductive glances of a harem dancer.

The moonlight was white. The clouds were gray. The night was pale and cold and bloodless, and off in the distance we heard a howl such as one might have imagined coming from the tormented soul of one who was truly both damned and insane.

Nancy Lee grabbed at my elbow. "What was that?" she whispered.

"I don't know," I whispered back, trying to pretend to myself that I hadn't heard it. "Probably just some wise guy trying to scare his mother-in-law. Don't forget, it's Halloween."

We followed Mike Laffy and Melanie Graice in silence. She led us through the mangled branches and over or around deep ruts and gullies without a backward glance and with no hesitation. Mike carried a flashlight, and kept its pallid gleam constantly centered on Melanie's back.

Dr. Humphries carried another flashlight for the three of us. I don't know if he was as frightened as we were, but after about ten minutes, when we arrived at the entrance to the asylum and stood beside the door and heard an ominous scraping beneath our feet, it was he who had the presence of mind to train the flashlight on the ground. Nancy Lee screamed and I threw my arms around her and almost strangled her in a desperate embrace of fear.

"It is nothing to be afraid of," Dr. Humphries said calmly. "We have here only the rats," and his flashlight revealed a rodent easily the size of a well-fed cat.

Nancy Lee gasped and frantically unwound my arms from around her body and dashed to a place about six feet away. There she stopped for a moment and turned back to face us. "I'm not going in there, Mathew Wylie. Not for you. Not for Laffy. Not for Cynthia. Not even for the eternal salvation of my soul. I am absolutely scared to death of rats."

I didn't like rats any more than she did, so I couldn't come up with any arguments to dissuade her. But I didn't want to stay out there keeping her company, either.

"What are you going to do?" I asked her. "You can't just wait out here all by yourself."

"I don't plan to. There's enough moonlight to get over to the riverbank. I'll wait for you guys by the railing near the water. Just try not to let whatever's in there get you. And if it does, don't tell it where I'm standing."

Nancy Lee turned, and in an instant she was gone.

Mike Laffy and Melanie were already in the double stairway leading into the basement, and as they descended, I saw their shadows grow huge and menacing, looming ever larger as the substance on which they depended moved slowly down the stairs. I turned for a moment and looked around. I was standing before what appeared to be the ruins of a medieval castle. Whole sides of the building had crumbled to the ground in a jagged diagonal from the gap-toothed crenellation at the summit to the formless pile of blue-gray rock out of which naked branches reached skeletal fingers to the sky. Turreted towers clung to brick walls that connected with staircases to nowhere. Gothic black windows arched over rooms without roofs, where the interior was as open to the elements as the exterior, and the question became academic as to which was which.

There were no sounds except for the wind and the rustle of rats scratching scratching scratching in the mortuary beneath our feet.

I shook my head and said dumbly, "I can't believe I'm in the twentieth century."

Dr. Humphries tapped me on the arm. "Come." I followed him down the stairs.

Melanie was standing in the doorway, staring at Mike Laffy, her face rigid with hatred. Her eyes bored into Mike's back with that lidless look that now appeared to be characteristic of her. Mike was brushing aside a snare of spiderwebs, and then lifting a long, large cylindrical metal tube out of what I knew in my heart of hearts had to have been a body drawer. The thought of what had once spent its time in there made me sick with revulsion, and for a moment I lowered my eyes and turned away.

Dr. Humphries said, "Yes. I recognize those journals," and I looked up in time to see Laffy pulling two thick notebooks out of the cylinder and laying them on a chunk of fallen concrete about a foot and a half away.

Melanie didn't even bother to look at them, so disinterested did she appear. However, she did state flatly, "There's also a metal file in there about as big as a shoe box. Dr. Solo pushed it all the way in the back of the drawer. On the right-hand side."

Laffy reached his arm in as deeply as it would go.

"I don't feel anything."

208

Melanie shrugged. "Well, it's in there."

Laffy turned to me. "Help me move this crossbeam, and I'll reach in from the back of the drawer on the other side."

Dr. Humphries moved in my direction. "I, too, will assist you."

And so, that moment when the three of us were heaving our shoulders into the massive fallen beam was the moment that Melanie chose to be the time for our dream's demise. For as we became more and more obsessed by the nearness of our treasure, we failed to realize that we had already attained it, and we forgot completely just how treacherous Melanie Graice, our guide, could be.

We pushed and shoved and heaved at the crossbeam, and we gained a little leverage and a little less headway, and just as we had managed to move the beam an inch forward, we all fell silent and stopped moving. For at exactly that instant, we heard the ominous sound of a movement behind us.

Mike lifted up his head.

"It's rats again," I reassured him.

But Mike shook his head, let go of the crossbeam, which crashed back in place, and pushed me to one side. He scrambled over the debris from the fallen ceiling, to the little clearing in front of the body drawer from which he had taken Julian Solo's notebooks only moments before.

"Oh, Christ," he said.

"What happened?"

But Mike didn't answer. He turned, leaped over some twisted metal ductwork, shouted, "Follow me!" and then shot up the mortuary's stairs. A second later he was gone.

"What happened?" I turned to Dr. Humphries.

The doctor was shaking his head fretfully as the two of us scrambled out of the cellar. "The journals are gone," he said as we ran. "I fear that the duplicitous young lady who led us here has stolen them and fled while our backs were turned."

I swore, but kept on running.

Off in the distance, I could see two silhouettes racing in the moonlight. The smaller, slighter figure held in its hand what were clearly Julian's notebooks, and as she got closer and closer to the balustrade overlooking the East River, it became obvious that the larger, more lumbering figure was trailing much too far behind and could not possibly catch up with her in time.

Melanie arrived at the embankment, crashing into the railing. She grasped the cold metal barrier with her left hand, and raised Julian's journals high over her head in her right, swinging her arm back over her shoulder to gather the momentum necessary to heave the notebooks far into the river, to get caught up in the turbulent tide.

Then, just as Melanie's arm swept forward through an arc . . .

"Ayeeyah!"

We heard a savage, homicidal shout reverberating through the silence. At the same instant, we saw a small, terrifying projectile of fury flying, apparently out of nowhere, and hurling itself at Melanie Graice's head.

Dr. Humphries and I ran toward the commotion.

We got there only seconds behind Mike Laffy.

On the ground, limp and lifeless at his feet, we saw the body of Melanie Graice. Half of it was jammed under the railing on the island side of the embankment and half of it had fallen toward a precipice of rocks and jetsam that arose out of the river below.

Not three feet from Melanie's unconscious body, and curled up in a ball with her eyes looking out apprehensively over her knees and her arms and legs squeezed protectively around Julian Solo's journals, was my mother's best friend, Nancy Lee Meyers.

Mike Laffy reached down his hand. Nancy Lee uncurled her body from around the journals and tried to get to her feet. But her leg buckled. Mike put his arm around her waist and steadied her. She held on to him, and then looked down at her legs.

"I think I scraped my knee." She pointed to her right knee, which was in fact scratched and bloody, but which somehow, in that cold and gruesome setting, looked so innocent and inappropriate that the incongruity of her statement must have struck Nancy Lee as funny, for she started to giggle. And I don't know why, but after I stopped looking at her bony knees, my eyes went up to look at her eyes, and I started to giggle too. Then Mike Laffy threw back his head, and he started to roar. And by the time Mike had begun to laugh, Nancy Lee had stopped laughing and had started to cry, and during all of this emotionalism, only one of us wasn't giggling or laughing or crying, and that person was Dr. T. Gideon Humphries.

"Come," Dr. Humphries said firmly but gently. He took Julian Solo's journals out of Nancy Lee's hands and turned toward the walkway that would lead us back to the tram, back to Manhattan, back to my mother, Cynthia Solo, wife of the colleague whom Dr. Humphries had come so greatly to respect.

"Come," he said again softly. "We may have time yet to save the life of the wife of my friend."

Final Words—by Dr. T. Gideon Humphries.

I am writing these last thoughts at the request of my young friend Mathew. I have read the preceding manuscript with close attention, and it has stirred in me emotions of great sadness. Over these pages, I have shed many tears.

During the reading of these journals and correspondence, I have pondered deeply, and now I am done. The episode has been concluded. Concerning it, one can only shake one's head, and sigh, and regret.

Toward the future, I look with hope, and trepidation. The district attorney, having also perused these pages, has concluded that our friend was a helpless victim of, indeed, tragic occurrences. The charges against Mathew Wylie for the murder of Julian Solo have been terminated; the case will never come to trial.

Of greater importance than the vindication of Mathew, however, was the outcome concerning Julian Solo's wife. Our examination of Julian's journals clearly indicated how we might revive her, and both the body and the mind of Cynthia Solo have recovered rapidly. I have seen her several times since she is no longer in the hospital, and neither her inner nor her outer beauty has diminished. She is always so unfailingly kind and lovely, her eyes so attentive, a soft smile always so sweet to touch her lips. And yet I cannot but look at her without feeling tears begin to assemble inside me, and as often as I approach her, just so often must I turn away. For inside this strong and luminous woman . . . inside her soul, I can feel that she is of a spirit both fragile and gossamer . . . of a spirit once kindred in perfection with her husband, and now utterly and completely alone.

And it is of her husband and my friend and colleague, Julian Solo, that I now come to speak. I wish that I had some of the facility with language that Mathew often displayed in the narrative sections he wrote. But I am only a semiliterate scientist. What I want to convey to you in words is the reverence and compassion that is in my heart for a man of great physical and spiritual beauty, and of tremendous intellectual and moral stature.

This manuscript . . . these papers that you have before you . . . they communicate to us all a tragedy, but I find it so vital . . . so momentous . . . so important that I convey to you also that the man around whom all of these incidents revolve be judged not for his failure to be omniscient, but instead for the commitment he had made, and for the intellectual courage that he displayed in forging new paths in science as a means of saving his beloved wife.

Oh, I know that here I am failing to communicate that which is so apparent to me. Perhaps this will make it clearer.

In earlier passages of this text, you read letters and memoranda that were written back and forth between Julian and me. In them, I often accused Julian Solo of inattention to the integration of the various branches of philosophy, of excessive enthusiasm at the expense of necessary caution, of attempting to find the secret of life "somewhere between a neutron and a conditioned reflex."

Yes, as I look back on these papers, I can find many things of which I accused Julian Solo for failing to do; and yet, in reality, I feel that he failed in only one way, and that even in that he was, perhaps, at the mercy of events that he could not control.

How did he fail?

By seeking to stretch the limits of science? No. To do so is an intellectual virtue, and his achievements made him but easier to admire.

By trying to reach into a realm that many consider the sole province of religion, and thereby attempting to manipulate death and life? No, again. For religion is but one branch of philosophy, and by his deeds, every scientist is a philosopher, and the philosopher's duty and obligation is the comprehension, beautification, and enhancement of human life.

By working in secret, and not sharing with other scientists his creative thoughts and ideas, and seeking from them perhaps time- and life-saving modification of his ideas? No, and here I say no for two reasons. One, I do not think it is any creator's responsibility or obligation to share. Surely some of man's greatest achievements were conceived by creators like Copernicus and Kepler, who not only worked at odds with other scientists, but who worked alone. And second, and most unusual for a man of his unquestionable brilliance, Julian Solo was not averse to sharing or communicating with others about his ideas. From the very beginning, *I* knew that Julian, with this great interest in hypothermia, was attempting to prolong life by simulating a state of cryogenic death. And the correspondence with Dr. Lilljigren in Norway also shows that not only was Julian fearless about divulging the purposes of his experiments, but he was also a seeker of the advice of one who might be even more knowledgeable than he.

And herein we have in the nutshell the origin of the tragedy. For had Julian but received the letter from Dr. Lilljigren, there is no question in my mind that he would have immediately desisted in his experiments, and that both he and Mrs. Solo would be alive and happy today.

However, there is evil in the world, and evil entered into Julian's life in the person of his secretary, Melanie Graice. She hid the letter to him from Dr. Lilljigren, and Julian was never to read these fatal words which could have saved us all from so much grief:

> Volunteers who were prevented from attaining the REM stage for over five nights in a row developed alarming symptoms of mental degeneration. They lost control of their impulses, became antisocial, irritable, uncoordinated, listless, and inefficient; they experienced hallucinations, blurred visions, lack of memory, anxiety, and entire personality alterations.

Had Julian but read that letter, he would have known that he could not perform experiments on himself. Had Julian but read that letter, he would have seen immediately that any time spent at all in a deathlike state of sleep would deprive him of his REM dreaming, and thus of his judgment, and that all additional experiments from that time forward would be of absolutely no value. For, if a scientist cannot evaluate the results of his experiments from a position of objectivity and reason, then a scientist cannot go on.

My poor friend Julian.

He was never to know how adversely his lack of REM dreaming would affect him. Oh, at times one sees hints in his journals of how relieved both he and his wife were to get a good night's sleep, but from the first time that he injected himself with his Cryogenic Catalystic Serum to the last, if no

214

one had come out of the very heavens to save him, he had become incapable of saving himself.

My young and hasty friend Mathew . . . he continues to blame his stepfather for Cynthia Solo's brush with death. For he says that Julian's decision to save Cynthia without consulting her first about the method or treatment deprived her of her options, deprived her of the choice, and that in doing so, Julian behaved immorally.

Could Julian Solo behave immorally?

As we are all creatures of free will, then of course Julian had that possibility to do so, as we all do.

But was his behavior immoral in this instance?

I beg of you, my young friend Mathew, to remember that when Julian made the decision to use the Cryogenic Catalystic Serum on your mother, his judgment and ability to reason had already been deeply impaired by his prior use of the CCS treatment on himself . . . a course of action that he attempted so bravely and sadly and lovingly in order to share any risks that his wife might be incurring by his treatment of her disease.

As I relate these thoughts and feelings now, I cannot help but be put to mind of a childhood poem I learned so long ago:

> For want of a nail the shoe is lost,
> for want of a shoe the horse is lost,
> for want of a horse the rider is lost,
> for want of a rider the war is lost.

The nail that Julian Solo lacked was Dr. Lilljigren's letter informing him that the treatment that Julian was projecting would jeopardize the powers of his brain.

The nail that Julian lacked was deliberately stolen and hidden from him by Melanie Graice because she thought that in so doing, it would cause the death of Julian's wife.

For want of a nail, Julian Solo was lost. Let us therefore please not malign him. Let us please not think of him or categorize him as "a good man gone bad" or "a brillliant scientist gone mad." Let us please revere this man for his commitment to science, for his devotion to a beloved woman, for his ebullient nature, his elegance, his joie de vivre.

There is a saying that the higher they fly, the harder they fall. Please let us prevent this splendid individual from any fall at all in our esteem. But if in your estimation, there must be some descent, let it be ever so gently, and may we bring him down only far enough to rest on his laurels, and may we do so with infinite tenderness.

Bibliography

Coleman, James, and William E. Broen, Jr. *Abnormal Psychology and Modern Life*, 4th ed. Glenview, Ill.: Scott, Foresman, 1972.

Gallup, George, Jr. *Adventures in Immortality*. New York: McGraw-Hill, 1982.

Galvin, Ruth Mehrtens. "Control of Dreams." *Smithsonian*, August 1982.

Hubbard, Linda. "In Search of 40 Winks." *Modern Maturity*, April–May 1982.

Rand, Ayn. *Philosophy: Who Needs It*. Indianapolis, Ind.: Bobbs-Merrill, 1982.

Restak, Richard M., M.D. *The Brain*. New York: Doubleday, 1979.

Silverstein, Alvin. *Conquest of Death*. New York: Macmillan, 1979.

Thompson, Carole. "Catching Up With Sleep." *Cosmopolitan*, April 1982.

Tucker, Jonathan B. "The Brain: Something to Think About." *Cosmopolitan*, May 1982.